THE HOLBORN SCROLL

James Fitzsimons

Book Guild Publishing

Sussex, England

First published in Great Britain in 2010 by
The Book Guild
Pavilion View
19 New Road
Brighton, BN1 1UF

Typesetting in Baskerville by
Keyboard Services, Luton, Bedfordshire

Printed in Great Britain by
CPI Antony Rowe

A catalogue record for this book is available from
The British Library

ISBN 978 1 84624 474 2

For Kathleen.
Thank you for all your love and support.

To David, Claire and Kirsty.
Swim always in the right direction.

Prologue

Palestine 1944

The horse's hooves pounded fiercely onto the hard, parched track as it sped eagerly toward the border. The rider lashed the reins from side to side, his knees and feet pumping hard against the animal's flanks, driving it harder, faster, into the fading light. He glanced back occasionally, frantically, to check for pursuers. He could see only dust rising high into the air behind him. He was not yet safe. He could not afford the luxury, the certainty, that his mission had been accomplished until he had delivered his precious package.

Up ahead, the two men standing lazily by the side of the hard-baked track smiled at each other and nodded knowingly. The skin on the back of their hands and face was weathered, like distressed leather, through years of exposure to the dust-laden wind and baking sun. The taller one slowly removed a rope from under his tunic, and handed one end to his accomplice. They both knew the routine. They moved to either side of the road and tied the rope around the two large white rocks that they had already rolled into position. They left the rope lying limp across the path of the oncoming horse, and waved at each other to confirm that the trap was set.

Crouching down behind the rocks, they pulled their hoods over their heads, their dusty tunics blending in with the arid desert around them. It had been a barren week for them, and they needed a decent return for all

1

their efforts. Their adrenalin rose as they anticipated the spoils to come.

The rider did not ease up, relentlessly pushing his mount on, both man and beast exerting maximum effort as they sought to escape from certain death. Only a few kilometres more and the rider would be safe, his future secure. An hour had passed, but time had stood still for him. He had become the only person alive. It was on his shoulders, and his alone, to ensure mankind's future.

The two men signalled to each other again, surprised at the speed of their fast-approaching prey. They grabbed the rope tightly, wrapping it firmly around each large rock to ensure its rigidity, and watched carefully as the horse, head nodding almost grotesquely now, approached the marker lying at the side of the road some ten yards away. They knew that by the time the rider caught sight of the obstacle – *if* he caught sight of it – it would already be too late.

It was over in seconds. The horse let out a loud, high-pitched, echoing shriek as it tumbled forward, breaking its neck on impact with the ground as it threw its rider forward, high into the air. The rider landed head first on the hard rubble off to one side of the track, sending a great plume of dust high into the blue silent sky.

The two men winced. It was a spectacular kill. It wasn't often they encountered someone travelling with such speed along this road from nowhere. Their curiosity was aroused, their sense of anticipation heightened. Their expectation of success made each of them involuntarily lick their parched lips.

Quickly, they both stood up and waited for the dust to settle. The horse lay motionless in the middle of the road, its head bent under its body at an impossibly acute angle, flesh ripped away from much of its neck, the dark sticky fluid of life flowing rapidly from the warm carcass. They walked along the path toward the rider. He was lying on his back, motionless. As they reached him they could see he was still alive, but a pool of blood was slowly gathering behind his head. They would not have any trouble from him 'Well, what do we have here?' the taller of the men asked, turning to his friend who had gathered in the rope and was feeding it back into the belt below his tunic.

The rider groaned and spluttered, blood seeping slowly from between his lips. He weakly reached down with his right hand toward his side. The smaller man crouched down slowly beside him, watching the painfully slow movement.

'Wow! Look at this, Simeon, a pistol!' He looked at his colleague and pointed at the gun, safe in the knowledge that the rider was too injured to cause any sort of threat. He looked back at the rider. 'And what are you going to do with this, my friend?' The men laughed. The smaller man ripped open the pistol holder and removed the weapon, holding it up to the sky to inspect its silhouette.

The rider groaned again, his body taut and straining to find some last strength with which to engage the enemy. He was clearly tall and muscular, Arian, with a sharp, lean face that, even through the dirt and the pain which was now etched heavily into his face, was clearly distinguishable. He wore a khaki safari jacket, laden with pockets, a leather belt tied tightly round his waist from which the pistol holder was suspended. The right leg of his dark trousers had been ripped away at the thigh, exposing a bloodied leg just above the black knee-length boots. They could clearly see his knee had been shattered by the impact.

'A military man, eh?' said the taller one. 'But not from these parts!' They both laughed.

At the rider's other side lay a leather satchel, the strap hanging diagonally across his chest. The taller man bent down to inspect the bag, flicking open the two leather straps at either end. He pulled out his knife and quickly broke the lock on the metal catch that was in the centre of the bag and had been damaged by the impact. He tore the bag open.

'Careless,' he said, smiling. 'You're obviously the trusting sort.' The other man laughed.

Suddenly, gathering all the strength he could muster and letting out a muffled grunt, the rider shot out his hand and grabbed the taller man's arm, which was now exploring the bag. He sent out a loud, pained cry as he pulled himself slightly off the ground, and stared hard into the man's face. The rider's eyes were no longer dull and weak. Instead they were wide and focused, piercing blue, brimming with a passion and fire that made the tall man pull back slightly.

The rider swallowed hard, holding on desperately to the man's arm. In his mind this was not happening. It could not be happening. He could not fail, not at this point and in this way. He parted his dry, bloodstained lips slowly. The words came out painfully in stuttering Hebrew, a language that he guessed his assailants would understand. They did.

'What you have done can never be forgiven... You know not what you do...'

The rider felt the life slowly ebbing from his broken body, his mind trying desperately to summon some strength from his disconnected limbs. Far away he could see a light and hear the sound of triumph, a crescendo of noise building to celebrate the great victory. He had to awaken from this dream. He began to shake as his body convulsed, then suddenly he straightened, rigid, and almost peacefully fell back down onto the ground.

The two men stood silently looking at him for a few moments. They felt cold and uncomfortable, both repeating in their own mind the rider's words. They were hardened men who valued no life but their own, but something in the man's words, his intense final stare, even in the face of death, made them feel uneasy. Who was this man?

'Come on, let's get on with it,' said the smaller one finally, a frown now replacing his previous merriment.

'Yeah ... right. Take a look in the bag,' said the taller one, unconsciously rubbing his arm where the rider's grip had dug into the muscle only seconds before. 'Come on, come on! What's in it?' he said impatiently. He just wanted it to be over, to take the money and go.

The bag's contents were emptied onto the dirt and the men crouched over them.

'Where's the money?' asked the taller one, now brimming with frustration. 'Search his jacket!'

The smaller man did as he was told. He found a small leather pouch with a few coins inside.

'Shit! Is that it? There's not enough to buy a decent chicken!' said the taller one, grabbing the money from his colleague and pushing him over. He looked down again at the contents of the bag. The rider's words had got to him. What did he mean by them? Who was this man? He spoke Hebrew well, but he was clearly foreign – a tall, blond Westerner. He sifted through the contents, mostly papers, which meant nothing to him as he could not read.

He picked up what looked like an old cloth bag that had been held in the satchel. It was carefully tied with a thin cord at the top. The faint but unmistakable emblem of an eagle, its wings spread wide apart, had been drawn freehand on the front. He looked at the line drawing quizzically for a moment, then opened the bag, and pulled out a thick roll of parchment that was wrapped around an old wooden stick.

'A scroll?' said the other man, moving over to his side.

'Can you read?' asked his accomplice.

'No, but I've seen this sort of thing before. My uncle has some...'

'Shut up!' shouted the taller one, stuffing the scroll back into the bag and tying the knot. 'We'll take it into town. Perhaps we can sell it for some food.'

He tucked it into the belt around his tunic and flicked through the rest of the rider's valuables. He noticed a small hardback book covered in dust. He picked it up carefully and ran his hand over the cover, removing the dirt from the surface. He smiled and gave a little laugh.

He held the book up to his colleague. 'Look at this,' he said, pointing at the insignia on the front. 'A Nazi!' Both men laughed for a few seconds.

The taller man turned slowly and looked back down the road. As he casually flicked the dust off his tunic, he began to wonder what on earth the rider had been doing there.

London 1997

The compound gate swung open and rattled wildly as it bounced off the wire-mesh fence circling the site. The night watchman casually waved to the entering workman, and immediately pulled on his jacket, walked out of the Portakabin and locked the door.

'She's all yours,' he shouted, as he made his way quickly through the gate and jumped into the rusty old Montego parked at the side of the road.

The workman just smiled. He closed the gate, taking care not to drop the Tupperware sandwich box and flask he was carrying. He whistled quietly to himself as he strolled across to the JCB parked where he had left it the previous night – at the bottom of the 30-foot embankment.

He couldn't remember how many sites he had been on, how many offices for rich City gentlemen he had built, but this was just one more. Nothing special. It was work, and that's all he needed.

He climbed up into the bright-yellow cab, placed his box and flask behind the seat and pulled off his regulation black donkey jacket. *Four hours to go*, he thought to himself, suddenly remembering with pleasure that today was Saturday. The warm morning air promised a hot sleepy afternoon. Reaching forward he placed the key in the ignition and pressed the red button to fire up the engine. It started at the third time of asking.

He reached up above him and pulled the red hard hat from a hook on the cabin ceiling. As he put it on, out of the corner of his eye he caught sight of a reddish-brown object about ten feet away, sticking out of the side of the embankment. Almost unconsciously he dismissed it as an old brick or stone of some kind and placed the digger into gear. He lowered the bucket, ready to scoop up the first mass of clay and soil directly ahead of him. Casually, he glanced again at the object.

This time he could see that it had a rounded end, protruding at a 45-degree angle from the face of the embankment. Only two inches or so stood out, but he was now sure it wasn't a brick or stone. He put the machine into neutral and sat back in his seat with a sigh. Why the hell was he wasting his time with this, he thought, as he climbed down from the cab.

Chapter 1

The phone rang. Nick Stephenson rolled over slowly and, without opening his eyes, reached out and grabbed the receiver from the small bedside table.

'Hello, Nick here,' he croaked before loudly clearing his throat of the excesses of the night. He wasn't really the sort to frequent London's trendier bars, but the occasional Friday night out with the office staff was good for morale, he had decided. Anyway, it made a change to have some company occasionally.

'Sorry to call so early,' said the gruff northern voice, 'but we've just dug up something I think you should have a look at Nick.'

'What time is it?' asked Nick, ignoring the statement. Why the hell was he being woken up on a Saturday morning by a site foreman who had seen and done everything on a multitude of building sites all over the country?

'It's er ... ten to nine,' said the voice, almost apologetically. 'I'm sorry Nick, but I really do think you should see this. I've had to tell the boys to stop working...'

'What!' Nick bolted upright, beads of perspiration glistening on his naked torso. 'What the hell is it, a bomb?' It was the only thing he could immediately imagine would cause such a step to be taken, and Nick knew that finding buried wartime bombs were not unheard of in that part of the City.

'No,' came the hesitant reply. 'I'm not really sure what it is.'

Nick paused. It wasn't the sort of response he expected from his old associate. His mind started to focus, realising he was not imagining the exchange. He lowered his tone. 'Come on, Joe, what's going on? I don't care what it is – you get those diggers back working.'

'It's not as easy as that,' replied the foreman, sounding like a nervous trainee who couldn't find the answer to a simple, obvious question. There was a brief pause while both men assessed their situation. 'Look, I really think you should come down here.'

There was silence for a few seconds on the other end of the phone. Nick had known Joe Stone for ten years, and if something was bothering him then Nick knew it was serious. They had worked together on enough construction jobs for both of them to trust one another's judgement, even – no especially – thought Nick, if it meant giving up a Saturday morning to justify the trust.

'OK, Joe, I'll be straight over, but for God's sake find them something to do! It's Saturday, and those guys are on double time!'

He replaced the handset and ran his right hand through his sandy-coloured hair, a nervous habit which he had acquired in his schooldays, and which, he had once convinced himself, accounted for the greying streaks which swept back, with the rest of his hair, from his forehead like a great mane, finishing well past collar length. He wasn't particularly tall, but the mass of well-groomed hair and athletic frame, which he didn't seem to have to work too hard to maintain, made him seem somewhat bigger, and the cheeky schoolboy grin and perfect white teeth ensured that there was never any shortage of female admirers.

At thirty-five years of age Nick had settled into the sort of routine he always promised himself he would avoid. He had reached that point where comfort came too easily, but every now and again a gnawing sense of disquiet about the future path of his life would jump into his thoughts. He felt he had everything he really wanted, yet there still seemed to be something missing, or at least a feeling that there would at some point be something, or someone, in his life that he would wonder how he had lived without. Or maybe he was just growing up.

He threw back the single sheet and landed, walking, on the cool wooden floor. Morris, his cat – named after the first car Nick had ever owned – shot off the bed and ran through the spacious living room and into the open-plan kitchen, hiding under the breakfast bar. He was hungry even if no one else was.

Nick made for the bathroom. Somehow he knew today was going to be a little different. He turned on the shower and picked a clean towel from the immaculately stacked pile on top of the pine dresser. Red, white, red, white. Nick smiled. Mrs Johnson was an Arsenal fan and always left Nick some little reminder of the fact when she had finished cleaning his flat. Not that the flat needed a lot of cleaning. Nick didn't spend a lot of time there, even although it was his pride and joy. He preferred to work long into the evening most nights, and have dinner on the way home at one of the few quiet hostelries he frequented. He was happy in his own company, and being waited on and befriended by restaurant managers gave him all the social interaction he needed. He enjoyed paying to eat well and was comfortable buying companionship.

The smile didn't last long as Nick remembered the urgency of the situation. He decided to skip breakfast, stopping briefly in the kitchen to open a can of food for Morris before slipping out of the towelling dressing gown and into a pair of light trousers and a Ralph Lauren polo shirt.

Nick glanced back at the empty bed. He smiled to himself and shook his head. He tried to remember the name of the girl in the bar last night. Cute, but far too young, he thought. He glanced again at the bed. Nick had been through the pain of feeling lonely. Now he had convinced himself that he positively enjoyed solitude. Besides, as far as he was concerned there was no getting away from other people, not really. The loft was *his* place and *only* his, bought with *his* savings. It was an extravagance, he knew, but what else did he have to spend his well-earned cash on? The Morgan wasn't his, although it would be in three months when the loan was repaid. Not even Morris was his. You don't own a cat, he had once told a friend, you cohabitate. It was the closest he had come to living with someone.

He opened the blinds which covered the full-length arch window looking onto the Thames. He covered his eyes as light gushed in, the heat of the sun already strong on the London morning below him, causing the brickwork walls to glow almost orange, like the entrance to a glasswork furnace. He picked up his Ray-Bans and the keys to the Morgan. It was going to be another hot day.

The drive from his apartment in Chelsea Harbour to the site in Holborn was completed in record time. It was a game Nick liked to play, timing the journey on a small stopwatch stuck onto the dashboard. This morning, though, his mind was far too preoccupied to remember to set the watch running and he felt no sense of pride or achievement.

On any other car, he had surmised, the little brown stopwatch would have looked completely ridiculous. Not on the Morgan. That's what he liked about it. It looked *built*. You could see the individual pieces that had been used. OK, some didn't fit together to the tolerance of a Mercedes or some other luxury German car, but it was an individual. All the bits had an obvious function – no bland rounded or plastic edges from dashboard to door panel, or light fitting to bonnet. No, the Morgan looked like a small building on wheels, and buildings were what Nick was all about.

The Morgan came to an abrupt halt outside the site office. Nick quickly scanned the site and saw a group of workmen standing idly around a large digger at the other end of the compound. He felt his jaw tighten, ran his hand through his hair and removed his glasses. He strode into the Portakabin and made straight for Joe Stone's office, kicking up dust from the hot dry ground that just six weeks earlier had been an endless sea of mud.

The office was small and, like most site offices, very basic and untidy. Nick's building plans hung around the walls like some giant jigsaw wallpaper pattern – colourless, but finely detailed.

Joe stood up and, before Nick could open his mouth, he pointed at the cylindrical object lying on a small table underneath the room's only window.

Nick looked at Joe. 'This had better be good,' he said in a threatening tone that Joe recognised. He walked over to the table to examine the problem. A terracotta holder of some kind, caked in clay and about twelve inches long, lay on the table. It had been broken at one end, and several small pieces lay on the table beside the main part, which, although intact, had a crack running down its length, breaking the ornate pattern of what looked to Nick like a very old pipe of some sort. Not a good first impression.

'What the hell is this?' he asked in an angry voice, looking at Joe.

Joe put his hands out in front of him as if to stop Nick saying any more. 'I know it don't look like much. It's what we found inside that's got me worried.'

Nick looked at him in disbelief. 'Inside? What do you

mean, *inside?*' He looked at the object again and for the first time realised that the cylinder was sealed at one end like a jar. He picked it up and looked inside the open end. 'Was this closed off too?' he asked Joe, his curiosity becoming more aroused.

'I think so, but that end must have broken off as we were pulling it out of the embankment. We got as much of the damn thing out intact as we could,' said Joe.

Nick looked at him. 'The embankment?'

'Yeah, it was about three feet up from the base. Ray still doesn't know how the hell he missed it yesterday when he dug into it. Not like him ... but that's where it was found, sticking out like a bloody sore thumb.'

Nick looked into the cylinder, staring at the contents. It was probably just an old piece of junk that someone had thrown down a hole at some point when the site had been exposed before, maybe while the previous building was under construction. If it hadn't been sticking out like that, he thought, it would have ended up in a bucketful of earth and been sent on its way off the site like all the other rubbish. Yes, that was all there was to it. A bit more interesting than the norm, but so what?

'Everything's there ... we put all of it back,' said Joe. 'Strangest thing I've ever found on a site.'

Nick sighed and shook his head. He might as well indulge his curiosity. He reached in carefully and pulled out the contents. He replaced the cylinder on the table and looked at the strange waxy material in his hands. It was rolled up tightly, and what appeared to be an old wooden stick ran down through the centre.

'I reckon it's some sort of old script, like a scroll thing...' said Joe.

Nick stared at the foreman and shook his head. 'I think I can see that, Joe.'

Nick slowly opened out the scroll, carefully holding the

wooden handle at the bottom and pulling the jagged end of the scroll itself. He looked at the blurred, faint writing. He shook his head, thinking out loud as he scanned the document from top to bottom. 'It doesn't look like English ... or Latin ... or Greek...' he remarked, now peering intently at a more prominent section. 'Looks like Hebrew or some other Middle Eastern language to me.' He slowly rubbed the scroll between his fingers. 'Feel's like ... like parchment.'

Joe watched his boss intently as he slowly unrolled more of the scroll. Once he had unrolled about six inches, the brittle parchment suddenly cracked, and the exposed piece tore away from the rest, causing both of them to jump slightly.

'Shit!' said Nick involuntarily, instinctively rolling back the part that was still intact. He placed it down gently on the table and turned his attention to the piece that had separated.

'It's pretty old-looking,' said Joe, peering over Nick's shoulders as he held it up to the bright sunlight streaming through the window. Nick decided to ignore the comment. 'What are you looking for?' he continued.

Nick lowered the parchment, but said nothing. He didn't really know what he was looking for – a watermark or perhaps some more comprehensible writing that would give away its identity. But there was nothing there – only the small, fine letters, faded but defined, carefully laid out row after row, words written in a language Nick couldn't even start to understand.

'You said it was found buried in the embankment?' said Nick, turning round to face Joe as he carefully rolled up the parchment.

'Well,' said Joe, 'sticking out of it to be precise.'

'Show me exactly where,' said Nick, walking toward the door.

They emerged into the sunshine, Nick removing the sunglasses from the breast pocket of his shirt and placing them back on his face as he followed Joe across the site.

Joe stopped at the embankment and pointed to the hole from where the cylinder had been removed. 'This is it. Ray saw it first thing this morning. He was in the digger, about to start moving the loose soil over there to finish the western trench, when he noticed it sticking out.'

Nick looked at the hole and then cast his eye up to the top of the embankment. 'That must be twenty feet to the top,' he said.

'Nineteen feet two inches to be precise' said Joe.

Nick ran his hand through his hair and then shook his head. He knew that anything buried that deep must have been there for a very long time. The size of the planned office building had meant they had had to dig foundations much deeper than those of any previous buildings on the site. The old shops and flats that had been demolished only had foundations to a depth of eight or nine feet. No, to be buried so deep this would have to be *hundreds* of years old, unless there was some other explanation he couldn't imagine at that moment. He convinced himself that there must be. It couldn't be genuine.

'What do you think?' asked Joe, looking at the vacant expression on Nick's face.

Nick turned to him. 'Look, I know what you're thinking, but we're not stopping work.' He turned and walked back toward the car. Joe followed him.

'Christ, Nick! You know the rules! If that thing is genuine we could all be in the shit if I carry on!'

Nick stopped and looked at him intently. 'Who else knows about this?'

'Only us and Ray have seen it,' answered Joe. 'The rest of the boys know something's up, but they ain't seen it.'

'Well, keep it that way!' Nick paused for a moment,

trying to think his way through the options. He turned around and walked back into the Portakabin.

'OK, let's think' said Nick, removing his sunglasses and replacing them once more in his shirt pocket. Joe closed the door and stood opposite him. Without thinking, Nick picked up a bundle of plans sitting on the desk in front of him. 'If this ... thing is of special scientific or historical interest,' said Nick, exaggerating the words as though reciting straight from some hated rulebook, 'I should notify the planning officer immediately ... yes?'

Joe didn't answer. He decided Nick wasn't actually asking a question.

'The planning officer would then have the power to slap an enforcement notice on the site, stop all work, and carry out further investigations as he or she sees fit ... yes?' Again Joe didn't answer. He knew Nick *definitely* wasn't asking a question.

'Well, I think we both know that our paymaster, Mr Forster, would be delighted. He would come down personally to congratulate us on our find ... and then we could all go home! No bloody way, Joe!' He slammed the plans onto the desk.

Nick glanced at the wall, the picture of himself, Charles Forster of Forster Developments and Mrs Margaret Essex, the Mayoress, smiling back at him. It usually amused him to see the Mayoress awkwardly perched on the seat of the JCB. Now he looked again at Forster, his fat, bulging stomach hanging over the ill-fitting trousers, his tie, as usual, hanging all of six inches short of his waistline. Nick could almost sense the stale smell of cigars from his jacket, mixed in with the hair gel that completely flattened his thinning grey hair and which at times seemed to Nick to have the odour of a burning tyre.

He was everything Nick hated in a client. A northern contractor who had struck rich in the 80s boom and had decided to take on the big boys in the City at their own game. He wasn't interested in buildings or how they looked. Initially, he had bullied and forced his way into acquiring potential development sites in run-down parts of town, cutting corners on building contracts to build up a modest fortune. He used it to gain recognition, wining and dining with the rich and famous, throwing lavish parties and insisting on buying expensive gifts for those who could help his cause – namely, Forster Developments. Over time he had attracted the less scrupulous in the investment world who needed somewhere to launder their ill-gotten gains, and property offered an easy route. He became the latest development guru. 'Bricks and mortar, son...' he told Nick at their first meeting '...can't be hidden, so they must be honest!' Nick didn't understand what he meant when he said it, but he knew now. Nick hated him, and he was sure that Forster hated all of them too.

Joe interrupted Nick's thoughts. 'Do you want me to get them back to work?'

Nick looked at Joe. He knew what Forster's reaction would be if Nick issued an instruction to stop work. Nick had the power to do it, and he wasn't altogether against the idea of landing Mr Forster in it, but he was too big a client for the firm, and not many developers paid his level of fees. Nick hated it, but there were mouths to feed. No, he would have to tread carefully if he was to make *that* decision.

'What's left to be done on the excavations?' he asked Joe, folding his arms and trying to sound positive.

'Well, apart from the area around the embankment, not a lot. On Monday we could start laying the foundations at the top end,' Joe answered.

'How long will it take to get the steel?' asked Nick.

'The supplier said he can do it in a week. Things are

pretty slow. But we really need to order now, Nick, like we agreed yesterday.'

Nick thought about it for a moment. Joe was right. They were on a hell of a tight schedule. OK, it was the middle of summer so weather wouldn't be a problem, but one delay somewhere along the line and Forster's deadline wouldn't be met.

'How late could we leave it?' Nick asked casually.

'Jesus, Nick. You know how critical that is. If it's delayed at all then it's time lost. We can't do anything else while it's going up.'

Nick looked at him straight. 'OK, Joe, but how much time *could* we buy if we delayed it now?'

Joe shook his head. 'If you want me to stay away from the embankment, I've got maybe five days' work before we get in there. After that, we take it away and the steel's got to be here.'

'How long will it take to finish off the embankment?' asked Nick, sensing an opportunity to buy some time.

Joe looked at Nick. 'I'm not comfortable with this, Nick', he stuttered, shaking his head. Nick didn't answer. 'OK, a week,' Joe conceded.

Nick smiled. 'So, I've got until next Friday before you need to order the steel, yes?'

Joe nodded his agreement in slow motion, emphasising his reluctance. 'One week, and not a day more!'

Nick continued, 'And in the meantime your men can pour the foundations round the north, west and south sides?'

Joe nodded again. 'I don't see what difference it makes though,' said Joe. 'Forster's not goin' to be too chuffed if we spend more money now just for him to find out that the site gets closed down a week from now if that things genuine, is he?'

Nick looked at Joe. 'There's a hell of a difference

between pouring concrete and ordering steelwork, Joe – you know that. There's at least eight hundred grand in the steelwork and I don't want to have that on my head – do you?' Joe nodded sheepishly. 'That will give me a week to check this out, and when I get to the bottom of it, we haven't lost any time on the critical path.' Nick smiled again at Joe and patted him gently on the shoulder. He had made up his mind that there had to be a simple explanation – one that he would find quickly – once he had decided where to start.

He went into Joe's office and picked up the scroll from the table. 'Keep the pot here…' he said to Joe, picking up a plastic bag and carefully placing the two pieces of parchment inside before wrapping it tightly around them. 'But, for God's sake, keep it locked away!' he added, pointing to the desk as though it were a safe.

'Now, Joe, get your men back to work. There's a good two hours left this morning,' he shouted back as he strode out the door, once again putting on the Ray-Bans and jumping into the Morgan.

For a brief moment he realised that he was actually excited by the thought of the object being genuine – perhaps some piece of ancient history, a significant find that would transform historians' knowledge of some famous event or person. He allowed himself a brief grin. Well, it *was* a Saturday. But how would he start to unravel the mystery? He smiled to himself. Of course! He would speak to Robert.

Chapter 2

Robert Stanhope was sixty-three. He had formed the firm of Stanhope Architects in 1971 after breaking away from a dour Norfolk practice that seemed to him to be interested only in designing imitation windmills, ziggurats and public conveniences. The young Robert Stanhope had wanted to master his art, to break new ground and be able to take on commissions that *he* wanted, and by the age of thirty-seven he had just enough money to take the risk.

After a few barren years, the eighties had been fairly kind to Stanhope Architects – a number of small-scale but prestigious office and retail schemes in London and the Home Counties – and Robert Stanhope had invested in young ambitious talent – though not always wisely – to develop his own ambition of heading up a creative architectural practice of *'quality and innovation'*, as the firm's brochure proudly stated.

Nick had liked Robert from the moment they met. Of course, as Nick realised later, it was like Robert meeting himself at a younger age, but Nick had never let him down. He was determined never to do so. Then, in 1991, on Nick's thirtieth birthday, Robert had offered him a partnership and he had become the heir apparent. Nick felt like his apprenticeship was up and accepted without hesitation. Together the two men had developed an enviable record of designing buildings around the City, not the largest, but certainly some of the most striking, and their ability to deliver projects on time and to budget had quickly attracted the lazier of the property developers who needed a safe pair of hands to deliver their little palaces.

After a long illness Robert's wife, Katherine, had died of cancer and, as is the case with so many devoted men, the spark had left Robert's work. He was content to let his younger prodigy assume the mantle of responsibility and guide the company through the troubled times of the collapse of the property market, and ride out the problems that the associated professions – architects, surveyors, engineers – were left to deal with.

Like many practices in the early nineties, Stanhope Stephenson had contracted, shedding staff, good staff, and reinvesting capital to keep itself afloat, and now, with Robert's contacts and Nick's growing reputation, it was finally slowly recovering. But the last few years had seemed to take their toll on Robert. The fire in his belly finally seemed to have been extinguished. It wasn't just the death of Katherine. He had tired of the constant need to seek out new contacts and new commissions in a world that seemed to have become less interested in the qualities he strived for, and more in an instant and cheap fix. His journey into an uncertain retirement had begun.

The Morgan raced its way along the country lanes, Nick soaking in the smell of freshly cut grass and the scent of summer flowers. It had been some time since Nick had taken the Morgan out into the country, and he could sense the engine running freely, purring as it kept itself in top gear for an eternity longer than it could in town. As he turned into the gravel drive, Nick allowed himself the briefest thought that he, too, would one day live in such style, or at least own a house with a lawn and a garage. He drove the one hundred yards or so to the front door of the Victorian mansion, the screaming harshness of Meatloaf suddenly cutting as he removed the keys. The marked tranquillity of the surroundings somehow accentuated the difference in the partners' lifestyles. Nick smiled. Maybe the time hadn't yet come. He carefully picked up the bag and stepped out of the car.

Nick rang the doorbell, wiping the remaining dust off his shoes on the 'welcome' mat. Robert came to the door.

'Nick!' he said, smiling in surprise at seeing his partner on a Saturday morning. 'I thought Spurs were at home today' he added, fully aware of Nick's normal Saturday pursuit.

'They are, Robert, but I've something I'd like to show you first,' said Nick, once again feeling agitated by the interruption to his weekend, and that of his old friend.

Robert smiled and led Nick into the house, through the ornately decorated hallway and into the oak-lined drawing room, whose walls were covered on three sides by row upon row of neatly arranged books of every size and colour. He gestured to Nick to sit down, but instead Nick wandered toward a large highly polished drawing table in the centre of the room.

'I want you to look at something, Robert.' Nick opened up the bag and emptied the contents onto the table.

'Where did you get this?' said Robert, his eyes widening with interest.

'Just tell me what you think it is,' said Nick, shrugging his shoulders and hoping to get the matter sorted out as quickly as possible.

Robert slowly and very deliberately leaned forward and lightly ran a palm over the display. 'Well it's clearly some type of old parchment ... like a scroll of some kind.' He carefully unfolded the main part of the parchment. 'It's very good,' he added, looking up at Nick and smiling like a kid with a new toy.

'Very good? What do you mean "very good?",' Nick asked, puzzled, watching the older man's face intently.

'Well, I mean, it's a good copy of an old scroll – better

than the ones they sell in museums.' He grinned. 'Come on, where did you get it from?'

Nick set his gaze on the older man's face. 'Are you sure it's a fake?'

Robert slowly stopped smiling. 'What do you mean? Are you telling me this is genuine?'

Nick made no reply. 'What's going on, Nick?' Robert's face became a little more serious. 'Where did you get it?'

Before Nick could answer, the door opened and an attractive young blonde woman, dressed casually in jeans and a loose pale-blue blouse, came breezing into the room. Rachel Stanhope was twenty-five years old, going on nineteen, and since the age of fifteen had been madly in love with her father's partner. Oh, she knew Nick would never make a play for her, but she also knew he secretly shared their unspoken love – at least she liked to think so. Anyway, somehow Nick had lately become more like a big brother. They would meet at office parties or at dinner in her house, or occasionally she would even accompany him to a client's dinner or function. She had resigned herself to the fact that they would always be friends, but never lovers.

As always, she noticeably brightened on seeing Nick. She bounced up and down once on her toes and locked her fingers behind her back, almost laying her head on her left shoulder as she smiled in an exaggerated manner. 'Hello, Nick, it's nice to see you again.'

'Hi, Rachel,' Nick said in a monotone voice. Although he was very fond of her, somehow she was always that fifteen-year-old girl whom Nick had first met in Robert's home.

He turned back to Robert. 'You probably won't believe it...'

'What's this, Daddy?' Rachel asked, like an inquisitive

five-year-old, leaning forward to pick up a piece of loose parchment.

'Don't touch!' shouted Robert in a voice that startled both Rachel and Nick. Rachel stood up straight, her pretty face suddenly creased by the rebuke. 'This has nothing to do with you.' He threw his arm upwards. 'Why don't you go and make us some tea?' he said, without turning his face to look at her.

Rachel looked at Nick, who said nothing but smiled and gave the merest hint of a shoulder shrug. She turned and swept out of the room, making as big a sigh as she could manage to indicate her protest.

'That was a bit strong,' said Nick, suddenly feeling sorry for Rachel, who could now be heard opening and banging closed cupboards in the kitchen. He had never seen his partner shout at Rachel like that before.

Nick had seen a change in his old friend over the past few months. It was only just over a year until Robert's retirement, and Nick knew that soon the burden of carrying on the practice would be entirely down to him. All right, there were only twenty-four people employed by Stanhope Stephenson, but he knew how much Robert wanted to make sure that, when he left, the firm was on a secure footing for the future. It was still as precious to him as Rachel. After several years of threatening to retire, and never actually doing so, perhaps his final decision to call it a day was taking just a little too long to happen.

'Look,' said Nick in a deliberately quiet tone, as he gently laid his hand on Robert's arm. 'I don't want to worry you, but Joe found these in an old terracotta container on the site this morning.'

Robert stared at Nick and thought for a few moments. 'And you think this could be some historical find?' he eventually offered. It sounded like a statement, not a question.

'I don't know,' said Nick, throwing his hands open and casting his eyes around the room at the various bookshelves and cabinets stuffed with artefacts of one sort or another. 'You're the expert on this sort of thing. Your house is full of old relics and books. What do you think?'

Robert picked up a piece of the parchment. 'It's a hobby, Nick, not my profession. Besides, my interest is more in paintings and carvings.'

'Yes, but religious ones. Aren't scrolls like this normally some sort of ... of holy writing,' said Nick aware he sounded completely uninformed on the subject. He leaned on the table and looked up at Robert.

He looked back at Nick and gave an awkward little laugh. 'I think you're getting carried away, Nick. Those sorts of things are found in the Middle East, not in some hole in Central London?'

Nick snapped back at him. 'It was found 28 feet underground, Robert. How do you explain that?'

Robert looked intently at the scroll pieces. 'If we assume for just a moment that they are genuine,' said Robert, 'and I only said "assume",' he added quickly, 'you know what this could mean for the site.'

Nick slowly stood up straight and picked up the broken piece of scroll, looking at it closely as if hoping to find some flaw or date stamp that would confirm it as a fake.

Robert moved over to Nick and placed a hand on his shoulder. He looked deeply into Nick's eyes, in a way that Nick had not felt before, and in a manner that sounded like he was giving an instruction. 'I have always admired and respected your integrity, you know that. I know you will do the right thing.'

Nick looked at Robert directly. 'My client may see it differently. What do you think Mr Charles Forster would say if I told him I had closed down the site and reported to the Planning Authorities that he owns a site of potential historic interest, instead of a development site for 100,000 square feet of offices?'

Robert looked at Nick with a worried frown. 'Look, Nick, don't be too hasty. You have no evidence whatsoever to suggest that this is genuine. What have you done so far? Who else knows about this?'

Nick put the scroll back on the table and ran his hand through his hair, looking for all the world like a man who didn't have a clue what to do next. 'I've stopped all excavations, moved all work to the western end and issued an instruction to start pouring the foundations at that end from Monday.'

Robert interrupted. 'What about the steelwork? Have you stopped it being ordered?'

Nick nodded. 'Yes, but that's the problem. We can only delay it for seven days, otherwise the contractor is into claims, and even Forster couldn't live with fifty grand a week costs for too long. Anyway, we'll be back at that end of the site by next Friday. This has to be sorted by then.'

Robert walked over to the window. He stood for a moment, looking out at his manicured lawn, to the rose garden where the blooms gently rocked back and forth in the gentle summer breeze. He looked at the Mercedes soft-top parked in the drive next to Rachel's BMW. Simon, the gardener, waved to him as he picked up the loose apples from the lawn. He had everything he had ever wanted, but no longer someone to share it with. His life was becoming a never-ending dream, but one he wished he could wake up from. Without turning round he hesitantly remarked in a questioning tone. 'You could always just ignore it.'

Nick paused for a moment then said slowly, 'Yes, Robert ... I could.'

The drawing room door opened and in came Rachel,

carrying a large tray with a pot of tea, three cups and a tin of biscuits. She smiled radiantly as if the rebuke of a few minutes earlier had never happened. 'There we are!' she said, placing the tray on the table. 'Can't you tell me even a little bit about these things?' she teased, pouring out the tea.

Nick laughed. He had always loved the way she could casually dismiss a crisis as if she didn't even know there was one. She was a girl who could fall in a river and come out with a pearl in her mouth. He picked up the scrolls and carefully put them back in the bag. 'Come on,' he said, 'pour me some tea. I don't get paid to work Saturdays!'

Rachel smiled at Nick. 'Well, if it's that important I don't think a polythene bag is appropriate!' Nick looked at her. Of course she was right. If this was genuine, then he had to protect it. He realised that he may indeed be holding some important, not to say, valuable piece of history – something that made another insignificant City office block somewhat irrelevant.

'You're right, Rachel.' He started looking around the room. 'I need something that will protect it.'

Rachel looked down at the table. Her eyes opened wide and she bounced again on her toes. 'I've got it! The biscuit tin!'

Nick looked at it. The tin was the long red cylinder type made to hold digestive biscuits. He smiled again at Rachel. 'Sometimes you are the smartest girl I've ever met Miss Stanhope!'

He opened the tin, took out the packet of biscuits and placed the scroll pieces carefully inside. 'Perfect!' He leaned over and kissed Rachel on the forehead. He always kissed her on the forehead, as a father or an uncle would kiss a child. Rachel took what she could get.

Robert came over to the two of them and poured out the tea. 'What are you going to do Nick?'

The smile disappeared from Nick's face as he remembered why he was there. 'Well, I have to find out if this is genuine or not.'

Robert looked at Nick and took a deep breath. 'What you could do is take it to the British Museum. There's a Dr Weisman who is based there. He specialises in these sorts of things. He could probably tell you if it is genuine just by looking at it. Even if he can't, he'll have access to the right type of equipment to test it. I'm sure he could do it within a few days.'

Nick's face brightened and he stood up straight as if a great weight had suddenly been taken off his shoulders. 'Why didn't I think of that? Of course, the British Museum. How do you know this Dr Weisman?'

Robert looked down at the table. 'Oh, I met him once at an auction. He helped me pick a painting... I can't remember which one.'

'Well, that's great,' said Nick, picking up a tea cup. 'I'll go to the museum tomorrow and sort this out.'

Rachel looked at Nick. 'Oh, can I come with you, Nick? I love going into town, and I've never been to the British Museum.'

Nick looked at her. He knew he would be happier if he went by himself, but somehow his problem had turned into a great adventure. He would go to the museum, meet Dr Weisman, who would laugh and tell him it was a fake and then ... well, he could take Rachel for lunch.

He smiled at her. 'Why not?' he said.

Rachel bounced on her toes and clapped her hands. 'I'll phone the museum and pick you up tomorrow morning,' he added.

'Great! What time will I meet you?'

Nick smiled. 'Well, I better check with Dr Weisman first, don't you think! I'll phone you once I've spoken to him. We'll meet at Holborn Tube Station.'

'OK, I'll be waiting,' she said, a wide grin exploding across her pretty face.

'Well, I must be on my way,' said Nick, gently waving the biscuit tin as he stood up to go

Robert looked at him. 'You *will* let me know how you got on, Nick?' He watched Nick's face intently. 'Phone me tomorrow night, won't you?' he added.

Nick looked at Robert. 'Don't tell me you'll be disappointed if they're not genuine, Robert. Or do you want me to donate them to you if they are? Is that it!' he laughed. 'I'll tell Dr Weisman you recommended him,' he said as he turned to walk to the door.

'Oh don't bother,' said Robert. 'I'm sure he won't remember me – it was a few years ago now and I'm sure he meets dozens of people like me, looking for a piece of free advice.'

Nick carried on toward the door, with Rachel following close behind, her hands once again clasped behind her back, and her steps now bouncy and matching Nick's. 'OK,' he said, as he opened the front door. 'I'm glad you've got such a good memory though, Robert.' He waved nonchalantly as he started to walk down the path.

'Don't forget to phone,' shouted Robert, as Nick climbed into the Morgan and gently placed the tin on the passenger seat. He picked up his car mobile and called directory enquiries. He wanted this unexpected mission out of the way as quickly as possible. He took down the number for the British Museum and then entered it into the phone. It rang for what seemed like an eternity, Nick remembering finally that it was a Saturday. Eventually he was put through to Dr Weisman's 'assistant'.

'I would like to arrange to meet Dr Weisman as early as possible,' stated Nick in a businesslike manner, realising that he had to avoid sounding like some crank who thought he had just discovered the Holy Grail. 'I have an artefact that I am sure he would wish to have a look at.'

'Does Dr Weisman know you, Sir? Are you calling on behalf of a museum?' asked the assistant, sounding equally businesslike. Nick put the key in the ignition, and then picked up his Ray-Bans. He decided that there was no time to waste, but that he needed to at least sound credible.

'No,' answered Nick. 'Dr Weisman was recommended to me as the best in this particular field,' he added, guessing that such praise was less likely to illicit a negative response. It worked.

'Well, it is fortunate that Dr Weisman's trip to South America was cancelled last night. I am sure he can see you some time next week, now that his diary is free for a few days.'

'Is he available tomorrow?' asked Nick, eager to sort out the problem as quickly as possible. The voice on the other end began to sound irritated. 'Dr Weisman doesn't work Sundays. In any case, he has decided to visit friends in the country this weekend.'

'Would it be possible to see him on Monday first thing then?' asked Nick, trying hard not to sound *too* pushy.

'Well, Sir, I'm sure Dr Weisman will have a number of things to do first thing on Monday,' answered the assistant, her voice reverting to a defensive tone. 'The murder of the Chilean Director of Cultural Affairs has come as a shock to all of us, and we don't know what will happen to the several pieces we were to receive on loan for the South American Tribes exhibition next month.'

Nick couldn't think what to say. He had always imagined museums and museum curators as rather dull and uninspiring – dealing in dead objects but not death itself. Although he thought of himself as cultured, Nick would rather spend his time at White Hart Lane or in the West

End. Most times he had visited a museum he had found himself wandering round looking at the buildings themselves, the spaces they created, the grand scale and the use of materials he could never hope to work with. To him the exhibits were mere temporary occupants, and usually never made good use of the building's space anyway. But maybe life in a museum wasn't so dull after all.

The silence was eventually broken by the assistant. 'Look, I will pencil you in for 10.30 a.m.,' she said, sounding for all the world like a doctor's receptionist. 'But I suggest you phone first thing on Monday morning to check that he can see you.'

'That's great,' said Nick, immediately deciding not to phone first thing on Monday. 'I'll do that, and I appreciate your help. Thanks.'

Nick pressed the 'clear' button and started up the engine. Perhaps he still had time to make the Spurs match if the traffic wasn't too bad. As he sped along the country lanes back toward London he glanced at the tin and smiled. He thought about Rachel.

Chapter 3

As arranged, Nick met Rachel outside Holborn Tube Station at 10 a.m. sharp. He had phoned her on Saturday night and had decided that the less Robert was worried about this the better. He told Rachel not to mention their meeting.

As he walked toward her he noticed how grown up she had become, the short miniskirt accentuating the length of her slim legs, and the tight-fitting T-shirt exaggerating her curves. He felt slightly awkward at his own thoughts, like an older brother suddenly realising his kid sister wasn't a kid any more. It passed and he felt good as she grinned widely and waved at his approach.

'Ready, Indiana!' she joked, putting out her hand for Nick to hold, and setting off in the direction of the museum.

Nick laughed. 'Rachel, this is important! I could have a lot of trouble if this thing is real!' His attempt to sound serious failed miserably. Somehow with Rachel things never were serious.

'Oh come on, Nick, if this thing *was* real it would be far more interesting than another boring old office building. Think of the adventure! Who knows what the story of this scroll might be?'

Nick smiled. For a moment he let himself go, and he too wondered what would happen if it were genuine. He imagined some great hoard of archaeological storm-troopers descending on the site, a great plastic bubble thrown over the area to prevent the new world infecting the past –

huge diggers replaced by small trowels and toothbrushes as grain by grain, the hole, his hole, was sterilised, catalogued and removed. Then he pictured Charles Forster.

They entered the museum and approached a stern-looking man in a dark uniform. 'Excuse me, could you point the way to Dr Weisman's office please?' asked Nick.

'Yes, Sir,' replied the commissionaire. 'If you take the lift to the second floor, come out and turn left, the Ancient Relics department is third door down on the right.'

'Thank you,' replied Nick. As they walked towards the lift Rachel started to laugh. Nick looked at her. Did she find everything funny?

She looked at Nick. 'I'm sorry, but this guy sounds like a real bundle of laughs.' Nick looked back at her with a puzzled expression. 'The *Ancient Relics* department?' she spelled out. 'Sounds like the kind of guy I normally end up going out with!'

Nick looked at her with a surprised expression. Somehow he hadn't imagined Rachel 'going out' with 'guys'. He felt stupid. As they stepped out of the lift their footsteps echoed around the great empty space. The marbled walls and floors brought a welcome coolness to the hot day.

'God, it's like a hospital,' remarked Rachel, once again grabbing hold of Nick's hand. 'Do you think many people have died here?' Nick looked at her and shook his head. They reached the third floor on the right. It was wooden with a frosted-glass window, the word 'Reception' barely legible in worn-out letterset. Nick knocked and entered. Facing him was a great wooden desk, behind which sat a frail-looking woman dressed entirely in black, with her hair pulled back severely into a bun, and a pair of horn-framed glasses perched precariously on her nose.

Rachel, standing slightly behind Nick, whispered slowly, 'I think we've found the right department.' Nick tried not to react.

Nick smiled at the woman. 'Good morning, I have an appointment with Dr Weisman. I'm Nick Stephenson.'

Without responding the woman stood up, gave the faintest of smiles and walked back toward the door. 'Follow me, please. Dr Weisman is expecting you,' she stated as she brushed past them.

Nick and Rachel turned to follow her. Rachel's lips parted slightly as if she was about to speak. Nick looked at her and squeezed her hand. 'Not another word!' he whispered. Rachel shut her mouth and smiled.

The woman opened another door further down the corridor and beckoned Nick and Rachel inside. As they entered she closed the door behind them. A small bald man stood up from behind the desk, the half-moon glasses barely gripping the end of his nose as he bent his head to see over the top of them.

'Dr Weisman?' said Nick, as much to satisfy himself that this was the important historian Robert had spoken about, as by way of greeting.

'You must be Mr Stephenson,' he replied with a smile, offering a handshake to his guest, who duly obliged. 'And you must be ... Mrs Stephenson,' he added, looking at Rachel approvingly, and offering her his hand in turn. She shook it briefly, smiled but said nothing.

Nick looked at her and then back at Dr Weisman. 'No, no,' he said. 'This is Rachel Stanhope... She's ... a friend.' He grinned self-consciously. In all the times he had introduced Rachel to friends or business associates she was always his partner's daughter. Somehow it didn't work any more. She was a somebody ... but he wasn't quite sure who.

'Ah, I see,' said Dr Weisman with a smile and in a manner that Nick would somehow have expected from a small Jewish academic. 'So, you have something to show me I believe.'

'Oh yes,' said Nick, remembering the purpose for his being there. 'I would like you to look at something. I'm sure it will probably be a waste of time, I'm afraid, but I need a very quick and expert opinion on something I ... found,' said Nick. He had decided it would be wise not to give away any information that could be traced back to the site. 'A colleague suggested that you were just the man!' said Nick, trying to sound as though the whole thing was some wild goose chase.

'And where is this mysterious object?' asked Dr Weisman, trying to appear enthusiastic.

Nick slowly reached into the plastic bag suddenly conscious of the fact that the scroll was sitting inside the biscuit tin. He did not want to look a complete idiot in front of his clearly very learned acquaintance. Somehow he managed to quietly pull off the lid and slip out the scroll without Weisman noticing the receptacle. He glanced at Rachel, who smiled back apologetically.

Nick carefully emptied the contents into his hand, then placed both pieces on the desk.

Dr Weisman looked at them briefly without opening them up, and then at Nick. 'What do you *think* these are Mr Stephenson?' he asked, as he removed his glasses.

Nick looked at him. He felt rather foolish. This wasn't the *Antiques Roadshow*. Here he was with one of the world's foremost archaeologists, probably handing him a piece of old parchment worth £1.50 made in China or Hong Kong ... or Bradford, yet he still couldn't explain how it had been discovered. He had to *hear* it was nothing more than a worthless fake.

'The truth is I don't know what it is. I think the writing on it is Hebrew, but I don't know what it says ... or how old it is. I thought perhaps you could confirm it for me.' Nick glanced at Rachel. 'I know this sort of thing probably happens to you all the time.' He grinned. 'I'm sure you get lots of people who think they've found some treasure in their attic!'

Dr Weisman's expression remained unaltered. 'Is that where you found it?'

Nick looked at him. His smile disappeared. 'Well ... no, not exactly. I ... inherited it,' he said, trying to give some reason for his enquiry that sounded realistic and was remotely truthful.

Dr Weisman gave an audible sigh and put his glasses back on. He picked up the main part of the scroll like a man simply going through the motions. As he unrolled it he glanced occasionally at Nick. 'If I looked at every sheet of parchment, every piece of broken pottery, every potential "treasure" that comes through this door I would have no time to do my job.'

Nick began to feel agitated by Dr Weisman's tone. He didn't need the rebuke. He looked straight at him. 'And what exactly is your job?' he asked.

Dr Weisman looked up. 'My job, Mr Stephenson, is to educate, to inform, to impart knowledge on the British people – to make them learn from history, from great triumphs and disasters.' He stared intently at Nick, the vein in his neck clearly visible and pulsing quickly, pushing blood to a face that now suddenly appeared animated.

'This is an ignorant nation, Mr Stephenson,' he continued, his tone softening. 'They see history as some great treasure trove, reduced to a mere commodity to be sold like some unwanted piece of junk.'

Nick looked at the curator. 'I am not interested in the monetary worth of this parchment, Dr Weisman.' He meant it, of course, but somehow he doubted whether he would ever convince *him* of that.

Dr Weisman looked back at the parchment. 'Then you are indeed a man in a million, Mr Stephenson, and it is a long time since ...' He stopped in mid sentence and touched the edge of his glasses as if trying to adjust his focus. He lifted the parchment closer to his face. Nick looked at him and then at Rachel. Dr Weisman carefully rolled out another twelve inches of the scroll. Nick watched him with growing interest, the silence suddenly seeming to become meaningful. Almost under his breath Dr Weisman muttered, 'The Qumran Brotherhood!' his expression signalling disbelief.

Nick moved closer to him. 'The what?' he asked.

Dr Weisman didn't answer. He continued to stare intently at the scroll, his eyes wandering up and down the script, his forefinger now tracing the path of his eyes.

Nick looked at Rachel. She silently mouthed the words she had heard, shrugging her shoulders at the same time. 'Dr Weisman, does this mean something to you?' asked Nick.

He looked up at Nick and, as if suddenly woken from a trance, changed his expression completely. 'No ... well, yes,' he said, correcting himself. 'What I mean is I have seen something similar a long time ago,' he added, somewhat hesitantly.

'Does that mean this could be a genuine historical article?' asked Nick, his worst fears beginning to resurface.

Dr Weisman hesitated for a few moments, as if searching his mind for some memory filed away at the back of his mind. 'I am not sure. I would like to investigate this further. Is this all you have?' he asked.

Nick looked at him, his alarm growing. 'Yes,' he answered, hesitantly. 'Do you think there should be more?'

'Perhaps,' answered Dr Weisman. 'Where exactly did you get these from, Mr Stephenson? Did it come in ... any sort of ... container, or was it wrapped in something...? Most items like this are packaged in some way.' His voice tailed off, anticipating a response.

Nick was now on the defensive. 'I'd rather not say to be honest.'

Dr Weisman persisted. 'It could be very important. You see, most archaeological detective work can be done from a desk. We can check reference books, other manuscripts, contact other museums, but we need a starting point, and that is where the object was discovered. Now, where *exactly* did this come from?'

There was a long pause. Nick's mind was racing. What did he do? If he told him where it was found he would very likely have Dr Weisman and a whole team of archaeologists and planners, not to say lawyers, all over the site immediately. Yet, if he didn't, it might not be possible for Dr Weisman to check its authenticity and indeed confirm it was a cheap fake for some time. He ran his hand through his hair.

'Look, I can't tell you that at the moment. But I need to know quickly if it's genuine. How long do these things take?'

Dr Weisman groaned loudly and looked at Rachel. 'The man walks into my building, he asks for my help, I offer it and he does not return the compliment? Then he asks for a deadline!' Dr Weisman looked at Nick directly, his face betraying anger. 'I want to know where you got this from!'

Nick was alarmed at his reaction. He bent over the table and picked up the pieces of the scroll. Dr Weisman grabbed his arm. 'What are you doing?'

'Thank you for your help, Dr Weisman,' said Nick. 'I'm sorry to have troubled you.'

'No, wait! Please,' said Dr Weisman, his whole demeanour suddenly changing completely once again, as he realised Nick would not back down. 'All right, all right,' he pleaded. 'I will do what I can. It should only take me two or three days to carry out some checks. Please, give me the scroll.'

Nick stood up slowly as Dr Weisman let go of his arm. He looked intently at the bespectacled old man who suddenly appeared very keen to investigate his find. At least he could live with the timescale, although he was beginning to fear the worst.

'What is this Qumran...?' Nick couldn't remember the second word. Dr Weisman just stared back at him.

'Brotherhood,' added Rachel who had moved forward to Nick's side, her eyes also fixed on the curator, her face also now showing seriousness and concern.

Dr Weisman looked at both of them. Then he smiled and gave a small shrug of his shoulders. 'Your "scroll" has a mark, a symbol that looks like one used by an ancient religious sect ... the Qumran Brotherhood. It is this I would like to investigate further, Mr Stephenson.' He smiled again and his posture became more relaxed. 'I promise to look after your scroll very carefully. I can see it is a "treasured" inheritance, although I still believe it is probably a worthless fake I am afraid.'

Nick looked at Dr Weisman for a few seconds before separating the smaller part of the scroll and placing it carefully on the desk. 'You can keep this part. I'll hold onto the rest for now,' said Nick.

For a moment Dr Weisman moved forward as if to protest, but thought the better of it, Nick glaring at him intensely as he replaced the main part of the scroll back in the tin. 'Very well, Mr Stephenson, I will make the most of what you have given me. Where can I contact you?'

Nick instinctively reached for his wallet to produce a business card, stopping only after his hand had reached inside his pocket. 'You can get me on my mobile phone at this number.' He reached down onto the desk and picked up a pen, scribbling his number on the top of a yellow Post-it pad. 'If I don't hear from you by Wednesday, I'll call you,' he added, now feeling back in control of events. Dr Weisman nodded.

'Thank you for your assistance, Dr Weisman,' he remarked as he took Rachel's hand and led her to the door. 'We will see ourselves out.'

As he opened the door to leave, Nick glanced back and saw the old man already huddled over his desk, peering intently through his glasses at the parchment spread out in front of him. Nick frowned and ran his hand through his hair.

Chapter 4

Rachel talked non-stop on leaving Dr Weisman's room, all the way along the corridor, down the marble staircase, across the entrance hall and out into the street. Once outside Nick turned to her, placed his arms on her shoulders and looked straight at her. She stopped talking.

'Thank you,' he said, his face betraying neither amusement nor displeasure. 'I have to think about this, Rachel – it's not exactly what I expected to happen'.

'But Nick, it's so exciting. A mysterious brotherhood, a loopy old professor...'

'He's a doctor,' interjected Nick. Rachel ignored him. She was loving the whole business.

'Why should we leave *him* to enjoy himself?' she queried, her eyes wide open, and a large smile on her face. Nick looked at her, bemused.

'Look, he's given us the key! We could find out about this Qumran Brotherhood ourselves. It can't be that hard. Let's go to the Library now,' she added, grabbing Nick's arm and starting to walk down the street.

Nick grabbed her. 'Rachel, this isn't a game any more. If this thing's genuine I have a real problem. This could shut down the site and the firm could lose its most important client.' He brandished the tin at her. 'This *has* to be a fake.'

Rachel looked at him, the feeling of disappointment written all over her face. Then the beam reappeared. 'OK,' she enthused. 'Let's prove it's a fake! It's the same thing!'

Nick looked at her and shook his head. 'I give up. Let's go and have a coffee.'

As they walked down High Holborn through the busy commuter traffic and seemingly endless streams of black cabs and black suits, Nick began to reflect on the meeting with Dr Weisman. Perhaps Rachel was right; perhaps he should look into this himself. After all, it could take longer than a couple of days to clear it all up, and he couldn't afford any delay.

There was something about Dr Weisman as well, he thought, that went beyond the 'nutty professor' or fanatical archaeologist. Nick was sure that Weisman had dismissed the scroll as soon as he saw the parchment. Yet his reaction on finding the reference to the Brotherhood seemed almost over the top, like finding the Holy Grail. He didn't think Weisman was going to let this go easily.

Nick decided Rachel was right. He would have to continue his own search for the truth.

'Do you want to share your thoughts with me?' Rachel asked as they turned into the brightly lit coffee shop, the door wide open in an attempt to allow whatever breeze there was reach inside and cool the customers and waitresses alike.

'No, not at the moment,' Nick answered, deciding to keep control of the situation, at least for a few minutes more.

They sat down and started to chat over coffee and the two Chelsea buns that Rachel had insisted were pleading to be eaten. It was a long time since Nick had eaten a Chelsea bun.

The conversation started with Rachel explaining how she would redecorate the British Museum – 'Give it a bit of a woman's touch' – and by the time they had finished their second coffee, she was on to where to find the freshest ingredients for the perfect *Palatschinke*, an Austrian crêpe she had learned to cook at night school.

Nick said very little. He didn't get the chance. He

considered briefly the mixed emotions of being comfortable in an attractive woman's company again, and being potentially on the brink of bankruptcy. Both, he concluded, were exaggerations.

'Come on,' he said finally, after Rachel had stopped for breath and finished the final piece of bun. 'Where's the nearest library?' he added, in a manner which suggested he hadn't heard her suggest it in the first place. Rachel smiled broadly.

'We've just been to it. You can't get much bigger than that!'

Nick sat back. The British Library. Of course, they had just been in one of the biggest libraries in England. He hesitated.

'I don't know if I want to go back there.'

'Why not?' asked Rachel.

Nick couldn't think of a logical answer. He shrugged his shoulders. 'Isn't there a ... public library near here?'

Rachel smiled again. 'There's one ten minutes from here. Holborn Library. Used to be a church ... off High Holborn. Mummy took me there when I was a child.' She frowned as she thought suddenly of her mother's face. 'It's a bit downmarket from the one we've just come from though. What's wrong with...?'

Nick interrupted as he shot out his hand toward her. 'At least it won't be full of tourists. It'll be perfect. Come on!' Rachel grabbed his outstretched hand and gave a small skip as they headed off.

The library was dark and grey, even although streams of light poured into the room through the long, narrow windows, catching dust particles suspended in the air and creating the effect of a great silent solution filling the space. At least it was cool.

They found the reference section and approached the smart-looking young woman at the desk, who smiled eagerly at Nick as though desperate to help another customer with some life-saving information.

'Can I help you, Sir?' she asked in anticipation.

'I hope so,' answered Nick, trying desperately to look confused and lost.

'I'm looking for information on ... scrolls,' said Nick, realising that this wasn't really very precise.

'Scrolls? Ah, you want Henry' replied the young woman, the smile still there, but beginning to wane.

'He's our expert on that sort of thing.' Suddenly she had the air of disappointment, like a waitress in a posh restaurant who has just been asked for a chicken sandwich.

She moved over to a wooden table behind the desk and very gently tapped a small brass bell, which gave an apologetic sounding 'tring' that echoed gently through the quiet room.

Nick and Rachel looked around the room instinctively, wondering what would happen next. The young woman came back to the desk and smiled formally at them. She said nothing.

Within a matter of seconds, a tall gawky-looking young man appeared at the side of the desk, an eager look on his speckled face. Nick knew immediately this was Henry.

'This lady and gentleman have an enquiry about scrolls, Henry,' the librarian stated, in a way that suggested he was not the brightest of individuals.

Henry's eyes lit up and he nodded gleefully. Nick surmised that if Henry were a dog, his tail would be wagging.

Henry turned to Nick. 'Any particular scrolls, Sir? Or just scrolls in general?'

Rachel shook her head. 'We're interested in the Qumran Brotherhood.'

The young man's eyes lit up even more. 'Ah, you want the Dead Sea Scrolls!' he said victoriously. 'Fascinating subject.' He leaned toward them, a serious frown on his face indicating the imminent delivery of some very important fact. 'Do you know they've still only translated a fraction of the Dead Sea Scrolls?'

Nick, who had instinctively leaned toward the young man in anticipation, raised his eyebrows. 'Really?' he stuttered, trying to sound interested.

Henry continued. 'Very strange. Here we are at the very end of the twentieth century, and it takes nearly fifty years for some of the world's eminent authorities and organisations to translate just a fraction of perhaps the greatest collective work of literature ever written?'

Nick glanced at Rachel. Her eyes were large and focused intently on the young man.

'Where does the Qumran Brotherhood come into it?' she asked.

'They wrote them, basically – or, at least, wrote some of them. Look, I'll give you some books to look at. What is your particular interest?'

Nick paused for a moment. 'Oh! I came across a reference to the Qumran Brotherhood in some old papers I found, and I wanted to find out more information.'

Henry smiled back at Nick. 'Well, try these two to start with. They're the most up-to-date translations of the manuscripts and commentaries that have been written. Now that the Americans are on board maybe we'll get somewhere!' He noted some titles on a piece of paper.

Nick looked at him. 'The Americans?'

'The Huntington Library in San Marino,' answered the young man. 'Five years ago the Israeli's allowed some American colleges access to the Scrolls, and they've been busy piecing them back together again. There's a hell of a lot of them in one hell of a mess, as they would say!'

he added in his best attempt at an American accent and then chuckled loudly in a manner that Nick thought was rather incongruous with the surroundings.

Nick took the piece of paper from the young man and thanked him for his help. As soon as he had taken it, Rachel grabbed it out of his hand and headed towards the relevant section. She found both books within a matter of minutes, kept the thick one for herself and handed Nick the other with a smile.

'I'll read quicker than you,' she remarked as she brushed past him and headed for one of the library's old wooden desks.

Nick followed and sat down opposite her, producing the small notepad that he invariably carried with him in his pocket. He removed a pencil from the binding and placed it neatly on the desk next to the book. He had carried the pad and pencil ever since university, his artistic bent filling many pages and several books with small sketches of interesting details from buildings that he had visited or simply passed by in his travels. He had often considered architecture to be the biggest form of plagiarism – on the other hand, he had rationalised, why reinvent the wheel?

He sat the pad and pencil on the desk beside the book and opened the first page. He started reading the introduction, but was interrupted almost immediately by an excited whisper from Rachel.

'Here it is. Look!' She was pointing at the page in front of her which appeared to Nick to be about a quarter of the way through the book. He was impressed by how quickly she seemed capable of reading.

'It says here that the Scrolls were written by the Qumran Brotherhood who lived in Jordan over two thousand years ago, and that there are over six hundred of them'. She looked up at Nick. 'No wonder Weisman looked surprised.' Nick just shook his head.

She went on: 'There are over ten thousand fragments that have been recovered from caves on the northern shores of the Dead Sea, but guess what?'

Nick looked at her. He had absolutely no idea what she was likely to reveal next. He cocked his head to one side. 'Go on, surprise me. They were all typed on a word processor perhaps?'

Rachel gave a sarcastic grin. 'Exactly the opposite it would seem,' she added in a superior sort of way.

There was silence for a few seconds. Nick looked at her in anticipation. 'Well,' he asked eventually. 'Come on, tell me.'

Rachel looked at him with a smile that indicated she thought she had won a little battle.

'It would appear that since they were found in 1947, just after the Second World War, only about 10 per cent of them have been translated and published, just as the librarian said. Don't you think that's strange?' Nick thought about it. It was.

'It says the Scrolls are made of parchment, although there were some which were written on papyrus and leather,' Rachel added.

Clearly their scroll was neither leather nor papyrus and although Nick had never held something made of parchment before, the material didn't seem that old to him. He felt himself concluding, with some relief, that it must be a fake. But Weisman would have known that immediately. It wasn't until he read the scroll that he started to act peculiarly. Nick didn't feel satisfied that he had got to the bottom of the mystery; in fact he was even more confused.

As he read through the book Rachel had given to him, Nick's wonderment at the story unfolding before him grew rapidly. He read how the Qumran Brotherhood had, over almost three hundred years from 200 BC, written a huge body of religious work ending in AD 68, about the time of the death of Jesus. The Scrolls had reflected beliefs held by many religions, but were particularly seen as the basis for Judaism. The Brotherhood had been set up along almost communistic lines as a kind of model House of Israel, the first kibbutz, perhaps, designed to prepare the way for the imminent coming of the Kingdom of God and the Day of Judgement. The Scrolls included manuals of discipline, hymn-books, biblical commentaries and apocalyptic writings, and included fragments of every book in the Old Testament.

Only a small group of people had been allowed access to study the Scrolls and translate them. The work had been carried out by a core team who comprised mainly Roman Catholic clergy and scholars who, for over forty years, had undertaken the painstaking task of assembling and piecing together the Scrolls, many of which were only tiny fragments. Several books had been published on the Scrolls by members of the group, but latterly some other historians and theologians had also published books interpreting the work that had been published, and criticising the fact that so little information had been released to the wider academic community and the world at large.

Nick was unsure whether this was either a very long and boring exercise in archaeology, or one of the greatest detective stories he had ever read. He looked up and noticed that Rachel was writing something down on his notebook. 'What are you writing?' he asked, by now convinced that he was at the wrong end of some elaborate hoax.

She giggled and lowered her head, almost touching the book as she held back laughter.

Nick looked at her blankly. 'What's so funny?

'It's a name,' she answered without looking up from

the page. 'Cardinal Cornelli, he's a world expert on the Scrolls. It says here he is one of only a handful of people and one of the first to have sight of them and he has spent his life studying them from his base at the cathedral in Milan.' She shrugged her shoulders and looked at Nick. 'Cornelli was the name of the guy who owned our local chip shop.'

Nick shook his head. He decided to ignore her humorous add-on. 'Look, Rachel, the scroll I have is neither leather nor papyrus and there is no way that it could have found its way to Holborn if it was real. I don't know what it is, but it's not a Dead Sea Scroll'.

Rachel looked at him, her face still beaming. 'Well, how do you explain it then? You saw Dr Weisman's reaction when he read it – Why did he do that, and why would he keep a piece to examine it?' Nick couldn't answer those questions either.

Rachel carried on. 'This is really interesting, Nick, I never knew about all this stuff. Pretty hairy really. I've always thought of the Bible as a sort of paperback first written a couple of hundred years ago, and yet here's the original proof copies hidden in a cave for over two thousand years!' Nick smiled at her – he wasn't a religious person, but the worth of such a find was not lost on him. He felt slightly uncomfortable at the strength with which the story first told in the Scrolls had manifested itself over the following two thousand years.

Rachel again interrupted his thoughts. 'What language did you think was on the scroll?'

I have no idea,' Nick answered. 'It looked as if it might be Hebrew.'

'Well,' replied Rachel, 'it appears that they were written in different languages – Hebrew, Aramaic and Greek, It also says that, as well as the biblical writings, other scrolls were found.'

50

Nick could see her drawing her finger down the page. 'Look at this,' she exclaimed, 'they found something called the War Scroll, which it says describes the final battle of good against evil.' She looked up at Nick. 'Don't you find this a bit scary?' she asked, clearly believing that all the Scrolls must be true because they were so old.

Nick closed his book. He looked at Rachel. 'Why don't you just look at these Scrolls as a big library? If we had been living two thousand years ago we would be sitting here reading the real thing, not a book about them. Anyway, you said it yourself, if you go to the religious section you will be able to read a *modern* version of them, a reprint if you like, so what's all the fuss about?'

Rachel looked at him, her face reflecting disbelief. 'How can you sit there and not be moved by this, Nick. Just think of the number of people in the world to whom these writings are everything. Don't you think they are important? Why do people pay millions for a Van Gogh when every student flat in London has a £5 poster of *The Sunflowers* on their wall?'

They stared at each other for a few seconds. Nick thought about it. They didn't seem important to him, merely an unwanted interference in the course of one of his jobs. But he could see their importance to millions of others and, as a result, their potential value. Perhaps, he thought, that was why it had taken so long to release information on the Scrolls or allow the wider academic and religious community access to them. All the same it did seem curious to him that such a small part of the writings had ever been released.

'Haven't you got any religious feelings?' Rachel added.

Nick thought for a moment. His life was too busy for religion. Whether there was a God or not seemed like a nice theoretical question which was best thought about after too much wine – a dinner-party game perhaps. He

51

had too much baggage from his past to believe that a 'higher being' would allow so much pain in the world.

Rachel asked him again. 'Don't you believe in anything?' Nick tried to shrug her question off, but Rachel continued to stare at him.

'Well,' he finally offered, 'I remember when I was young thinking that God was basically like a headmaster.' He stopped and stared ahead.

Rachel waited patiently for the next line. It wasn't coming. Eventually she prompted him. 'A headmaster?'

'Yes,' Nick continued. He knew he was sounding silly, but for some reason he didn't really understand, he wanted to get it out. 'You see, I knew that you had to be good, and that this was the basis for getting into Heaven, and, if you were bad, God decided you couldn't get in and you went to Hell.'

Rachel grinned. 'Pretty deep thinking, Mr Stephenson! Not very original, but I suppose the simplicity saves it!' Nick looked at her, but didn't smile.

'Yes, but what I couldn't get my mind round was how we are judged. If you look over the course of our lives none of us is really better or worse than the next person. I imagined Heaven as a sort of utopian city with a big wall round it and, like all such places, a finite amount of people can get in. So how are we judged? How does God decide?'

Rachel shrugged her shoulders. She hadn't really thought about 'Heaven' like this.

Nick continued, now seemingly recounting a childhood puzzle that he had forgotten about for a long time and was suddenly revisiting as a mature adult.

'How can God just keep adding people to this place? I used to think that if there were three billion people in the world at any one time only, say, half of them would get in. So God would have to set a standard to judge everyone against. As long as you scored over 50 per cent you were in.' He gave a little chuckle. Rachel said nothing.

'I decided that only 51 per cent would be enough, and I was going to do everything I could to make sure I used up my 49 per cent of sins! As long as I was the one billion, four hundred and ninety-nine thousand whatever, I was OK.'

He looked at Rachel and smiled. 'That's as religious as I get I'm afraid.' He looked back down at the book.

Rachel shook her head. Somehow she wished she hadn't asked the question.

'What do we do now then?' asked Rachel, deciding not to continue with that particular discussion.

Nick smiled at her. 'We could always have another Chelsea bun,' he replied.

Rachel smiled, 'I'd prefer a proper lunch!'.

The telephone was replaced slowly, deliberately, back onto its terminal, and the room was silent again. There was doubt, of course, and the message would need to be verified, confirmed and double-checked.

There had been false alarms in the past, but this time the source was far more reliable, almost perfect in fact. That simply made it all the more surprising. Nevertheless, he would need to be patient, cautious and have no doubt before they made any move. They would only have one opportunity, a single strike, or all would be lost and their dream, his dream, his *right,* would have passed them by.

Chapter 5

Nick tried to remember how long it had been since he had been in a woman's company for so long. The leisurely pavement lunch in Covent Garden had been short on food, but high in conversational topics. Rachel wasn't slow at expressing her opinions on everything from the iceberg lettuce in her salad, to the architectural merits of the surrounding buildings. Nick found himself laughing at everything.

She persuaded him to let her accompany him to the two buildings on his 'site visit' list, projects he had recently finished but were still subject to 'snagging lists' by the firm. Nick took great pride in ensuring that all of his projects were brought to a complete conclusion, and that the client was completely satisfied with the end result of each scheme. Someone else may be paying, but, to Nick, each building was his.

The first was a small shopping mall in Croydon, a long-term job that Nick had taken particular pride in since the developer had let him indulge his own fantasies in creating a design for the terrazzo flooring of the mall. Rachel, of course, thought this was wonderful. Nick imagined what weird and wonderful ideas *she* would have come up with. Probably not the subtly coloured mosaic design Nick had finally settled on featuring the head of the Medusa, her serpent hair spreading out from the central atrium to each of the shop units, leading the unsuspecting shoppers into the brightly lit money traps. The developer loved it, even if the perverse symbolism would have horrified the customers if they'd understood it.

Later in the afternoon they visited an office refurbishment scheme in Kensington. It wasn't on the scale of the Holborn job, but gave Nick a different sort of satisfaction. He had known the owner, a small-time accountant who treated the four-room office like his home, since his days at college. Nick was a friend and he wouldn't have trusted the work to someone he didn't know.

Rachel smiled her way through their visit as usual, drawing several admiring glances from the owner, something that did not go unnoticed by Nick.

By five o'clock Nick had finished his business, and was heading for the office to check his mail. 'Where do you want me to drop you then?' he asked Rachel as the Morgan wound its way through the stifling city roads, the hood down to let whatever breeze there was do its work.

'Oh, let's have a whole day together,' she pleaded, looking wistfully at Nick and cocking her head on her right shoulder.

Nick laughed. 'I'm only going into the office to check my mail.'

'I don't mind', Rachel responded. 'Let's go out to dinner.' She was nothing if not direct.

Nick thought for a moment. He had enjoyed the day, but he wasn't used to having someone around him all the time. It wasn't Rachel – he just liked his own space.

'You're thinking of a reason to say no, aren't you?' she added, looking straight at him.

'Come on, Rachel, we've spent the whole day together already! I'm working for goodness' sake!'

'You haven't answered me,' she added, ignoring his statement. 'You can't think of a good reason, can you?'

Nick smiled. He had enjoyed himself, but didn't want to feel pressurised. The funny thing was, though, that he *wasn't* feeling pressurised. He couldn't think of a reason not to say yes. He just felt that for some reason he shouldn't.

'Look, Nick, I'm not pushing. I've had a great day.' Her voice began to sound more serious. 'Do you remember when Dad used to bring me into the office and I would sit at your drawing board and sketch pictures of the things in your room?'

Nick laughed. 'As I recall it was usually sketches of George Michael!'

'I never did!' Rachel replied trying to sound hurt. 'Anyway, it was the other one I liked,' she added. 'I loved it when Daddy took me in. He always seemed so ... proud to show me *his* office, the place that he had created.' Her voice stiffened. 'Mummy always said it was the most important thing in his life, and that I should be very proud of what he had achieved.' There were a few moments of silence while Nick kept the Morgan purring along. 'She was wrong, Nick.'

He looked at her, the smiling face now gone, a sad reflective look making the porcelain skin look very pale and fragile. He had never really spoken to her about Elizabeth. The age difference at the time seemed too great, their relationship too remote for him to help her. Yet, she had always seemed in control, even then harbouring a resilience that was hidden behind the fragile-looking facade.

He touched her hand. 'I know, Rachel. She gave your father more strength and determination than she ever knew.' He felt warmth growing inside him that he didn't recognise. She seemed so vulnerable. 'Look, I'll tell you what, why don't we go straight out after I've been into the office and we'll have a light supper... Save us going home first.'

Rachel forced a grin. 'Don't do that, Nick. I'm sorry I sounded pushy. I'm sure you've got things to do,'

'Nonsense! I've got nothing planned.' He felt he sounded insincere, but he realised he meant it. 'Rachel, I really want to. I promise. I wouldn't have said so if I didn't mean it.'

Rachel just looked at him and smiled warmly.

The fun and laughter of the afternoon rolled into the evening. The 'light supper' had ended up as a long meal, with both of them losing track of time. The outside table at Nick's favourite Greek restaurant added to the atmosphere of the balmy early evening, and the two bottles of house white sealed the feeling that they were both on some Mediterranean island.

Nick decided to leave the Morgan in the office car park, remembering to remove the biscuit tin, which had by now become a sort of running joke shared only by them. He persuaded himself that a taxi home to his apartment with Rachel for coffee was a logical end to the day. Rachel agreed.

They came out of the lift and walked toward the door of the flat, Rachel swinging the biscuit tin from one hand to another. When they were only two strides away Nick suddenly stopped. He reached out and grabbed Rachel's arm. She froze, looking straight at him. Nick pointed at the door. It was slightly ajar, and through the crack he could faintly see an occasional flash of light; he assumed, from a torch.

He looked at Rachel and put a finger to his lips, instructing her to be quiet. She nodded. He moved forward slowly and peered through the crack between the door and the frame. There was definitely someone in his flat. He put his ear to the crack, hoping to ascertain if there was more than one of them. There was no conversation, only the sound of drawers opening and closing, and the rustling of papers. Nick decided he could handle one.

He gently opened the door, hoping to see inside and

place the intruder before making his move. As he did so, the door creaked, just as Nick spotted the man, all in black and wearing a balaclava, his torch shining on the plans lying on top of Nick's drawing board. Startled, the intruder turned and shone his torch straight at Nick who had now burst into the room. Nick put his right arm up to screen his eyes, and rushed toward the light. The intruder made for his pocket and pulled out a short, black-handled knife, the blade momentarily flashing in the moonlight streaming through the arch window of the flat.

As he lunged, Nick caught sight of the blade and thrust out his forearm to cushion the blow. The intruder struck out, catching the arm of Nick's jacket and ripping the material cleanly from wrist to elbow. The momentum of Nick's lunge took him straight into the intruder's body, the pain of the deep cut inflicted on his arm only becoming suddenly noticeable to him as he tumbled forward onto his drawing table, the intruder momentarily pinned beneath him. As he started to scream under the sudden pain, the noise was stifled by a fist that caught the side of his face and sent him tumbling onto the floor.

The intruder, shaken by the attack, leapt to his feet and ran towards the door. Just as he reached it, Rachel came rushing in, finally succumbing to the stifled noises coming from within the dark room.

The door flew open and caught the intruder full in the face. For a split second Rachel looked into his eyes, dark and cold, staring intently and, it appeared to her, in fear as though begging for forgiveness. Rachel froze, and before she could come to terms with the situation before her, the intruder sprang to his feet and barged his way past her, fleeing out of the apartment and down the stairs, knocking the biscuit tin out of her hand and onto the floor of the flat.

Rachel looked around the dimly lit apartment. 'Nick,

where the hell are you? Nick, are you OK?' she asked, still frozen to the spot, her hands behind her pushed against the apartment wall.

There was a dull sound from the floor about five yards in front of her. The noise suddenly made her more aware of the situation, and instantly she knew he was all right. Reaching to her right she lit a side lamp and immediately saw Nick lying on his side holding his right forearm, blood flowing from a long gash creating a small pool of blood on the flat's wooden floor. Stifling a gasp, Rachel quickly ran to Nick's side and, tearing back the sleeve of his shirt, lifted his arm to quell the flow.

'It's OK, Nick,' she gasped, 'it's not deep. We'll soon fix this.' She looked ahead and noticed a towel hanging from the kitchen wall.

'Hold your arm up like this,' she said, pushing his hand as high in the air as she could before running to the kitchen, grabbing the towel and soaking it under the cold tap.

She returned to his side, took a deep breath and then pushed the towel against his arm, holding it as tight as she could.

Nick sat up, orientating himself for the first time since the attack. He looked at Rachel. 'Are you OK?'

She smiled, suddenly feeling more relaxed. He was safe. God, how she was glad.

'I'm fine, how do you feel? I don't think this cut's too deep,' she answered, trying her best to sound calm.

Nick looked at the towel. He winced as he suddenly felt the pain in his arm. 'Bastard!' he said, pushing the towel harder against his forearm. 'Probably after my Springsteen collection!'

Rachel smiled. She couldn't laugh. Being with Nick for twelve hours had been everything she had ever dreamed of – intriguing, fun, unpredictable, and ultimately also dangerous. Oh sure, it made it all the more exciting, but there was something vulnerable about the guy. What if she hadn't been here? What if she hadn't hit the intruder with the door? Would he have finished Nick off? He was vulnerable, and that's where she fitted in. In that split moment she decided that he needed her, even more than she needed him.

'I think you'll live,' she said calmly, her hand pressing against his forehead. She leaned forward, her face slowly closed in on his and taking control of the moment she gently and slowly moved her fingers down his cheek and across to his partly open lips. Rachel instinctively closed her eyes and delicately kissed his cheek and then moved slowly to his mouth.

Nick didn't flinch. He closed his eyes, and as he felt the gentle kiss on his lips he put his left hand behind Rachel's head and drew her toward him. The sensations flooded through him. The sharp pain in his arm subsided briefly as the warmth and feeling of Rachel's kiss seemed to flow through his body, his mind seemingly bouncing around the room, out of control yet confined to some tiny space.

He suddenly felt a sharp pain and broke away. 'Aagh, it hurts!'

Rachel pulled back. 'I'm sorry!' she spurted, suddenly remembering the predicament that Nick was in. 'I think we should get you to a hospital – this may need stitches.' She stood up, still holding the towel against his arm.

Nick slowly climbed to his feet, giving her a little smile as she removed her hand from his arm. Concern spread across her face and Nick thought that this made her look even more attractive and desirable.

'Where's your phone, Nick? I'll call the police,' she asked.

Nick nodded in the direction of the kitchen. 'It's over there on the wall beside the...' He stopped. He scanned quickly around the room. Without saying a word he walked to the bedroom door, pushed it open and switched on the light.

'What is it?' Rachel asked, watching him intently.

'Notice anything strange?' he asked, his eyes still wandering around the flat.

Rachel looked around. 'Nick, I've never been here before. It looks like most flats I've ever seen.' She paused. 'No, it's a lot nicer than most flats I've ever seen actually.'

'Exactly!' said Nick. 'Nothing out of place. No drawers emptied onto floors, no lamps toppled over onto tabletops.' Rachel stared at him and shrugged her shoulders.

'Perhaps you just disturbed him as he was getting started.'

Nick ignored her remark. 'Why was the front door open?' he asked, almost in a whisper.

He looked up at Rachel who had walked across the room toward the telephone.

'Don't phone the police,' he said in a firm voice. Rachel looked at him, a puzzled expression on her face.

'What is it?' she asked.

Nick hesitated. Was he becoming paranoid? 'I think he was looking for something,' he offered slowly and to himself. Could there really be a connection?

Rachel gave a nervous laugh. 'Yeah, your Springsteen collection; you said yourself...'

He cut her off. 'Not on my drawing board.' He walked quickly to the board. Several large drawings lay on top, just as he had left them. To the side, though, he noticed two legal documents, old title plans showing the site at Holborn that he knew he had left with the other papers on a shelf next to the drawing board. They were printed on parchment. He picked them up and replaced them slowly on the shelf, his mind racing.

Rachel was now standing beside him, the girlish grin gone completely, as she looked intently at Nick's face.

'What is it Nick?' she asked. 'Do you know what he was after?'

Nick looked at her and smiled. He glanced round the room and caught sight of the biscuit tin; he walked over to it and picked it up off the floor. He couldn't tell Rachel what he thought. Anyway, it was pretty unlikely and far-fetched, just the sort of thing Rachel would want to believe. But if it was true, he realised that they could both be in a lot of danger. He had to take control of the situation quickly.

'Look', he said, putting his 'good' arm around her shoulder. 'I think it's time we said goodnight. I'll call you a taxi.'

'What?' interrupted Rachel, pushing him away. 'Please, Nick, I'm not a child! Besides I'm not leaving until I'm satisfied the bleeding has stopped.' She made her way to the bathroom and found some bandages. When she returned she firmly placed the bandage around the wound; she remembered reading somewhere that pressure on a wound would stop the bleeding.

Nick looked at her as she worked at stopping the blood flowing. His mind flew back to the thoughts that had raced through him as she kissed him.

'You think it's got something to do with the scroll, don't you?' Rachel asked, interrupting his thoughts.

'Don't be silly,' he answered, trying to appear as though it had never crossed his mind.

'Then tell me what you do think?' she answered. 'I think I deserve that at least.'

'Look, Rachel, I don't want you to get involved in this any further. I don't know what I think. If it has got something to do with the scroll, then I certainly don't want you getting mixed up in it.' He lifted up his arm.

'I'm already mixed up in this,' Rachel said, looking directly at him and releasing her grip of his arm. 'That should stop the bleeding. How does it feel?'

Nick looked at his bandaged arm. 'The pain's not so bad, I'll be all right, but I think it would be safer if you went home!'

He could see disappointment in Rachel's eyes. He knew deep down that she wanted to stay the night and he then realised how much *he* wanted her to stay.

'I'm not leaving you alone tonight, I ... I'll sleep on the couch,' Rachel replied.

'No', said Nick firmly. 'I'll call you a taxi, Rachel ... please. I'll be fine,' he added, softening his tone. 'I'll call you ... I promise.' He reached out and gently brushed her cheek with the back of his hand. He had waited this long for someone to penetrate his life. He could wait a few days longer if it was to become more permanent.

Chapter 6

As soon as Nick opened his eyes the pain was there. He grimaced and instinctively held his forearm with his right hand. He looked down at the bandage. At least there was no sign of blood. Rachel's first-aid training had passed the test. Slowly he got out of bed and walked over to the kitchen area. The hot London summer showed no sign of abating. Nick enjoyed the heat, but somehow today it belonged somewhere else. For once it just felt uncomfortable, an unwanted guest.

He took a tin of Kitekat from the kitchen cupboard and pressed it hard against the automatic tin opener on the wall. Morris purred around the bottom of his legs and licked his toes. Nick's mind wandered back to the previous night. He suddenly remembered the scroll. His eyes shot across to the black ash table in the dining room. The digestive biscuit tin sat motionless where he had left it the night before. Of course it was, he thought to himself. But he couldn't help connecting the two things – the break-in and the scroll. Was someone aware of it? Were they trying to get it? If so, why?

Morris scratched at Nick's foot, a gentle reminder that the tin opener had done its job and Morris was ready for breakfast. Nick poured the contents of the tin into Morris' bowl and placed it on the tiled floor. As he bent down, his eyes caught a brilliant pinhead of light on the floor about three feet ahead of him. Nick bent over slowly and picked up the object carefully. He sat it in the palm of his hand. It was silver, and no more than two centimetres in size, shaped like a triangle sitting on top of a circle.

On the back, a small pin protruded no more than one centimetre. Nick decided that it was a stud of some sort, a lapel badge or perhaps even an earring. But where had it come from? He played with it in his hand for a few minutes. It could be Mrs Johnson's. No, it didn't seem the sort of jewellery she would wear. Perhaps Rachel had dropped it. He thought back to the night before. He tried to picture her face. He pictured her hair, the little kink above her left temple, and the neat way it toppled over her shoulder like a cascading waterfall, the natural highlights adding to the effect. He could envisage her cute little nose, and her infectious smile, with the slightly crooked eye tooth on the right. Then her eyes, blue, steely blue, like a child's marbles.

He was pleased with himself for remembering so much, but then he *was* trained to notice detail. He couldn't see her earrings though, if she wore any. He lingered on his vision, his mind wandering back to the Tube station, the café, the Chelsea buns, and the laughter. He recalled the library and the look on her face when she realised that he was cut. He liked that look. More importantly, he thought to himself, there was no feeling of guilt. Perhaps he *would* call her today.

He walked over to the table, opened the digestive tin and dropped the object into it. He replaced the lid and went back into the bedroom. He caught sight of himself on the bedside mirror. He touched his arm, but decided not to touch the bandage as he wasn't sure he could get it back on if his arm was still bleeding.

He thought back to the previous night and realised that they had both been lucky, yet he remained convinced the intruder was after something in particular. He ran his hand through his hair.

* * *

The large, strong hand reached down slowly in the dim light and touched the silver handle on the oak desk drawer. He tapped the ornate metal gently, but did not open the drawer. He knew it would still be there, waiting patiently for its moment. He wondered whether this time that moment was almost upon them. He could picture it in his hand, like a prophet holding the words that would bring deliverance to his people. He closed his eyes for a few moments. He knew that there would be much work to be done, preparations made, favours called in and a truth unleashed that would change the world for ever. He took a long, deep breath and held it for what seemed like an eternity, blocking out all noise to allow him to concentrate his mind. It felt as though the world was suddenly rushing toward him, and he was ready.

It was time.

As he drove into the site Nick was pleased to see a group of six or seven workmen busily pouring concrete at the far end. Their bare backs and chests glistened with perspiration. The noise of the Morgan stopping sharply on the dusty compound car park brought Joe out of the office before Nick could reach it.

'Everything OK?' asked Nick, half expecting to hear of further finds, or some other problem.

'Well, it might be, or then again...' Joe didn't finish the answer, merely shaking his head slightly and wiping sweat off his brow.

Nick looked at him. 'What does that mean?'

'It's probably nothin', but we've 'ad a visit from the building inspectors' office today,' said Joe.

Nick waited for him to go on, but Joe just looked at him. 'What happened to your arm?'

Nick just shrugged his shoulders. 'Oh, I ... had an

accident last night.' He moved swiftly on, eager to change the subject. 'So? This visit wasn't scheduled?' he asked.

Joe shook his head. 'No, that's the thing. We're not due to 'ave a visit till we let 'em know the foundations are complete.'

'Well, what did he want?' asked Nick.

'He said he wanted to check the drawings as they had heard that we had made some changes to the plans without informing the Council,' answered Joe.

'What did you say?' asked Nick, his curiosity now changing to concern.

'Well, I told him there hadn't been any changes and the planning drawings were still the ones we were building to.' Joe looked for reassurance. 'There ain't been any changes, have there?' he added.

'No, of course not, Joe. I would have given you them. Did he say who told him this?'

'No. But he asked for a full copy of all the drawings for the site,' added Joe.

Nick looked at him in disbelief. 'What! Who the hell was this guy? That's over one hundred drawings. They've already got three copies down there. What was his name?'

Joe looked at Nick sheepishly. 'He said his name was Smith.'

'Smith?' repeated Nick in a sarcastic tone, instinctively putting both hands on his hips and darting a disbelieving look at his foreman.

Joe nodded his head. 'Look, I know what you're thinking. When he started looking at the plans on the wall and the papers on the desk I told him I had things to do and gave him your name and mobile if he wanted drawings.'

Nick thought for a moment. 'What time was this?'

'About 7.45 this morning,' answered Joe.

'Jesus, Joe! Do you think Council officers visit sites at that time of the morning?' Nick turned and walked back toward the car, running his right hand through his hair as he did so.

'I've been here since the back of six, Nick. I didn't realise how early it was until he'd gone.'

Nick picked his briefcase out of the Morgan and placed it on the bonnet. Flicking it open, he took out his mobile and address book. He looked up the Council's number.

Rowland Davies was an old friend. A Welshman who shared Nick's passion for cars, but whose job as a planning officer made him a spectator to Nick's player, even if he was a *senior* officer. 'Anyway,' he had once said to Nick, 'wouldn't do for a public official to be seen in a flash car, even if it was every penny of his life savings!'

Nick dialled the number. The switchboard at the Council's offices took the customary twenty rings or so to answer, putting him through to the Planning Department's reception. The girl there answered after the usual thirty rings, and promised to contact the City section 'as soon as possible' if he could hold. Nick held. Eventually he was connected to Linda, whose bubbly high-pitched voice never failed to bring a smile to Nick's face when he spoke to her.

'Hey, how are you today, gorgeous?' asked Nick, who pictured Linda as a 21-year-old curvy, miniskirted brunette, about five feet two inches who read *Woman's Own* and *Hello!* magazines all day, only answering the phone to anyone with enough stamina to withstand the constant ringing tone – a sort of *Krypton Factor* for tele-holics.

'Oh 'ello, Nick!' screeched the cockney voice at the other end. 'That was good timing, 'ees just walked through the door.'

Nick looked at his watch, thirty-seven minutes past nine. That was more like it.

'Good. Can I have a quick word with him before he starts opening his piles of mail?'

There was twittering at the other end. 'Oh you are a one!' said Linda, amused at the ridiculousness of the suggestion. There was more ringing. After three rings Rowland's voice appeared.

'Hello, Nick. To what do I owe this call? Still having problems with Mr Forster's trolley park?'

Nick thought for a moment. He hadn't really thought through how he could check out 'Mr Smith' without raising too much suspicion, but Rowland's question had opened a door.

'Well, you know what these developers are like,' Nick joked, trying to buy some time.

'Oh, come on Nick. I'm surprised you haven't talked him round on this yet. There's no way we'll accept a planning application for a supermarket trolley park with an alternative use as a McDonalds! He's not fooling anyone.'

Nick cringed. This was one of Forster's brilliant ideas. A planning application for a structure that was clearly designed to take a fast-food franchise, but initially had no walls and was to be used for what the Council were demanding outside the supermarket – a trolley park.

'Well, it's not helping that one of your boys has asked Forster for more details, Rowland. Forster thinks you're taking it seriously,' answered Nick, hoping to get his information by putting Rowland on the back foot. Nick went on. 'Of course, off the record, Rowland, I agree with you.'

There was a brief pause at the other end, then Rowland went on. 'I don't believe it! Who's spoken to him? It can't be one of my lot surely? Did he get a name?'

Nick smiled to himself. 'I think Forster said it was one of your building inspectors. Smith was the name.'

'Smith?' said Rowland, his voice becoming more animated. 'Smith?' he repeated. 'We've got hundreds of bloody Smith's down here. What's his first name?'

Nick persisted 'Forster didn't say. How many have you got in your building section though?'

Nick could hear Rowland flicking through some papers on his desk. 'Eh ... here we are, building section.' There was a momentary silence. 'Ah, Smith, E.S. Oh, no. She's a typist. Don't have any more. I didn't think we had. Can't think of any myself, and I know most of them. Are you sure it was Smith, Nick?'

Nick had the answer he wanted ... and expected. 'Well, I'm sure that's what Forster said. Leave it with me and I'll check. Anyway, I think I can still persuade him to withdraw the application, Rowland. I'll call you back if he wants to push it. In the meantime, if you come across a Smith, get rid of him, will you!' he added, laughing.

'You're bloody right, I will!' answered Rowland.

Nick pressed the 'clear' button and looked at Joe. 'I don't know who our visitor was, but he certainly wasn't from the Council'.

Joe smiled a smile of relief. At least he knew he hadn't done anything stupid, and he would be on his guard from now on – although he didn't really know why. Nick opened the briefcase and replaced the mobile phone, glancing at the biscuit tin and unconsciously shaking his head. He closed the case and turned back to Joe.

'What did this guy look like?'

Joe thought for a moment. 'Pretty average really. About five feet ten, slim, a dark-blue suit.'

'Any type of accent?' asked Nick.

'No. None really. I don't really think there was anything unusual about him. A typical young man really.'

Nick stopped him. '*Young* man? What makes you say that? Was he in his teens?'

Joe smiled. 'No, it's just that they're all so trendy these days. You know, smart suits, bloody aftershave, earrings.'

Nick straightened. 'Earrings? Was he wearing an earring?'

Joe looked at him with a quizzical look. 'Well, yes. There's a few of the boys 'ere do. But I ain't seen too many suits with 'em.'

'What did it look like?' asked Nick, suddenly excited by his own initiative.

'I ain't got a bloody clue, Nick!' answered Joe, any relevance totally lost on him. 'It ain't the sort of thing I take in!' straightening himself up as if to reinforce his manhood.

'Christ, Joe, if it wasn't important I wouldn't ask you! Of course you weren't *looking*, but did you *notice*?'

Joe shook his head, but gave no answer. Nick knew he didn't want to discuss it any further.

He thought about the pin from the flat. He opened up the briefcase again and took out the biscuit tin. Removing the lid he tipped it and gently shook the contents towards his palm. The pin dropped out.

'Did it look like this?' asked Nick, extending its head out toward Joe. He looked at it for a few seconds and then lifted the hard hat from his head and wiped his brow with his wrist. 'Well, I couldn't swear by it mind, but it does look like the sort of thing he was wearing. Just one, in his ... right ear'.

Nick closed his fingers round the pin. He had made a connection. Well, maybe. But at least it might back up his thought that someone else wanted the scroll. He put the pin back in the tin, replaced the lid and placed it carefully back in the case.

'Anyway,' added Joe, 'he didn't look around the site. He just walked out of the compound, handed the trainee his bag and got into his car.'

'What trainee? You never mentioned a trainee?' said Nick impatiently.

'Well I presume it was a trainee. Dressed casual, he was. Young bloke, I think.'

Nick threw his hands up in frustration. 'Jesus, Joe! What did *this* guy look like?'

'Foreign. Dark, like an Arab or an Iranian, Middle Eastern, you know. I only saw him from a distance. He was just standing by the car, though I did think it was odd he hadn't come into the compound.' He shrugged his shoulders, realising he was sounding even more unobservant.

Nick thought for a moment. 'Describe this ... trainee. What exactly was he wearing?'

Joe thought for a moment. 'Actually, that one's easy. He was all in black. A black polo neck and black trousers. His hair was jet black too.'

Nick was convinced he had definitely made a connection.

Joe looked at him. 'What's goin' on, Nick?'

Nick put the case into the passenger's seat and put his Ray-Bans on. 'Well, Joe, let's just say that your Mr Smith thinks we have something he wants, and I don't think it's drawings of the site. Look, if anyone else turns up, give me a call on my mobile. Doesn't matter who, or when, just call me.' He glanced down the site. The workmen were still busily raking the fresh concrete into shallow ditches, the pile driver continuing its steady rhythm as it thrust inch by inch into the dry, firm London ground. He looked at the embankment. What other surprises did it hold, he wondered, as he slowly ran his fingers through his hair.

Nick jumped into the car. 'I'm going into the office. I'll drop in again tomorrow. Don't worry. One way or another we'll be ordering that steel by Friday.'

Chapter 7

As he drove to the office in Mayfair, Nick's mind wandered back to the previous Saturday morning. He tried to relive every detail of the three days since then, desperate to stumble on some detail that would get him out of his predicament. Was the scroll genuine or not. He would just have to wait on Dr Weisman, although that thought didn't give him much comfort.

Nick parked the Morgan in his space, grabbed the briefcase and strode through the front door into the reception. The offices of Stanhope Stephenson weren't the plushest in Grosvenor Square. Indeed, like many architect's offices, they tried to make a virtue of austerity. The occasional painful-looking chair for waiting visitors designed by one of the practice's younger 'designers' – all chrome with patches of leather – sat scattered around the highly polished wooden floor. The large reception desk, looking for all the world like some giant wooden Meccano set built by someone who was determined to use every piece in the kit, was the only other item of furniture in the foyer.

Nick hated it. He always had, but Robert insisted on 'dressing' the area himself, and Nick knew which battles not to fight.

'Good morning, Mr Stephenson,' announced the receptionist as Nick entered.

'Morning, Maggie. Everything OK?' he asked as he breezed past.

'Yes, thank you,' she answered, smiling in an almost

adoring manner. She knew Nick was being conscientious rather than friendly, but she didn't care.

Nick walked through the large double doors that led into the airy open-plan offices, dotted with drawing boards and colourfully decorated partition boards displaying the latest achievements of the various architects.

Nick's office was at the far end of the room. As he approached it, his secretary, Keri, stood up and held out a piece of paper. Nick could see even from a distance that she was unusually worried-looking. He smiled.

'Morning, Keri. Everything OK?'

'Morning,' she replied, her tone immediately betraying concern. 'Rachel Stanhope phoned. She sounds very upset. She tried earlier and I told her to try you at the site, but she must have missed you...'

Nick stopped her. He took the piece of paper from her hand and looked at the number. It wasn't Robert's home number. 'Where is she?' he asked.

'She's at Westminster Hospital.' She hesitated and took a longer breath. 'I think it's Robert,' Keri said, clearly as worried as she knew Nick would now be.

Nick could see her distress and gave her a gentle smile. He knew that all the staff were very fond of Robert, and Keri had been with the firm almost as long as Nick.

'Don't worry. I'll phone her right now,' he said as calmly as he could manage. He headed for the office door, realising suddenly that there were at least eight pairs of eyes watching him disappear inside.

He picked up the phone and dialled the number. Rachel answered it immediately. 'Nick?'

'Yes, Rachel, it's me,' he answered.

Before he could say any more she added, 'Oh thank God I got you.' Nick could hear the distress in her voice and could tell she had been crying just before the call.

'What's happened, Rachel?' Nick asked hesitantly and as calmly as he could.

Her voice quivered, and she started to sob, clearly trying to hold back the tears. 'It's Daddy, Nick. He's had a heart attack.' Nick could just make out the last two words before she broke down.

'Look, you stay there, I'm on my way,' he said as clearly as he could, hoping she had heard him. He listened for a response. The telephone clicked.

Dr Josef Weisman sat alone at his desk and peered yet again at the closely packed digits in front of him, guiding the magnifying optic up and down the page slowly, careful not to miss the slightest detail in the text. He shook his head gently from side to side. His first instincts had been correct, he was sure of it, and yet the sense of excitement and elation he had felt in the first minutes of being alone with the words were tempered by the knowledge that it was clearly not genuine.

Hour after hour he had studied the small piece of parchment, such a *frustratingly* small piece after all this time. He cursed himself again for not insisting that this Mr Stephenson leave the rest of it with him. No, he should have *forced* him to leave it. He should never have been allowed to leave the building without first giving it up. But he knew they would eventually prevail. God was on their side. They would have it soon enough.

Rachel was sitting in the corridor of the ward being comforted by a nurse when Nick eventually arrived. He sat down beside her, and she immediately hugged tightly into him and started to cry. Nick ran his hand down her back and held her tightly. The nurse looked at Nick. 'Are you a relation?' she asked.

'No, I'm his business partner. How is he? Is he OK?'

'He's comfortable,' she said, falling immediately, Nick thought, into hospital speech.

'What the hell does that mean?' Nick asked instinctively, the pent-up frustration of not knowing how serious Robert was finally coming out.

'Is he going to be all right?' he added, trying not to sound annoyed, if only for Rachel's sake.

The nurse looked at him somewhat embarrassed. 'Mr Stanhope has had a heart attack. He is in intensive care, but his situation has stabilised. Look,' she added softly, 'I'll get one of the doctors to speak to you. They can give you more details.' She smiled sympathetically and got up from the seat.

'Thank you,' said Nick quietly, as he lifted Rachel's head to look at her face. 'He's OK, Rachel. He'll be all right.'

Rachel looked up at him. 'He's all I have, Nick. He frightened the hell out of me and I don't want to lose him.' She sat up in the seat, holding onto Nick's hand. She smiled at him. 'Thanks for coming. I didn't know who else to call.'

Nick smiled back. 'For goodness' sake, Rachel. I'm glad you phoned.' He wiped the tears from her cheeks.

Rachel's face turned serious again. 'There's something wrong, Nick, something seriously wrong.'

'What do you mean?' asked Nick, not following the obviousness of the statement.

'Daddy...' she began, her gaze staring blankly beyond Nick's face. '...He's in trouble of some kind, I think. I've never seen him like that before.'

Nick looked at her 'What do you mean, Rachel? What happened?'

Rachel shook her head slowly. 'This morning at breakfast

his hands were shaking and he hardly spoke to me when he came down. I asked him if he was OK and he just snapped at me. He didn't even open the mail or read his newspaper. I thought I would make conversation with him, so I told him about our visit to Dr Weisman.'

'What did he say about that?' asked Nick, wondering himself how Robert would react to him taking Rachel with him.

'He said he didn't believe me!' answered Rachel.

Nick looked at her. 'What? Why not?'

'I don't know,' answered Rachel, 'and it got worse. When I told him what Weisman had said he just kept saying it was impossible and the scroll couldn't be real. I told him that we had thought it could be one of the Dead Sea Scrolls that were found in the Middle East after the war, and he started shouting at me.'

'Rachel, we *don't* think it is one of the Dead Sea Scrolls,' interrupted Nick.

Rachel just shook her head. 'That's not the point, Nick. He kept saying the date proved it couldn't be, and that I should have nothing to do with it. That I should keep out of it and...' She hesitated.

'What else did he say?' Nick asked. Rachel looked at him, her eyes beginning to well up with tears. She bit her lip to fight them back. Nick put his hands on her shoulders. 'It's OK, Rachel, it's OK.'

She shook her head and took a deep breath. 'He said I should stay away from you, Nick,' she whispered through her tears.

Nick looked at her in disbelief. 'What?' He couldn't think of anything else to say. As Rachel began to sob again, Nick pulled her to him and held her gently in his arms. He felt completely empty inside. Robert had been like a father to Nick for all these years. It had helped Nick come to terms with the circumstances of his unhappy teenage years. They had shared their dreams and their love for their craft. They confided in one another and trusted each other beyond question – they had to. Nick felt confused but at the same time suddenly realised how much he wanted to be with Rachel.

Nick felt totally confused. Robert sounded *very* ill, although Rachel's recollections were baffling.

'Are you a relative of Mr Stanhope?' Nick looked up to see a rather stern-looking young doctor standing over him.

'No, I'm his business partner.'

Rachel interrupted. 'It's OK, Doctor, I want him to know everything. You can tell us both.'

The doctor relaxed slightly and looked at Rachel. 'Your father has had a mild stroke. He's sedated, but we have stabilised his condition. Is he under any stress at the moment?'

'Nothing particularly out of the normal, as far as I'm aware,' answered Rachel.

'He's the senior partner of an architecture business,' added Nick, as if that would explain everything. He looked at Rachel. 'But, I'm not aware of anything which could trigger this on its own.' He squeezed her hand.

The doctor shrugged his shoulders slightly. 'There isn't a great deal more we can do at the moment. Time and rest are the best healers, and your father needs both. You're welcome to stay, but it may be some time before you can speak to him, and you look as though you could do with some rest yourself.'

Nick looked at her. If anything, the tired and emotional look on her face seemed to make her even more attractive. She looked vulnerable, and he wanted to take care of her, comfort her and tell her things would be OK.

'Come on, I'll take you home … and don't argue with me,' he added as she started to plead with him that she should stay.

The whole way back to the house Nick listened as Rachel laid out her life in front of him. The shock of losing her mother, and her later realisation of how much Robert had shielded her from the pain and torment that both her parents had gone through had hit her hard, almost hurt her. They had hidden Catherine's cancer from her for nearly two years. As an only child, they had decided off their own back that she couldn't ... wouldn't cope with the realisation that her mother was dying.

When she had discovered the truth, she initially reacted with bitterness, then, realising that by that time her mother had only weeks to live, she had given up her university course to be with her, to squeeze every ounce of time she could out of her last days with her mother.

'No one is ever going to surprise me again, Nick, not like that. I love my father, and I want to look after him, but I will never let myself feel as bad as I did when Mummy left us. Never!'

Nick smiled at her and reached over to squeeze her hand.

'I'd like you to come in,' she said quietly as they pulled up in front of the house.

'OK,' answered Nick. He looked up at the vine-covered walls, which somehow didn't seem quite as solid as they did a few days before.

Once inside, Rachel made straight for the drinks cabinet in the drawing room. 'Do you want one?' she asked, pouring herself a large vodka.

Nick looked on in surprise. 'No thanks, I'm driving.'

'Well, I'm having one,' she said defensively. She came over to the large couch where Nick had sat himself down, and curled herself up into the opposite corner. She took a large mouthful from the glass and swallowed hard. Her eyes screwed up involuntarily, followed by a small cough. Nick chuckled, even although he was feeling more concerned than amused.

'Aren't you going to tell me not to do this,' Rachel asked, sounding like a little girl waiting to be scolded.

Nick shook his head and smiled. 'You're old enough to make your own decision on that.'

They looked at each other as if absorbing the importance of his comment. He had finally accepted that she was no longer the little girl he had first met. She was a woman, with a woman's emotions and needs.

Rachel slowly moved toward Nick and held the hand resting on his knee. She looked hard into his eyes as her face moved closer to his, as if challenging him to pull away or tell her to stop. He didn't. Their kiss was silent and long. It did not feel to Nick like passion or lust. It was warmth, and feeling, and he wanted it to last.

Rachel slowly broke away and stood up in front of him, still holding his hand. She took another sip from the glass, then leaned down and placed it on the glass coffee table at her side. Nick stood up beside her, and without either speaking Rachel led him through the hallway, up the stairs and into her bedroom. Nick could not understand why his thoughts were calm and uncluttered. No guilty feelings, no regrets or concerns about the consequences. They both wanted this to happen, and it felt right. That was all that mattered.

Chapter 8

The phone rang. Nick put down his toast and lowered the newspaper. It was Joe.

'We've had a break-in. The pot's gone,' he said in a matter-of-fact way.

Nick thought for a moment. 'Anything else taken? Any damage?' he asked.

'No, nothing else taken, but they forced the lock on my desk drawer and smashed the window in my office where they got in. They must have been pretty persistent. I've got ... had, a bloody great grille on it. They've ripped the whole thing off.'

'What about security? Didn't he hear anything?' asked Nick, shaking his head at the same time.

'He says he heard a noise outside that sounded as if it was coming from the JCB at the other end of the site. He went out to look around, but saw nothing. They must have got in while he was out.' There was silence on the other end of the phone.

Joe continued. 'How are we doing with the scroll thing? Can I do anything about the steelwork, or has this made it more complicated?'

Nick laughed nervously. 'Well, it hasn't helped! Someone else wants it, Joe – at least I think they do.' He thought for a moment. 'Are you sure no one else knows about it?'

Joe hesitated 'Well, I ain't told anyone, and the boys have been busy at the far end of the site the last few days. You know how they are. I'm sure Ray didn't have a clue what he'd found, and as long as they're working they don't care.'

'OK. I'll get back to you as soon as I can, Joe. I'll be in the office today if you need me.'

He hung up the phone. Morris purred at his feet, his black-and-white markings looking even more pronounced than normal. Nick picked him up and smiled at him, stroking the fur across the top of his head and down his back. He thought of Rachel ... and ... Robert. He picked up the phone and called Rachel. She answered almost immediately. 'Yes?' Nick realised he had probably alarmed her.

'It's me, Rachel – Nick. Are you OK?'

He heard her sigh out loud. 'Oh Nick! Yes, I'm fine. I'm OK. Daddy's still in intensive care, but they say he is improving. He's regained consciousness, but they would only let me speak to him briefly. He just kept saying he was sorry.' She paused.

There was an awkward little silence, neither one of them wanting to say anything that would embarrass the other. They had both known each other for so long that the previous night had seemed already like a dream, something to be cherished, but in the current circumstances almost inappropriate. Best not to mention it, not at the moment anyway.

'Have you had some sleep?' asked Nick, trying to break the silence.

'No, not really. I only got back about an hour ago. I'll take something now and go to bed.'

'OK, I'll drop in later to see how Robert is.'

'Nick,' Rachel added in a quizzical tone, 'I've been thinking about what Daddy said. Why do you think he said that I shouldn't see you?'

Nick had thought about it too. Several times. It had made him feel even greater guilt, but on the other hand had probably been partly to blame for what had happened at the house. He couldn't believe it was personal ... Daddy protecting his little girl from the dangerous pursuer? He had thought too about Robert's comment on the scroll – that it couldn't be a Dead Sea Scroll because it was 'too late'. What did that mean and how could Robert know?

'Oh, he obviously wasn't feeling well, Rachel. I wouldn't read too much into it. After all we only had lunch and dinner together,' he added.

Rachel gave a little laugh. 'Yes, but he knows you a lot better than I do, Mr Stephenson! You're not secretly married, are you?'

'Certainly not, Miss Stanhope. Perish the thought!' Nick added loudly, feigning disgust at the prospect. There was another uneasy silence before Nick continued.

'I'd better get into the office. I'll see you later at the hospital. There are a few things I'd better clear up first.'

'Be careful!' Rachel said suddenly, in a worried voice. Nick was about to protest, but thought better of it.

'I will,' he said and then hung up the phone.

The heat of the summer continued to rage, the lack of any wind on the dusty London air adding to the feeling that the city and its inhabitants were being slowly roasted. Nick kept the hood down and pushed the Morgan into short sprints between the crawling traffic when he could. It helped a little.

When he reached the office he noticed a large Rolls-Royce parked in Robert's space. He ran his fingers through his hair.

Charles Forster had only ever been to the offices of Stanhope Stephenson once before. That was six years ago when the firm had first been approached by him to carry out a refurbishment project in London's Docklands. Ever since, he had always insisted that they came to him. As Nick entered the office, the smell of cigar smoke wafted toward him. Keri stood up and started to apologise for not being able to stop Forster from waiting in his office. Nick just smiled at her and raised his hand as he strode past her and through the door. She didn't have to explain.

Forster was standing looking intently at one of Nick's pictures adorning his otherwise bare white walls.

'This is pretty good,' he said unconvincingly, throwing his hand out toward the picture, flicking ash onto the floor as he did so. 'You do it?' he added.

Nick put his briefcase down on the side table and walked behind his desk. 'It relaxes me, when I get the time.' He looked straight at Forster. 'Yes, it's a hobby.'

'Always buildings?' asked Forster, his eyes scouring around the room at the other seven pictures, all of which were either line drawings or watercolours of facades or other details of buildings Nick had come across and admired. They were good. He had a talent for noticing detail, and the patience to be able to record it on paper. Nick didn't consider it art; it was merely writing down in pictorial form what he saw.

He looked at Forster and feigned a smile.

'I'm afraid the imagination of an architect does not stretch beyond the building line,' he said, more than a hint of sarcasm in his tone.

Forster chuckled. 'That's why you're the consultant and I'm the client!' He laughed, convinced he had won that little encounter. Nick just kept smiling.

'To what do I owe this pleasure?' asked Nick, keen to get rid of Forster as quickly as he could.

'I heard about Robert,' said Forster, lowering the cigar. 'Is he OK?'

Nick looked at him in surprise. This wasn't the Forster he knew.

'Yes. He's fine now. I'm going to the hospital later today.'

'Tell him not to worry, everything will be fine,' added Forster. 'These things can take it out of you, drain you, but you can always bounce back.'

'Yes,' replied Nick. 'I'm sure that's what the doctors will be telling him.'

'Doctors?' Forster blurted. 'Ha! What do they know? They're worse than lawyers! Tell you how you feel, what you can and can't do! If you don't know yourself, you *deserve* to be ill, that's what I say'.

Nick looked at him and decided he loathed him even more than before. It was clear that Forster's lifestyle was conducive to a heart attack, and it seemed to Nick that he might have had more than his fair share of experiences with doctors. He didn't feel like entering into a discussion with Forster on the subject. He picked up the papers from his in-tray and placed them in front of him on the desk, hoping that Forster would take the hint.

'How's the Holborn site doing then? On schedule?' Forster asked as he took another puff from the cigar and looking Nick straight in the eye.

Nick tried not to look concerned. 'Yes, fine.'

Forster continued. 'Must be getting close to seeing steelwork.'

Nick looked at him. 'We are. I didn't realise you took such an interest in the programme Mr Forster. I'm impressed,' he said, lying.

'Oh, I like to keep my hand in. Don't want any slowdown on this one.' Forster leaned over and stubbed out his cigar on the plant pot next to Nick's desk, having decided that no ashtray in a room was a sign of bad manners for guests.

'Well, I'll be on my way then, Mr Stephenson. Mind and tell Robert what I said.' He let out a huge crackly cough.

Nick walked toward the door to make sure Forster would not pause any longer. 'I didn't realise you knew Robert that well,' he remarked.

'Oh, I don't know him *that* well, but our paths have crossed from time to time.' He put out his hand and shook Nick's as he stepped out of the room. Nick nodded.

After Forster had left, Nick sat at his desk and thought about the visit. As far as he was aware Robert had met Forster only two or three times, and even then it had been at parties or receptions. Nick had always dealt with Forster, and he couldn't imagine Forster coming round to the office to check on him if *he* was ill. He decided that Forster must have been in the neighbourhood and had just decided to drop in, perhaps to check that the company was still functioning in Robert's absence.

He started reading his mail, but his mind wandered almost immediately to their discussion about the Holborn site. It suddenly occurred to Nick that Forster might have heard something about the scroll, and that was the real reason for the visit. But how could he? He didn't mention it; that wasn't his style. If he thought the project would be held up he would have confronted Nick, surely?

He had to get this problem sorted. He buzzed through to Keri. 'Could you get me Dr Josef Weisman at the British Museum please.'

'Right away, Nick,' answered Keri.

Chapter 9

It didn't take long for Keri to connect Nick through to the Museum. 'Mr Stephenson,' said a bright, loud voice. 'I was going to phone you today. You beat me to it.'

'Do you have some news for me?' asked Nick, suddenly feeling that something was going his way.

'Possibly' came the careful-sounding reply.

'What does that mean'? queried Nick.

'I have a colleague in Jerusalem. He has a facsimile of the piece of parchment you gave me. He says he has seen something similar in a museum in Morocco.'

There was a silence. Nick eventually broke it. 'Well, what does that mean? Is this the real thing or not?'

'That depends on what you call "the real thing",' replied Weisman. 'It is my belief that what you have is old. But is not what I believed it might be. What you have makes reference to the Qumran Brotherhood, but it is not one of their own manuscripts.'

'Well, what does that mean'?

'It means that we need to investigate it further to trace the source, but we do not start at Qumran.'

Nick's frustration returned. 'Look, I don't really care where this thing came from. I need to know if it has historical value. Now, can you answer me that?'

Weisman gave an audible sigh at the other end of the line, and Nick could picture the small man's shoulders sag. 'Mr Stephenson, you have given me a tiny part of what I believe to be a long and, perhaps, important historical document. It would allow me to do my job a lot quicker if you gave me the rest of the scroll so that I can learn more about it. If you want me to help you, *you* have to help *me.*'

Nick thought for a moment in silence. It seemed a reasonable request, but giving the entire scroll away was a big risk, particularly if it *was* genuine. Letting it get out of his control could close the site down within hours.

Weisman interrupted his thoughts. 'I really do need to know where this came from as well. If I can trace its history from a physical point, it may be even simpler. Where did you find it, Mr Stephenson?'

Nick thought about the site and his conversation with Rachel at the hospital. He just couldn't take the risk. He straightened up.

'I'm afraid you'll have to work with what you've got, Dr Weisman. Let me know if you come up with anything.' He heard a muffled shout as he put down the phone.

Nick ran his fingers through his hair. He was an architect. He didn't need all this hassle and didn't really know how to deal with it. But it seemed even more important that he got on with things now that Robert appeared to be heading for a long convalescence. He picked up the pile of letters and set them down in front of him again. For forty minutes he made his way through clients' instructions, suppliers' bills and junk mail offering the promise of some revolutionary new building material or another. His mind kept wandering – the scroll, Robert, Forster ... Rachel. How can your life change so much in four days, he thought. He smiled wryly and placed both hands behind his head. It was no use. Today was not going to be one of his most productive.

'Keri. I'm going to see Robert. I don't think I'm going to be back for the rest of the day,' he offered casually as he walked out of the room and passed her desk.

'OK, Nick. Tell him we're thinking about him.'

'I will,' he answered.

*   *   *

Robert's eyes opened slowly, blinking in an exaggerated way as he tried to focus. Rachel squeezed his hand gently and moved forward on her seat next to his bed.

She smiled at him. 'Dad. It's Rachel. How do you feel?' He turned his head to the side and, seeing his daughter's face, smiled back at her, his eyes now fully opened. He glanced behind her, attracted by the movement. He saw it was Nick, and his expression changed, his body suddenly trying to lift itself as he opened his mouth to speak. The words came out blurred.

'Are you all right, Nick?' he eventually muttered, catching sight of Nick's bandaged arm.

Nick came over to the bedside. He smiled at Robert.

'Yes, I'm fine. Couldn't be better,' he answered, looking briefly at Rachel and giving a wry smile.

'You had us worried, partner,' he added, nervously patting Robert's leg. Robert's expression changed again. He licked his lips.

'I'm so sorry, Nick,' he said, shaking his head slowly from side to side.

Nick looked at Rachel. 'Hey, I can handle things,' he joked. Robert shook his head faster.

'No, Nick, the scroll thing.'

Nick's smile faded. 'Don't you worry about all of that, Robert, just you get better...'

Robert took his hand from Rachel's and grabbed Nick's arm.

'This should never have happened. I don't understand it. Forster must be behind it Nick. It must be Forster.'

Nick looked at him intently. He was desperate to learn more, but Robert was still seriously ill and Nick didn't like what he was hearing.

'Look, Robert, you had a real warning yesterday. Try to get some sleep'.

'No, Nick. Listen to me. The scroll's a fake. I know. I planted it there myself.'

Nick looked at him in disbelief. 'What are you talking about?'

'It's a fake, Nick. Forster knows all about it. But it's got out of hand. I never thought anything like this would happen. It was only meant to get you to slow down – buy Forster time.'

Nick leaned closer to his partner, incredulous at the story unfolding before him.

'Why, Robert? Why did Forster need time?'

'His pre-let has backed out, and Forster's company is nearly bust. If you had ordered the steel he told me he could go under ... and so would I...' Robert paused.

Nick looked at Rachel. She sat like a statue, frozen to the chair, not wanting to stop her father, but scared that he would have a relapse. Nick absorbed all that he had heard.

'Why would you ... "go under"?' Nick asked.

'All my money is tied up in that development, Nick. When Catherine became ill I spent all our savings on treatment. I tried everything, Nick, but nothing worked.' He hesitated, then looked straight into Nick's eyes. 'I remortgaged the house, I took on loans through the firm.' Nick stiffened.

'Oh don't worry, I've paid off most of the loans now, but I have no pension, Nick, and all the money I have I sunk into the Holborn scheme. Forster convinced me I would get a 70-per-cent return as soon as he let it, and he had a pre-let set up. The banks wouldn't lend him any more, and he needed to start works to convince his pre-let that it would be built.'

'How much, Robert?' asked Nick, coming straight to the point.

Robert hesitated. 'Seven hundred and fifty thousand.'

Nick tried not to show his surprise at the figure. 'So what happened' asked Nick, his mind racing.

'The pre-let pulled out last Wednesday. Forster phoned me – told me that it was my money that had paid for the work to date and that I had better come up with some way of stalling any more spend until he could find another tenant.'

Nick sighed and shook his head. 'Bastard!' he muttered under his breath.

'Oh he convinced me he could do it, Nick. Said he had already instructed solicitors and all he needed was another week.' He turned away. 'I believed him. I had to.' He looked back at Rachel. 'I'm so sorry, princess'.

Rachel smiled at him, fighting back tears welling up inside her. 'It's OK, Dad... I love you,' she whispered.

Nick shook his head. 'Why didn't you tell me?'

Robert looked up at him. 'I didn't want to get you involved. Besides, I didn't know how you would react. I still have some pride, Nick. I tried to get myself out of it and ... well, what a bloody mess I've made of it.'

Nick thought back to the day the scroll was found. He recalled his visit to Robert's house.

'You knew I would come to you with the scroll.'

Robert nodded. 'Yes. I knew you wouldn't go straight to the Planning Department. Besides, it was Saturday, and you would have time to think.'

'But what about Dr Weisman? Surely he doesn't know?'

Robert shook his head. 'That's where it started going wrong. Dr Weisman was supposed to be in South America until Thursday this week. I thought it would stall you until then. Once he returned, he would immediately see it was a fake and you would carry on – or Forster would have pulled out and I would have lost my money.'

Nick's mind was racing. The trouble was Weisman hadn't dismissed it immediately as a fake. Why not? If Robert planted it, surely it had to be. Was that a coincidence? It sure as hell wasn't an accident. Nick decided it didn't add up.

'Where did you get the scroll?' he asked Robert.

As he spoke, a ward nurse walked into the room. Pushing herself in front of Nick she glanced at the monitors above the bed and then removed a thermometer from the breast pocket of her uniform. 'Mr Stanhope has had enough conversation for one day, I think. He would like some rest now, if you don't mind.'

Nick gave a nervous laugh. 'I just want another minute or so. It's important,' he pleaded, the understatement in his voice hiding his pent-up frustration at being so close to solving his problems.

'All in good time,' answered the nurse casually but firmly, as she thrust the thermometer into the patient's mouth. She picked up his right forearm, and trained her two forefingers on his vein.

'Robert, where did it come from?' asked Nick, ignoring the nurse's intervention. She stared at him intently, and he swore he heard a growl as she pressed firmly on Robert's arm.

Robert slowly removed the thermometer with his right hand. 'My father gave me the original. It started my interest in antiques and relics, but it's completely worthless as far as I know.'

Nick moved forward. 'When did he give you it, Robert? Can you remember?'

Robert smiled. 'Yes. The 12th of October 1944. It was my tenth birthday present. My father came into my room and gave me this little bag. It looked so old and mysterious with its little line drawing on the front. I was so excited.'

What sort of drawing?' asked Nick.

'A little roughly drawn eagle ... like the German emblem. I thought I was a spy!'

Nick thought about the date and recalled what he had read about the Dead Sea Scrolls. If they were only found in 1947, then what Robert had could not be genuine. He stood up. He thought back to the Portakabin. He could only envisage the pot and the contents spilled on the table.

'Where's the bag it came in, Robert? When it was found, the scroll was in a clay pot of some sort. Where is the bag with the eagle emblem?'

Robert frowned as he tried to remember, his eyes beginning to close as the drugs started to kick in again. He shook his head.

The nurse put down Robert's arm and took the thermometer from his hand. 'Mr Stanhope, I think you've done quite enough talking for one day,' she insisted, moving down the bedside and beckoning Nick to leave.

'You need to rest now. Your ... friend can come back tomorrow'.

Nick's mind was in turmoil. He knew Robert was ill and that, despite her manner, the nurse was right, but he had so many questions to ask.

Rachel stood up and took Nick's hand. 'Come on, Nick, I think Dad needs some rest.' Nick looked at her in surprise. Surely she knew how important it was that he got some answers.

She turned and leaned over her father. 'You get some rest and we'll see you tomorrow. I love you, Dad.' She kissed him gently on the forehead and led Nick to the door.

The nurse looked at Nick with a smug expression, or at least so he decided, as he walked out of the ward.

'Rachel!' he exclaimed.

She stopped him immediately.

'Look, I know you want to ask my father all sorts of questions, Nick, but he's very ill. I won't let you do it.' Her eyes were pleading with him, and he felt the grip of her hand tighten on his. 'He's all I've got,' she added, her look turning to one of fear, of loneliness.

Nick calmed down and took her in his arms, hugging her tightly to him. He thought of the mess he was in. The break-in at his flat and the site, his partner seriously ill, and the scroll. Was it the common factor? And Rachel, what must she be going through? Her father *was* all she had. They had been so close since Katherine died, and yet she was the one who had been the stronger of the two of them, refusing to let Robert wallow in his loss, even though she must have been devastated by her mother's death at a time in life when most girls needed their guidance.

Nick put his hands on either side of her face and gently raised her head to face him. 'Hey, come on, he's going to be fine,' he said, giving a warm smile, and surprising even himself at how much he meant it and wanted it to help. Rachel smiled back at him and sniffed loudly as she fought back a tear and swallowed the lump in her throat.

Nick hugged her back into his chest as he thought out loud. 'You're right. Robert's in no state to start worrying about things. The less he knows the better. I'll sort this out myself.'

'What are you going to do?' Rachel asked, suddenly concerned at Nick's direct tone.

'I'm going to pay a visit to Mr Forster. I think he's got some explaining to do,' answered Nick, still staring blankly over the top of Rachel's head. Rachel pulled back from him.

'Don't do that, Nick! You heard what my father said. It could be dangerous. Who knows what Forster's up to? He's obviously behind all of this. Believe me, I want to

94

get my hands on him as much as you do, but he's too devious for both of us, Nick.'

Nick thought about it. She was right of course. He had to be careful, and he was in no position to do the obvious thing – go back to the site and order the steelwork immediately. It might sink Charles Forster Developments Ltd, but the person who would suffer would be his partner. It never ceased to amaze Nick how many times he had seen development companies go bust, only for their so called *entrepreneurial* directors to pop up a few months later with another development scheme. He knew why, of course. They used – *gambled* – with other people's money. He shook his head. How could Robert be so stupid?

He looked at Rachel and stroked her cheek. 'Don't worry, I'm not going to do anything silly,' he said, shaking his head slowly. 'I'm not likely to land Robert in it, am I? If nothing else I want to make sure he gets his money back. I'm just going to have a chat with Forster. Get this mess out of the road.'

Rachel frowned. 'Please be careful. I want to stay here with Daddy...' She glanced into the ward and smiled. '... Even if he does seem to have his own personal bouncer!'

Nick smiled back. He looked again at Rachel's face and for the first time saw a vulnerable, frightened woman staring back. He thought how the scroll had brought them together. A silver lining perhaps, but an expensive one.

'Please phone me after you've seen him,' she pleaded.

'I promise,' said Nick, as he leaned toward her and gave her a gentle kiss on her lips.

Chapter 10

Nick looked at his watch. It was 6.30. He left the hospital and phoned Forster's office from the car mobile. The office security man had eventually been persuaded that it was a matter of life or death that Nick had to see Forster immediately. A small dinner party at Benson's was being held to celebrate another site purchase. Nick was not inclined to wait until tomorrow. He was sure Forster would have had little compulsion in using Robert's sudden, but understandable weakness to his own advantage. His loathing of the man had plummeted to new depths, and he could barely contain his anger.

Nick strode into the dimly lit restaurant and up to the front desk. The maître d'hôte puffed out his chest and approached Nick with a frown.

'Can I help you, Sir?' He looked straight at Nick, his tone making it clear he was convinced that Nick could not possibly be seeking a table for dinner.

'I'm here to see Charles Forster. I believe he's dining here tonight,' answered Nick.

The maître d' stared at him. 'What is your business with Mr Forster? he asked.

It was all Nick needed. He knew Forster was there. Brushing aside the waiter he pushed his way into the restaurant and looked around for his prey. It didn't take him long to spot Forster's table, the noise of animated laughter drawing him in the right direction as soon as he entered the restaurant proper. He headed straight for the table and stood behind a young woman sitting opposite Forster, her hair tied tightly in a bun behind her head.

Forster was still laughing as his eyes caught Nick's profile through the smoky haze. He took the cigar from his mouth and waived it toward Nick.

'This man's makin' me my next million,' he stated, flicking the ash in Nick's direction and immediately leading another bout of laughter around the table. Gradually all eyes looked at Nick. He wasn't smiling.

The laughter slowly died and Nick was left staring at Forster who by now had leaned back into his seat and was puffing contentedly on his cigar.

'Have a seat and join us, son,' said Forster, signalling to a nearby waiter to bring a chair. Nick looked around the table. There were three men and at least six women – girls, sipping champagne, eating seafood and generally adoring their paymaster. Nick decided he couldn't care less whether they heard what he had to say or not.

Forster looked straight at Nick. 'You look tense, son. Come an' 'ave a drink – what's your fancy?'

Nick feigned a smile and sat on the seat that the waiter had eagerly thrust into the small gap immediately in front of him.

'I'm sorry to gatecrash such a happy occasion, Mr Forster,' Nick said slowly, 'but I would like to discuss something with you. It could be important.'

Forster sat back in his chair, the buttons on his dinner shirt straining to contain his satisfied mass.

'Come on then, Nick, what's this all about?' Forster's tone was more serious now, as though he was becoming bored with the unwanted guest, and did not care for the tone in which he was being addressed.

Nick looked around the table at the rest of the party who were now looking rather uncomfortable. He clenched his fists and leaned forward onto the table.

'I know what you've been up to. I've just come from the hospital and Robert's told me everything.' Nick still wasn't completely sure what Robert *had* told him, but Forster was his only chance of digging deeper into the puzzle.

Forster stared straight at Nick for what seemed like an eternity. Nick didn't flinch. Slowly Forster moved forward and put his elbows on the table, the huge cigar smouldering, threatening between his fingers.

'And what exactly is that, Mr Stephenson?'

Nick thought about the reply. At least Forster hadn't denied anything. He thought he had enough information from Robert to extract a lot more from Forster.

'He told me about his ... "investment" in your company. It was every last penny he had, you know.'

Forster looked at him. 'So what? He's a grown man, he knows the game.'

Nick shook his head. 'The ... *game?* Is that what you call it?' He could feel the anger growing inside him.

Forster sat back again in his seat and puffed on the cigar. 'Of course it is. He took a chance on making a quick killing. He could have put the whole lot on the 1.30 at Newmarket. It's the same thing, you know. Those kinds of risks and rewards don't come cheaply.'

Nick leaned further over the table. 'Not when the race is fixed, they don't.' He stared intently at Forster who slowly removed his cigar, a menacing look suddenly appearing on his face.

'Now you look here. Choose your words very carefully, Stephenson. He knew what he was doing. In any case, he'll probably get his *reward*, despite his stupidity.' He looked around at his guests, who by now appeared to have shrunk to half their original size. He relaxed his shoulders and smiled, signalling that the interruption was about to end and the party would resume. 'Now, unless you've got anything else to say, get the hell out of here.'

Nick looked at him bemused. 'How is he meant to do that when your pre-let has pulled out?'

'Because I've just instructed my solicitor to draw up a contract with an alternative occupier.' Forster sat back again in his seat. 'And what's more, it'll make me even more money.' He chuckled to himself. 'Should have the whole thing complete in the next two days. So it looks as though Robert's little trick worked, eh?'

Nick stood up straight, suddenly feeling rather conspicuous. If what Forster said was true, then Robert's money was safe. He looked back at Forster. 'You can pull your monkeys off me then as well. I don't like the way you do business, Mr Forster.'

'What the hell are you talking about now?' Forster asked angrily.

'You know full well – your ... *black army*,' answered Nick.

Forster shook his head, his bushy eyebrows squeezing themselves together as he frowned. 'I don't have a clue what you're talking about. What do you think I am – a gangster?' He laughed and looked around him, indicating another cue for all those at the table to join in. They laughed loudly.

Nick waited until the laughter had died away. Forster's reaction suddenly seemed genuine, as though he really *didn't* know what Nick was talking about. The realisation rushed through Nick's mind like a bolt. He really didn't have any idea what Nick was talking about!

Forster leaned forward on the table again. 'Look, Stephenson, it was Robert's idea to plant the ... scroll thing. It did its job. It stalled you for a couple of days, and you should know I only agreed to it because it was Robert's money that was at stake.' He was staring menacingly at Nick, who realised that Forster really didn't know what he had referred to but was somehow unsettled by this turn in the conversation.

Forster continued. 'Now, get back down to that site tomorrow and get them working again. I want my building finished in nine months.' He rammed the cigar back in his mouth.

Nick thought about the last few days. It didn't add up. A piece of the jigsaw was still missing. In fact it seemed like a whole half of the puzzle was missing.

'Just so I'm clear on this, are you saying that you didn't have anyone ... following me to make sure Robert's plan worked?'

Forster sighed. 'Why would I do that? Robert knew you would go to him as soon as you found the bloody thing, and he was right, wasn't he? I couldn't give a shit whether it worked or not. None of my money was exposed.' He put the cigar down on the ashtray in front of him. 'Do we have a problem here, Stephenson?'

Nick looked back at him and took a deep breath. 'I'm afraid we do, Mr Forster. You see, I'm not convinced that this scroll's a fake and, until I find out for sure, your building doesn't exist!' He stood up and turned to leave.

Forster jumped to his feet. 'Don't you dare walk out of here!' he shouted. The whole restaurant fell silent. Nick walked toward the door, ignoring the threat.

'Do you hear me?' shouted Forster in an even louder and increasingly stronger northern accent. 'Get those bastards back at work now!'

Nick strode out of the restaurant. Once outside he took another deep breath and ran his fingers though his hair. 'Now what?' he muttered to himself as he walked to the car park.

He climbed into the Morgan and realised that he was sweating profusely. He loosened his tie, undid the top button of his shirt and threw his head back against the headrest as he closed his eyes. 'Think this through, Nick,' he said to himself.

His mind was spinning with the twists and turns that the last few days had taken. He forced himself to go over the facts and be logical. Robert's father had given him the scroll in 1944, but the Dead Sea Scrolls had not been discovered until 1947. Seemed clear, except Dr Weisman had definitely referred to the Qumran Brotherhood, the Scrolls' guardians and authors. Something didn't fit. Even if the scroll wasn't genuine, someone somewhere knew it had been found on his site and had stolen the pot to try to prove it. That in itself was probably evidence enough to have the work stopped if they chose to tell the authorities. He thought about the attack in his apartment. He had no idea whom he was dealing with, or what they wanted, but he decided he had to do something to bring it to a head. He needed help from someone who knew what this all meant. He wasn't quite sure what the consequence of his actions would be, but one thing he did know was that now he really did have to sort out the mess as quickly as possible. Weisman didn't seem to have much of a clue and, besides, Nick felt something was amiss with him. No, he needed to take a more direct approach.

He picked up the phone and called Rachel's mobile. It rang once. 'Hello, Nick. Is that you?' There was immediate concern in her voice.

Nick tried to sound as normal as he could. 'Yes, it's me.' He paused. 'How's Robert? Is he feeling better?'

'Yes ... yes,' she answered. 'He's sleeping. I've just spoken to the doctor and he thinks he could be out of intensive care by tomorrow. How about you? Did you see Forster?'

Nick hesitated. He wasn't sure how much to tell her, but he *had* made up his mind about his next step.

'Yes, I've just seen him,' he said calmly. He paused for a few seconds. 'What was the name of the priest you read about in the library ... the one in Milan? Can you remember?'

'What do you want his name for?' she replied.

Nick ignored the question. 'Rachel, can you remember his name? I think he was a cardinal.'

Rachel thought back to the library visit and remembered the chip shop.

'Cardinal ... Cornelli!' she stated triumphantly, chuffed that she had remembered the name. 'Why do you want his name, Nick. Are you going to contact him?'

'Look, Rachel, I've decided to go to Milan to see him. I'm...'

Rachel interrupted. 'Milan? Why? ... What did Forster say? Surely you don't still believe this thing could be genuine, not after what Daddy said!'

'Look Rachel, I don't think it's genuine, but I haven't got answers to all the questions yet. Forster knew nothing about our friends in black, so it appears someone else isn't sure either.' He knew he was probably not making sense. I need to show this scroll to him and clear this up.'

'For goodness' sake, don't say anything to Robert. I don't want him getting worried about this any more than he already is.'

'I want to come with you, Nick,' interrupted Rachel again.

'No,' replied Nick. 'There's nothing you can do and, besides, Robert needs you there more...' He stopped himself short. 'I'll catch the first flight out in the morning and be back tomorrow night. Are you going to stay at the hospital again tonight?' he asked, trying not to sound overprotective or too concerned.

'Yes,' replied Rachel. 'They've managed to get me a bed just along the corridor from Daddy.'

'Good, well I know where to get you then. I'll call you as soon as I get back tomorrow. Goodnight, Rachel.'

He pressed the 'clear' button immediately and then the

'power' switch. He didn't want Rachel to have time to ask him more questions. He wanted someone to know what he was up to, but she didn't need to know too much detail. At least, he thought, she would be safe in the hospital, although he still didn't really understand why he should be thinking about her safety.

As he started up the engine and sped off into the warm sultry evening, the two men in the small family saloon slipped it into gear and quietly followed the Morgan out of the car park at a safe distance.

Chapter 11

Nick rose early the following morning. The summer heat carried on relentlessly and Nick wondered whether he would ever feel cold again. He hadn't had a good night's sleep, though the heat seemed like a poor excuse. Morris, as usual, looked completely content with his world. Nick sneered at him as he headed for a cooling shower, glancing only briefly at the biscuit tin lying innocuously on the breakfast bar.

It took him only thirty minutes to shower, eat and pack his bags, the biscuit tin placed carefully in the centre of his overnight bag. He decided to take a change of clothes just in case. He called in at the office and as usual found Keri at her desk by 7.45. There were four yellow Post-its attached to his diary, all of them with Charles Forster's name written on them in bold. As Nick approached Keri's desk she picked up the diary and started to give him the message. Nick put up his hand to stop her.

'I don't want to speak to Mr Forster this morning, Keri.' She decided that relaying Forster's insistence on an urgent conversation was superfluous. 'I'm afraid he'll probably try another dozen times, but you haven't seen me, and I'm not available all day, OK?' Keri nodded compliantly. She knew when not to ask for explanations, and Nick knew she would think of a credible alibi.

'Right,' he continued purposefully, as he strode into his room, followed by Keri. 'Could you get me on the first available flight to Milan? This is important. I need to get out there today. I think they go out of Stansted.' He thought about how long he would need. 'Keep the ticket open.'

Keri looked at him quizzically. 'I take it you want me to cancel your appointments for today?' She didn't wait for a reply. She turned and walked back out of the room.

Nick sat at his desk and phoned Joe. 'Everything OK down there?' he asked casually.

'Yeah, fine, Nick, but I'm runnin' out of things for the lads to do. Any news yet on the steel?' replied Joe.

'No, not yet. Look, I won't be down to the site this afternoon. If anything comes up Keri knows where I am'.

'OK,' replied Joe.

Nick went on: 'Oh, by the way, if Mr Forster turns up we haven't spoken today, and so that you're clear, Joe, you have no instructions from me. Is that understood?'

Joe thought for a moment. It certainly wasn't clear, but it was understood. 'Of course,' he replied, sounding somewhat confused. 'Is there a problem or something?' he added. 'Anything I should know about?'

'No,' replied Nick. 'I just want you to be clear on the position. I haven't issued you with any further instructions. Got that?'

'Oh, OK then. I'm clear. You're the boss, Nick.' It was all Joe had to say.

Nick drove straight to Stansted Airport and caught the 11.30 flight to Milan. He spent most of the flight with his head tucked into a newspaper, only occasionally glancing around to scan the faces of the other passengers. They looked like a typical mix of businessmen and women with the occasional tourist and what he imagined was the inevitable fashion designer type thrown in. In the same way that Nick reckoned he could always tell an architect by his watch, he had decided that you could always tell a designer in one of two ways – either they had improbably close-cropped hair or they wore odd spectacles. He was convinced that many didn't need them, but simply wanted to make some sort of personal statement with their multicoloured frames and shapes so oblique that it appeared impossible to derive any benefit from them. He estimated there were at least six on the flight.

Milan was a city that Nick had always wanted to visit. The combination of international design houses and fabulous architecture, coupled with the fact that it was a far more commercial city than Florence or Rome, excited him. He promised himself that one day he would return under different circumstances, and found himself drifting into the thought of himself and Rachel entering La Scala to take in one of Verdi's masterpieces or visiting Da Vinci's *Last Supper*. He dismissed the thought from his mind and tried for the hundredth time that day to make sense of the last few days.

The journey from the airport by bus took twenty-five minutes, ending outside the Statione Centrale. His vision of the beautiful city was almost destroyed immediately as he encountered a group of teenage dropouts hanging around the station entrance, openly passing needles from one to another, apparently completely unaware of the passing commuters. He approached a kiosk in the piazza in front of the station and purchased a city map. The Duomo had its own metro station that was only four stops away. Nick decided to stick with public transport while he was in the city. He felt he wanted plenty of people around him.

As he emerged from the subway Nick looked in awe at the majesty of the Duomo as it rose in front of him like some great grey Gothic cake, its magnificent facade crowned with jagged peaks of ornate stonework and spires. As an architect student years before, Nick had always envied the medieval masons who had had the opportunity to work on the biggest building projects of their time, the great cathedrals of the world, unhindered by commercial and time constraints, free to express their own talents and ideas. What he would give to create such a legacy!

As he crossed the wide Piazza del Duomo the pigeons scattered. Nick smiled as he wondered if these were the same birds that visited Trafalgar Square or perhaps St Mark's Square, like some avarian grand tour. A photographer approached him. 'You wanna your photo, please Signor?'

Nick smiled. 'No thanks'. He looked suspiciously at the man holding the camera. How could the man tell he was English? He worried that he was fast becoming paranoid. *Relax*, he thought, *you're a thousand miles from home*. Once again he looked in wonder at the facade of the cathedral as he approached the front door. How many visitors, he ventured, could ever appreciate the fine detail, the craftsmanship that had gone into creating such a three-dimensional work of art, the way he could, and yet here he was, hurrying to meet its current custodian, with no chance to absorb its splendour or enjoy the vision that rose about him.

He walked into the church and immediately noticed the drop in temperature and the tranquillity of the place. He walked down a side aisle, all the time taking in the sheer scale of the building and the beauty of its form.

He reached the altar and spotted a priest to the left busily arranging hymnbooks in what he assumed was the choir. He approached slowly, looking around self-consciously as if he was stepping over some unseen barrier where interested visitors suddenly dared to become conspicuous.

The priest looked up, startled by the sudden approach 'Signor?' he exclaimed, looking directly at Nick with wide innocent-looking eyes.

'*Buon giorno, Signor,*' Nick stuttered in the best schoolboy

Italian he could master. It had been a long time since he had attempted the language.

'*Buon giorno!*' said the priest, standing up slowly and visibly relaxing. 'You are English, yes?' he added, clearly amused by the amateur's attempt at his native tongue.

'Yes, I am from London,' answered Nick, smiling deliberately.

'Ah, London' said the priest, his eyes looking upwards. 'You have such beautiful churches, such great cathedrals, but you have no faith.'

Nick raised his eyebrows, the young's priest's statement suddenly throwing him off track.

'I am sorry signor,' added the priest, smiling. 'I have spent one year in London, but I fear for your future. You have great history, but few believers.'

Nick thought briefly about the priest's observation. He thought how his own love of such buildings, of their architecture, had indeed overlooked how they had become, perhaps, monuments to some past way of life rather than living temples of human belief. Yet here, as he looked around him, there was a sense of comfort that such magnificence was somehow only a representation of man's faith.

The priest watched as Nick looked around the huge ceiling. '*Qual é la sua professione?*' he asked.

Nick looked at him and shrugged his shoulders.

'I'm sorry,' said the priest. 'You have an interested eye, Signor?'

'I'm an architect,' Nick answered.

The priest smiled and nodded. 'Ah, then you have a *trained* eye, Signor.'

Nick looked directly at the priest and decided that the conversation was in danger of sidetracking him from his only purpose in being there. 'I would like to see Cardinal Cornelli, please', he asked calmly and quietly.

The priest looked at Nick with a puzzled expression. 'You have business with the Cardinal?' he asked.

'Yes,' Nick answered, deciding that the less he said the more chance he had of meeting the Cardinal.

The priest's expression softened. 'You have come about the works, yes?'

Nick smiled but didn't answer.

'Follow me, Signor,' said the priest, as he lifted the cordon separating visitor from worshipper.

As they entered a small vestibule at the rear of the altar the priest pointed to a simple wooden bench and signalled toward Nick to sit down. He disappeared behind a doorway covered by a piece of purple velvet curtain. Nick looked around the small room, admiring the delicate wooden carvings on the walls and ceilings, wondering at the history behind the paintings adorning the walls. He convinced himself that, even although this was a small insignificant space in the church, they were probably masterpieces of great historical value.

After a few minutes a small white-haired man dressed in black with a purple cap on his head came out through the doorway and walked toward Nick. He smiled and put out his hand for Nick to kiss his ring. Nick leaned forward and took the Cardinal's hand, his Catholic childhood suddenly given meaning as he instinctively bent down and kissed the jewel. He stood up.

'Good morning, my son,' said the Cardinal, his English almost perfect, but with a distinct Italian lilt that somehow added a touch of warmth to the greeting.

'Good morning, your Eminence,' answered Nick.

'Father Di Canio tells me you are an architect.'

Nick nodded. 'It has long been an ambition of mine to visit Milan's cathedral.'

The Cardinal smiled gently. 'And yet you build supermarkets and petrol stations?'

Nick's eyebrows involuntary rose in surprise for the second time. Did he have *atheist* stamped all over his forehead?

'I mean no offence,' said the Cardinal, smiling. He reached out and guided Nick back towards the altar. 'You have come all this way to see our church, so perhaps there is hope.'

Nick looked at the old man. 'Actually I have come about another matter.'

The Cardinal looked at Nick with a quizzical expression as they reached the choir seats. Nick continued. 'I believe you have made a study of the Dead Sea Scrolls.'

The Cardinal stopped and his eyes lit up. 'One does not "study" the Scrolls, my son. They are the essence of religious life. One "learns" from the Scrolls.' He looked at Nick intently for a moment then a faint smile reappeared on his lips. 'What is your interest in them?'

Nick started to walk on, looking around him to be certain that they were not being watched.

'I am researching their history... It's for a project on pre-Christian civilisation and cultures,' said Nick, trying to sound convincing. I'm particularly interested in how the Scrolls were found, and what has happened to them since.'

The Cardinal looked at Nick. 'That is well-documented, Signor. The scrolls were uncovered in 1947 in the north-western shores of the Dead Sea.'

'Were all of them found in the one place at the same time?' asked Nick.

The Cardinal stopped and looked at him directly. 'This too is well documented, my son.' He paused and looked intently into Nick's eyes. 'You did not travel all this way to ask me such mundane questions surely? What is your interest in them? What do you *really* want to know? Why is the timing ... important to you?'

Nick looked at the Cardinal. Nick sensed that there was something that the Cardinal wanted to hear him ask. He had to take a chance. He thought of Robert. 'Some of them are missing, aren't they?'

The Cardinal's face changed to one of concern and he appeared to be looking far more intently at Nick's face. 'Who sent you here?'

Nick put his hands up and tried to look as innocent as a choirboy. 'No one, your Eminence, please believe me.'

The Cardinal looked at him for several moments, their eyes locked on each other like some desperate game of bluff. He straightened up. 'I'm sorry I have nothing to say. Good-day, Signor.' He walked back toward the vestibule.

Nick followed him. 'Cardinal, please, I have something to show you.' He held up the tin. 'Please, take a look at this.'

The Cardinal kept on walking without looking round.

'I believe it is from the Scrolls,' Nick whispered loudly.

The Cardinal stopped. He clasped his two fists and for a moment seemed to tense, then turned slowly to face Nick. His eyes were bright and intense, burning into Nick's as though he was searching the corners of Nick's mind to discover why he had come all this way.

Nick realised he had stumbled on something he did not understand. 'Before I look at this,' the Cardinal said, glancing at the object in Nick's hand, 'tell me where you think this came from.'

Nick looked at the Cardinal. 'All I know is that it was found somewhere they should not have been.'

The Cardinal fixed his gaze on Nick. 'When?'

Nick stared back at the Cardinal, knowing that his answer was likely to sound ridiculous. 'Last week,' he answered.

'Then you know nothing about its history or how it got to be where you *found* it?'

'No', answered Nick. 'I have no idea what it is, or where it really came from. But I do know that there are others who would like to possess it'.

The Cardinal straightened up. 'You are wasting my time, Signor. Good-day.' He started to turn away again.

'No, wait, please,' Nick pleaded. 'There is something else.' He opened the tin and tipped it up, shaking it gently. The silver pin dropped into his hand. He held it out toward the Cardinal and watched the expression on his face. It did not change for several seconds. Eventually he looked up at Nick with an intense stare. Nick didn't flinch. He had no idea what the connection might be if there was one, but it seemed to be worth a try. If the Cardinal recognised the symbol, then perhaps if may provide him with a link to those who seemed to want the scroll. 'Does this mean something to you?'

The Cardinal looked up. His expression had changed to one of concern, and his eyes darted around the church beyond Nick's shoulders. 'Have you come alone?' he asked.

Nick nodded.

The Cardinal paused for a few seconds and Nick could see he was weighing up the position. 'Follow me, Signor,' said the Cardinal, suddenly grasping Nick's arm and leading him toward a small door at the back of the vestibule. The door opened onto a small enclosed stairwell. Nick followed the Cardinal up the dark spiral staircase. He imagined that there must be over one hundred steps, his head beginning to spin as he climbed around the central pillar, up and up until at last they reached a small passageway that led to a large metal door. The Cardinal took out a key from under his tunic and unlocked the door. As Nick followed him through the door into the sunlight, he was struck by the magnificent view over the cathedral roof, the city spread out beyond him and the Piazza del Duomo far below. The spires of the cathedral reached up like ornate stalagmites all around him, several of them surrounded by scaffolding, yet still they maintained their beauty and sense of history.

Cardinal Cornelli stepped carefully over the rows of pipe work and loose stonework and walked toward the western face of the cathedral. 'I am sorry you are not seeing my church at its most beautiful. I am afraid even the most solid of buildings cannot compete with our modern ways,' he said, pointing at the cars below, and then the construction cranes that towered above the cathedral's roof.

He turned and looked at Nick. The Cardinal's expression had changed again. He had said nothing during the climb to the roof and Nick wondered what had been going through the old priest's mind, what information had been unlocked by the simple silver pin. Smiling gently, Cardinal Cornelli sighed.

'When I was a boy my father told me about the great writings that God had hidden in a holy place, and which man would find only in his darkest hour so that he might read, and learn, and believe.' The Cardinal turned away from Nick and looked out over the piazza below. 'When I was a young curate in Roma it was announced that the Scrolls had been ... uncovered. I hadn't forgotten my father's words, but somehow it seemed to me they had been found too late. My country had been liberated from the evil of fascism, but many had died. God had not kept His word.' He stopped and cast his gaze across the city in a long slow sweep.

Nick played nervously with the tin between his hands. He moved over to the edge and stood beside the Cardinal. He thought back to Robert's words, to something that had been bothering him ever since. He decided to push for answers as quickly as he could. 'Some of them were found earlier, weren't they?' he asked, searching the Cardinal's face for an answer.

The Cardinal looked at Nick intently, his face showing surprise, yet somehow also displaying excitement. 'What evidence do you have for this ... question?' he asked.

Nick pulled the lid off the tin and pulled out the scroll. He handed it to the Cardinal. Nick watched as he carefully rubbed his fingers over the surface of the paper and then held it up to the light. 'What is this?' he asked, looking straight at Nick, his expression suddenly changing. 'This has no relevance to the Scrolls,' he added. 'Are you trying to trick me?'

'No, I was hoping you might be able to help me. I don't know what this is, but I believe it may be connected in some way with the Dead Sea Scrolls.'

The Cardinal looked at the parchment again. His eyes squinted as he tried to read the writing. He turned to Nick. 'These are not genuine, my son, if that is what you believe. I have been a witness. The Scrolls are written mainly on parchment, some on leather and papyrus, and even one on copperplate, but none on this type of material. It may be parchment, but it is not like the others.'

Nick looked at the Cardinal, convinced that they represented part of the Scrolls' history. He was desperate to have the Cardinal give him some hope that the mystery could be solved. 'Some were found *before* 1947, weren't they?'

The Cardinal's expression changed completely, the knowledgeable look of an old man suddenly replaced by the expectant openness of a young scholar. Nick knew instinctively that the Cardinal believed him. The Cardinal handed the parchment back to Nick and then looked away. After what seemed to Nick like an eternity the Cardinal turned back to him. 'There is something driving you, my son, and I sense you are a good man. But sometimes there are things that are best left alone.'

Nick persisted, convinced this was the best, the only chance he had to solve the problem. 'Look, I am not a religious man, and I know our reasons to know are very different, but we both want answers to what has happened with the Scrolls. I know there is something not right here, and I have to find out what it is!'

Nick looked at the Cardinal and suddenly saw a very old and frail face behind the formal garments and serene presence. The Cardinal turned back to face the city. He sighed heavily and his shoulders fell as though giving way under some great weight that could no longer be borne. Slowly he lifted his eyes and, without turning to Nick, released his thoughts.

'In 1943 a Dr Marten led a secret German expedition to find the Scrolls. He had heard, through German Intelligence, a rumour of the writings of God at a place called Wadi Qumran in Jordan. He took a small group of handpicked SS men and sealed off an area no larger than a tennis court. After digging for eight months, and enduring regular attacks from local Jews his team found the dry caves in which they were stored. He was intent on taking his treasure back to the Führer. What a prize for an anti-Semite the great Jewish writings would have made. But before he did so, he spent over a month locked away with two of his assistants transcribing and noting as much as he could of the writings.

'Then, one night while guards slept, the site was attacked by Jewish extremists who had heard what was going on, and Marten and his guards were killed. Only one of his assistants, a man called Harold Gerber, survived. The Jews replaced all of the Scrolls in their original vaults and filled in the entire area so that no trace was left of the site. Of course, rumours spread and it wasn't until 1947, after the war, that they were 'officially' found by Bedouins. There was much confusion in the area at that time and many more Scrolls disappeared before their true importance was known.'

Nick looked at the Cardinal. 'Why were they filled in after Martens was killed? Surely a group of Jewish fundamentalists would want the Scrolls made public. They are the very foundation of their faith.'

The Cardinal looked at Nick, a serious expression on his face. 'They knew that what they had found was hugely important, but they could not take the risk of moving them in a time of great uncertainty in the world. The day after Dr Martens was killed Gerber was found dying at the side of a road five kilometres away near the town of Kallia. He had been attacked by some local bandits and all his possessions stolen. When they got to him he was almost dead, but he told them that Martens had found something which would end the Jewish state for ever, that would turn the whole world against them, and have Jew fighting Jew...' The Cardinal stopped.

Nick looked at him, astonished at what he was hearing, but completely lost as to its significance. 'Well, what was it?' he asked.

The Cardinal was silent for what seemed to Nick an eternity, his eyes seemingly searching behind Nick's entering the deepest recesses of his mind. Could Nick be trusted? He started talking without breaking his gaze. 'Gerber told them of a parchment stolen from him by the two bandits that, he said, would destroy the Jewish faith and bring victory to his homeland ... a scroll so powerful that it would change the course of history.'

Nick was struggling to grasp the enormity of what he was hearing, and the possible connection to the scroll in his possession, if there was one. 'So why has this never come out? I've never heard any of this before.'

'There is no *evidence* to support Gerber's claims. Believe me, I have worked on the Scrolls most of my life, and I have seen nothing to suggest it is true of any of the parchments. It may be the last testament of a dying man,

116

but none of it has ever been proven. He was a Nazi. He would have had reason to say such things.'

Nick was still struggling to cope with what he had heard. Why, he wondered, was the Cardinal telling him all this anyway, to a complete stranger, especially since he had rejected the scroll out of hand.

After a short pause Nick asked, 'Why are you telling me this?'

The Cardinal moved toward him. 'Where did you find the pin? Truthfully, please.'

Nick decided honesty was the only policy now if he wanted answers.

'I believe it was dropped by someone who tried to burgle my apartment.' He made a leap in logic. 'I believe it was someone who was looking for this.' He waved the biscuit tin at the priest.

The Cardinal stood motionless for a few moments and then signalled to Nick to open the tin once again. 'Let me see what you have again, Signor,' said the Cardinal, this time taking out a pair of reading glasses, and gently placing them on the bridge of his nose. Nick carefully removed the scroll and handed it over.

As soon as he touched them the Cardinal shook his head. 'This is merely paper, Signor.' He opened out the scroll and began to read the words written in Hebrew on the paper. It was clear to Nick that Cardinal Cornelli badly wanted these papers to be something else, something that he had hoped to find for many years. As the old priest studied the manuscript Nick's mind was racing, trying to fathom a possible link in the Cardinal's story, however tentative, with the scroll found at Holborn. If there was one, what could it be?

'You think there could be some possible connection, Cardinal?' asked Nick, not knowing what other question to ask. The Cardinal didn't answer. Instead Nick noticed his face begin to tense. His eyes flirted around the scroll at an increasing rate, and his grip on the scroll became more obvious.

'Is there something there?' asked Nick, feeling stupid at asking such an inane question, but hoping desperately to get an answer that would suddenly open the door onto whatever it was the Cardinal knew.

The Cardinal suddenly lowered the scroll. '*Meus Deus!*' he exclaimed, almost to himself.

Nick looked at him, his eyes open wide and his mind trying to translate a language he barely knew. 'What is it, your Eminence?' he asked.

The Cardinal looked up at Nick. 'Tell me please where *exactly* this was found.'

Nick looked at him, eager to give him any information he could that would help unravel the mystery. There seemed little point in holding any information back. 'It was found on a building site in London three days ago, buried twenty feet under the ground.'

The Cardinal stared at Nick with an incredulous look on his face. 'Then it is still out there my son. It...'

Before he could finish the sentence a huge stone pallet, suspended from the arm of one of the cranes, swinging thirty feet above their heads, came hurtling at them from the side. Out of the corner of his eye Nick spotted the deadly load and threw himself down and across, trying to push the Cardinal away from its path.

The Cardinal turned toward it, his eyes wide and his mouth instinctively opening, but only uttering a silent word as he dropped the scroll at his feet. The pallet struck the Cardinal full on the chest knocking him clean off his feet and over the small parapet. He fell straight back, in what seemed to Nick like slow motion, falling freely through the air before stopping suddenly, impaled on the sharp edge of a stone spire.

Nick looked in disbelief as blood started running down the spire and onto a grotesque gargoyle below, its open mouth and evil eyes adding to the horror of the scene. He rushed to the edge and, climbing over the parapet wall, lowered himself down the steep-sloping side of the church, clinging to a series of small stone pillars that ran the length of the roof. When he reached the Cardinal he could see that there was a slight flicker in his eyes. Nick realised immediately that there was nothing he could do to help him. The sharp point of the spire had pierced through the priest's back and out of his right-hand side, part of his ribcage clearly protruding beneath his torn tunic.

The Cardinal's body was completely still, but his eyes suddenly opened wide, staring blankly straight ahead. His lips moved slowly and Nick suddenly realised that he was trying to speak. Nick put his ear down to the Cardinal's mouth, desperately trying to make out the Cardinal's words. The sound was muffled, but after repeating three or four times, Nick could tell the Cardinal was repeating the same word, over and over. To Nick it sounded like *emet*. He had no idea what it meant. He glanced down and saw the index finger of the Cardinal's right hand flicking up and down, pointing toward the tin that had been left sitting on the parapet wall.

The Cardinal's voice suddenly stopped and Nick pulled away from his face. The Cardinal took a sudden deep breath and held it for what seemed to Nick like an eternity. The Cardinal's eyes flickered, then slowly closed. He gradually exhaled his last breath in an almost peaceful way. Nick dropped his head. Above him, the sun was momentarily blocked out by the swinging boom of the crane. Nick looked up at it and watched it swing back slowly, silently, above the roof of the Duomo. Suddenly remembering what had happened, Nick turned and scrambled back up the side roof and back over the parapet. He picked up the scroll, pushed it back in the tin and thrust it into his shoulder bag. He traced the line of the boom up and along the crane arm. His eyes caught the outline of a figure dressed in black scrambling down from the crane's cabin some fifty feet away.

Nick threw the image around in his head. The figure was now reaching the bottom of the crane's ladder, about five steps from the Cathedral's roof, and had stopped, momentarily looking toward Nick, then continued rapidly, faster, down the remaining steps. Nick's mind raced. *Could* this have been deliberate? Was he watching a killer escaping? He didn't think any longer, instinctively starting to run toward the figure as it reached the rooftop footpath and turned, swiftly heading toward another entrance door some fifty yards away from where Nick had dived to avoid the murderous load.

The figure disappeared through the door. Nick stopped where he was, realising that the door he had come through earlier was only a few paces away. He decided that both exits must lead back into the Duomo... perhaps he would be able to cut the man off. He pushed the door open and scrambled down the tight spiral staircase, the sudden darkness momentarily blinding him as he tried to take as many steps as he could with each bound.

When he reached the bottom he flung the small door open and leapt into the vast internal space of the cathedral, the sudden brightness briefly disorientating him. Several tourists stopped and stared at the sudden noisy appearance of the intruder. Nick had no time for explanations. His eyes searched the length of the western aisle of the church, desperately trying to locate the man in black. He could not be found. Nick moved across the aisle and started to head toward the centre, squeezing awkwardly along one of the rows of pews, stepping over the occasional knee-rest while gripping tightly onto his shoulder bag. His search became more frantic, his head now pivoting on his neck like a searchlight. Nick realised the longer the killer remained undetected, the more likely he was to escape unseen.

Nick reached the centre aisle and stopped. The tourists were no longer watching him, content, he imagined, to assume that he was searching for his lost child or wife. His heart was beating frantically, but he tried to concentrate on a slow sweeping search of the building, picking out each figure in turn and mentally checking it against the imprint of the killer's silhouette. It was no use. The seconds ticked by. Had the man doubled back and escaped through a third rooftop door? Had he removed the black top to reveal a brightly coloured one below, allowing him to blend in with the hordes of brightly garbed tourists? He instinctively made for the entrance door. He wasn't sure, but his brief visit hadn't revealed any other public entrance, although there were sure to be emergency or concealed escape routes around the sides.

He emerged back out into the Piazza del Duomo, looking down from the five or six steps that led to the cathedral entrance. The same mix of meandering tourists and busy workers went about their respective routines in the wide-open concourse. Nick scanned the crowd with a feeling of hopelessness, his eyes half closed as he adjusted to the bright sunlight. To his left a small flock of pigeons suddenly scattered and shot up into the air. Two children laughed as they threw their hands up in triumph.

Suddenly his eye caught a figure just beyond them. It was standing still, lighting a cigarette. Then it moved away slowly, and Nick watched carefully as the figure, a man, took out a pair of sunglasses and placed them carefully on his face. As he did so, the man looked around him in both directions and pulled down slightly on his black polo shirt.

It was him. Nick was sure of it. He ran down the stairs in the killer's direction, but stopped sharply when he reached the piazza. What was he going to do? He had instinctively wanted to shout. But what, and to whom? He had to get to the man, confront him, make a scene. The rest would work itself out.

He walked quickly in the man's direction, his eyes fixed on him like a laser. He got to within thirty yards from him, when the man casually glanced over his right shoulder and almost instantly spotted Nick homing in on him. Immediately, the man threw the cigarette to the ground and started running toward the underground station at the far end of the piazza. Nick responded and set off in pursuit as fast as he could. The crowds and pigeons scattered as the two men weaved their way at speed over the paved arena before leaping down the stairs that led into the station. Their pounding steps echoed wildly along the tiled tunnel. The killer reached the ticket hall and, without checking his stride, leaped over the ticket barrier and continued his run toward the stairs that led down to the platforms below. A guard watched in disbelief as the man disappeared into the mass of people and then let out a helpless yell as Nick followed the killer's lead and hurdled the barrier before he too disappeared from the guard's view.

Nick ran down the stairs, stumbling as he dodged through the crowds of tourists moving in each direction, still clutching his bag. As he approached the bottom he stopped, throwing his gaze out along the platform in front of him, vainly trying to relocate the man among the bobbing sea of heads. He tried to slow down his breathing, which by now had become conspicuous to passers-by to the point of distracting him from identifying his target. His eyes darted to and fro along the long narrow double-sided platform crowded with every nationality of visitor and the occasional lunchtime commuter. He was thankful at least that there were no trains in the station, but knew that unless he could identify the man quickly, he would surely disappear with the throng and achieve his getaway.

A gentle rumble suddenly caused a stir in the crowd below him as they moved toward the edge of the platform on his left. Nick caught sight of the dark curly-haired man wearing the black shirt through a small gap in the crowd about thirty yards ahead of him.

Without thinking, Nick shouted and leapt forward onto the platform. 'Stop him!'

Hearing the noise, the man turned briefly to look at Nick, before weaving his way as quickly as he could further down the platform.

The noise of the approaching train grew louder as Nick started to push people out of the way in a desperate effort to reach the man before it was too late. He stepped out toward the very edge of the platform beyond the green safety line. As he did so, the man similarly stepped over the line some twenty yards ahead, and saw Nick approaching at great speed. The man turned away from Nick, looked toward the end of the platform, and realised that he had nowhere to go. As Nick sped toward him, the man stood up straight, his body instantly relaxing and a calm smile breaking across his face. The incoming train emerged from the tunnel behind Nick with a thunderous roar and sped past him, buffeting him and almost blowing him off his feet as he continued his determined pursuit along the platform. He slowed momentarily, but kept his gaze fixed on the young man who was now a mere ten yards in front of him.

As the train drew level with the young man, he raised his left arm into the air and calmly took one side step off the platform, meeting the full force of the train head on as it roared to a halt at the station.

A single scream rang out from an older woman who had been standing close by, a noise muffled by the screeching brakes of the train. Then there was silence. The driver of the train bounded out of his cab and onto the platform, both hands holding his head, his mouth wide open but silent.

Nick was frozen to the spot, staring blankly at the space where a second before the young man had stood. The doors of the train opened and all around him the routine exchange of passengers burst into action. Nick continued to look down the platform. Through breaks in the blurred movement he could see the driver kneeling down and pointing at the track in front of the train, while two brightly coloured tourists were attending to a small middle-aged woman who was slumped against the end wall of the station.

Nick suddenly focused his thoughts and decided that, no matter what his next move was, it would not be to remain standing still on the platform. He looked around, now feeling very conspicuous. Surely, everyone had seen the young man step off the platform? Surely they had all heard *him* shout and run towards the man seconds before the fateful move?

Nick turned around, dropped his head and swiftly walked back toward the stairs. He tried to get as deep into the crowd as he could, as it made its way slowly, painfully slowly, toward the exit. He reached the stair. He took a step, then another, and another. He desperately wanted to look back, to convince himself that the man had not climbed back up onto the platform, and was by now heading for Nick. His heart raced. What the hell was he thinking about anyway? What if he had caught the man, the killer? What then? Even worse, what if the man wasn't a killer? Maybe the Cardinal's death was a tragic accident and he had just caused the death of an innocent man.

Another step ... and another. Nick took a deep breath, his head still bowed, his eyes staring at each step as he climbed slowly, higher toward safety. A whistle blew, then another. The crowd in front of him stopped. He heard voices above him, and tentatively raised his head and looked toward the top of the stairs. The crowd parted as three *carabinieri*, their whistles intermittently sounding out and echoing down into the platform and tunnels below, forced their way down the stairs. Nick held his breath and pushed his way further into the stationary mass to his side. He ran his fingers through his hair.

Nick decided that the quicker he got to the airport and caught a flight back to Stansted the better. The police were sure to find out sooner or later that the dead man had been chased across the Piazza del Duomo. A thousand people in broad daylight must have seen it, and were sure to be able to give the police a description that would eventually lead them to him. He needed to get home.

At the airport, Nick explained how his business trip had been shortened by a sudden illness at home and he desperately needed to return early. He was in luck. The 6.30 flight had two seats available on standby.

He sat on the plane feeling trapped. He was convinced that everyone around him knew his secret. He felt he *looked* guilty. But of what? The man had committed suicide. He couldn't have foreseen that. It wasn't his fault. His mind was racing. It still didn't make any sense. He thought about Cardinal Cornelli. By now he would have been found, and Nick knew that *his* death would be the more puzzling for the police. Perhaps it would be seen as a tragic accident, caused by a stumble over the piles of rubble and scaffold poles.

After an eternity the plane touched down and Nick's

heart raced even faster. Would there be a posse of police waiting for him on his arrival, to whisk him off to a local police station or march him straight back onto a plane for Milan? He scurried off as soon as the plane door opened, striding out along the long bare corridor, mixing in with passengers joining from other gates along the route. He reached the arrivals lounge, passed through passport control and emerged into the terminal building. He kept his head down and followed the exit signs, expecting at any moment to feel a hand on his shoulder. It didn't come. He emerged into the daylight, the bright sunshine momentarily blinding him. He quickly made straight for the car park and jumped into the Morgan. Once inside he sat back and felt the tension flow from his whole body. He was safe ... at least for the moment.

Chapter 12

The next morning Nick woke with a start. His inability to sleep had finally given way through sheer physical and mental exhaustion at some point in the middle of the night. For a split second he thought he had been having a nightmare. He quickly remembered he hadn't. The sweat was dripping from him, a result he decided, not only of the relentless summer heat wave, but also of his imagination, which, he felt, was draining him.

After showering he made some coffee and fed Morris, the only friend, he thought, who appeared untouched by the last few days. He tried to shut out the horror of the two deaths he had witnessed less than twenty-four hours before. His mind flashed back, for the first time, to the conversation with the Cardinal. If some of the Scrolls had been removed before 1947, could Robert's really be one of them? Yet, he had again had it confirmed that the document itself could not be genuine. He shook his head and ran his fingers through his hair, wishing he could somehow unwind time. His decisions, his persistence in finding answers, seemed to be doing little more than creating more questions.

He walked to the door and removed the morning paper from the letter box and sat at the brightly tiled breakfast bar. He suddenly thought of the Cardinal, and quickly started to scan through the pages of *The Times*. He reached page seven and his eyes were immediately drawn to a headline at the bottom of the left-hand column. He hurriedly read the article:

Milan Cardinal in Mystery Death
Italian police are today investigating the gruesome death
of Cardinal Gianfranco Cornelli at the Duomo in Milan.
The Cardinal was found late yesterday afternoon by two
workmen, impaled on an ornate sandstone column some
twelve feet below the cathedral's roof walkway. Early
indications are that the Cardinal may have been struck
by the boom of a crane carrying out work on the building's
crumbling structure.

Nick exhaled, suddenly aware that he had been holding
his breath as he read. He felt his heart pounding as he
read on.

The Pope broke off from his visit to Australia to express
his shock at the news, and his great admiration of the
academic work that the Cardinal had undertaken over his
lifetime. In particular he referred to his study of the Dead
Sea Scrolls, on which for several years the Cardinal had
led a team of religious academics from around the world.
The Pope said his counsel would be sadly missed.
   Police refused to confirm or deny any connection with
the apparent suicide earlier in the day of Abraham Stern,
an Israeli known to have links with the little-known Jewish
extremist organisation Shomrei Emet. The incident happened
in the Milan subway at approximately 2.15 p.m. (CET).
Eyewitnesses confirmed that he had stepped off the platform
into the path of an oncoming train. Unconfirmed reports,
however, suggest that he may have been involved in a
chase across the Piazza del Duomo shortly before his death.
   Police investigations are continuing.

Nick felt as though he was bolted to the seat, and that
any minute the door would burst open and he would be
led away. This had all got out of control and he couldn't

understand what was going on. He was convinced that there was a link between the scroll and the Cardinal's death, and, for that matter, the 'men in black'. But if they were out to get him, surely it wouldn't be that difficult. Whatever the answer it was clear that this had to be resolved quickly and now not only because of the Holborn building. He thought of Weisman. He seemed to be as lost as Nick, despite the surprise he had shown at their first meeting. Perhaps the librarian, Henry, could help. He didn't feel inclined to phone Weisman again, but perhaps Henry could help him with some of the Cardinal's comments. He had to try something. Nick decided not to carry the scroll with him. He left it in the biscuit tin and planted it carefully at the back of one of the kitchen units. Morris watched the interesting-looking object being slotted in next to his food tins.

Nick pointed at him. 'Don't you get any thoughts. It's past its sell-by date!'

Morris purred.

The four men sat at the long, walnut table in nervous silence. The grand, elegant boardroom was gloomy, only half-lit by daylight which managed to find its way in through the vast but heavily curtained window. It was not a place they enjoyed visiting, but the recent turn of events had left each of them both apprehensive and intensely excited.

They each wore simple black suits, no stripes or patterns, and plain dark ties, each a slightly different colour. One of them was a leading City analyst with a firm of international stockbrokers, and one a vice-governor of the Bank of England. A third was a member of the British Cabinet, and the fourth, one of the assistant governors of the BBC. They looked as unremarkable a group of professionals as could be found at any meeting in the City on any weekday. But this was no ordinary assembly. Earlier in the day each man had received a message, delivered by hand by a young man, to all intents and purposes the average bike delivery service rider, the only distinguishing feature being a small silver brooch on the left collar of his tight black cycle wear. The plain red manila envelopes bore no names or addresses. A piece of paper carefully folded once simply identified a time – 12.30 p.m.

Each recipient had simply acknowledged the receipt, not by signing, but by merely glancing at the brooch and nodding. It had confirmed their growing anticipation that the lifelong search that had been the centre of their lives could soon be over. But with it had come for each a nervous realisation of the enormity of the revelation, its implications and the effect not only on their people, on other nations and the world order, but also on themselves and their families. It was the day they had long awaited, but now that the possibility was upon them their mounting years had brought fear and apprehension. They knew such thoughts would pass, that the plans set out so long ago would ensure that they would be seen as strong leaders and guardians, guiding the country through the confusion and anger that would inevitably follow the revelations. Their patience and unstinting belief in the eventual discovery of the Scroll would finally pay off. Benjamin would lead them along the right path.

Just before 12.25 each of them had separately arrived at the imposing sandstone monolith at the heart of the City. It was unremarkable, but still had the unquestionable aura of wealth oozing from every stone in its facade and the imposing, if somewhat understated and anonymous, entrance lobby. The small brass plaque on the internal face of the entrance portico read simply –'The Truth Foundation'.

Each man had nodded politely to the concierge and proceeded to the furthest of the seven lifts in the lobby. To any other visitor or employee, the fact that this lift had a twenty-third floor button went unnoticed. The fact that the lift only accepted the instruction if the seventh and sixteenth floor buttons were depressed at the same time ensured that the chances of uninvited or involuntary guests reaching the floor were kept to a minimum. Once the correct sequence had been entered, each man turned to face the small, almost unnoticeable high-imaging camera in the crossbar above the lift door to allow verification of their image by the elaborate security system.

On reaching the building's top floor an efficient if somewhat stern-looking middle-aged woman sitting behind a small, uncluttered desk arose and greeted each visitor by name before turning away and walking swiftly in the opposite direction. It was a polite but mechanical exercise, a ritual that each one of them had undertaken dozens of times over the past thirty years. Today, however, had a completely different feel. The air of expectancy fell heavily around the building's very fabric. The understated grandness took on a new, seemingly higher level of power and importance.

Each followed silently along a dimly lit internal oak-lined corridor to its end, where two large ornate wood-panelled doors faced them. On entering through the imposing, but eerily silent doors, they acknowledged the others already present. Not since their first meeting had they been so apprehensive, so unsure of what lay ahead, even allowing for, or perhaps because of, their own experiences over those long years.

One of the group, a small stout man with rimmed glasses and a sallow complexion, gave a nervous cough and moved forward slightly in his seat. He placed both his palms on the table, his short fat fingers stained with the telltale signs of a heavy smoker, spots of perspiration clearly visible on the back of his hands. The others looked intently at him.

'I...' he started, but his voiced tailed away as he looked at each of them in turn. He dropped his shoulders as if too weary to even start his sentence, and gave a small sigh.

'My friends,' he said, smiling nervously and looking again at each of them. 'I have ... *we* have all waited a long time for this day, or at least for what we think we may hear today. I am sure that Benjamin will guide us through the days to come and...'

He was interrupted by a louder, shorter cough by the balding, distinguished-looking man sitting directly opposite him.

'Samuel, my good friend,' he started in a calm deep voice – the voice of a seasoned politician that had authority and experience etched in every tone. 'I think we should wait for Benjamin to tell us exactly what we know about the situation.' He raised his hands slightly as if trying to stop the conversation before it went any further.

Samuel looked at the other two members of the group, one sitting beside him, the other diagonally opposite. 'But you saw the papers this morning, Paul.' He looked at all three for confirmation.

'Yes, and all I know is that this Stephenson may, or may not, have what we want,' he proffered, his volume slightly louder, his tone more assertive.

Samuel leaned further forward in his chair. 'As far as I am concerned Stephenson is being given too much leeway. We should...' He cut short his sentence at the sound of the large wooden door at the opposite end of the room slowly opening. Each man instinctively straightened up and sat back in their chair, eyes now fixed on the door.

After a few seconds, a tall, physically powerful-looking man dressed in a sharp, dark suit strode into the room. He had the look of a man in his late fifties, but Benjamin Goldberg was almost in his seventieth year. His hair was thinning, an attractive mixture of black and silver, but his striking face had retained the taut, glowing skin of youth, with a jaw line that looked chiselled from rock and had given him so many admirers over his lifetime. He exuded an aura about his person which others found hard to ignore. The very way he carried himself stated his authority and gave the impression he lived his life on a higher plane from the onlooker. He had the look of a born leader. The almost exaggerated rigidity of his posture, the way he comfortably accentuated the width of his shoulders, and the immaculate way in which he wore his Savile Row suit, left no one in any doubt that he was a man who knew what he wanted, and knew exactly how to get it. Today it seemed he had succeeded.

He stopped at the end of the table and straightened up his large frame, dropping a small black folder onto the table in front of him. He looked sombre, but relaxed. Slowly he undid the single button on his suit, all the time his penetrating deep brown eyes watching the four expectant men at the other end of the table. He sat down slowly and placed both hands on top of the folder.

'Gentlemen...' he began, in the deep calm voice which the others had come to recognise over the years as if it were their own father's, '...it is time for us to prepare for our work. The time of our deliverance and for the freeing of our people is drawing near.' He spoke in calm, measured terms, looking at each of them in turn, assured that they were riveted to his every word. They were dramatic words, but, spoken by him, they sounded natural and believable.

'When each of us came to this country we came with

a belief, and in search of the evidence that would vindicate that belief. Today, gentlemen, we are closer to achieving that objective than we have ever been. We must make the preparations for the revelation. I will shortly send out the instructions to Washington, Rome, Moscow and Jerusalem. We must have coordination. There must be no gaps, no panic. You must ensure that your individual networks are kept intact and that your politicians, your banks and press are contained. Control must be swift.' The four men nodded to indicate their compliance with his instruction. Benjamin picked up the folder and slowly stood up. He walked down the room toward the four expectant men, and as he reached each one he opened the folder, pulled out a small bound report with an unmarked cover and placed it in front of them on the table. They remained closed.

'The instructions for each of you are set out in these papers. Make sure your people are fully briefed, then destroy them in the usual way. There must be no trace of our meetings. Our strength, gentlemen, as ever will lie in our lack of connectivity.' He placed both hands on the table and leaned forward, slowly moving his gaze from one to another. 'Now is the time for each of you to play your part. You must each be ready when the time comes to challenge, to persuade and finally to lead.' He rose slightly away from the table, and his voice took on a lower, more threatening tone. 'This is why you are where you are today, and I know you will not fail in your tasks.' He looked again at each man, their faces transfixed to his own, their bodies totally still. The moment seemed to last for an eternity, until he suddenly straightened upright and clapped his hands. The four men were startled by the sudden change in mood, each jumping slightly in their seats.

'Good!' exclaimed Benjamin as he made his way back

to his seat. He sat down, clasped his hands in front of him on the table and gave a faint smile. 'The next time we meet you will each have more power and wealth than you have ever dreamed of. You will each achieve your lifelong ambitions, and our people will have the recognition that they truly deserve.'

The four men, still sitting uncomfortably after the sudden change in their host's demeanour, glanced cautiously at each other. Samuel, the merchant banker, began to move uneasily in his seat. He opened his mouth unconsciously in reaction to the swirling questions inside his head.

Benjamin looked straight at him and smiled, leaning forward in his seat. 'Samuel. You look as though there is something you would like ... clarified. Please, share it with us. I am sure the others may be wanting to ask the same question.' His approach had changed to that of the concerned headmaster.

Samuel looked at the others. In all the time they had known Benjamin none had dared to question his instructions or challenge his authority over them. Beyond being the head of one of the world's great conglomerates they knew very little about him; what he did from day to day, his interests, and where he had come from. Indeed, like the rest of the outside world they knew next to nothing. But they had never queried his belief in finding the truth, and, after all, they each owed him a debt that they could never repay.

Their whole personae, their careers, their way of life were entirely down to him. Each of them, at an early age, had been handpicked and set off on rapidly rising careers in their respective fields, none of them sure why they in particular had been chosen. Even at times when mistakes were made, Benjamin had been there to sort them out. Enemies had often vanished suddenly or had rapid changes in fortune. Their rise to the top had been unprecedented.

They were favoured members of the community, quickly rising through social ranks to become Establishment figures with unblemished records, and highly respected by their peers and the public alike. The press had only kind words, and indiscretions had never become cause for public scrutiny.

And, yes, there had been times when each of them had, quietly, on their own, questioned Benjamin's power, his ability to ensure their continued success, but none spoke to another on the matter. They each accepted his guiding hand. He was their benefactor, someone who could see their abilities, and simply helped them make the most out of their lives. The occasional doubt about his methods had crept in from time to time – the disappearance of a rival; the sudden change of heart by an interviewing panel – had it been him?

But their success had, after all, eventually been through their own efforts. They had deserved what they had earned themselves. Over time the zeal and unbending belief in their common purpose had waned. When they were young they were convinced it would not be long before the evidence that Benjamin had promised them would be found and Christianity and Western civilisation would be rocked to the core. They had not truly understood how this would unfold, but it was their blind understanding of how it could be harnessed to bring each of them untold riches and power that had set them apart from Benjamin's other followers. They had only too willingly become part of his network, sleepers, quietly awaiting the day.

'Come, come, Samuel. Share your thoughts with us,' Benjamin insisted.

Samuel felt his throat tighten as though his body did not want him to say a word. 'I suppose it has been such a surprise to us all,' he stated somewhat unconvincingly, looking around the table for a glimmer of support. 'This sudden ... breakthrough.' There was little evidence of agreement from the others. He decided his choice of words wasn't quite appropriate, and the shift in Benjamin's body seemed to indicate a controlled displeasure. He tried to recover his position. 'What I mean is...'

Paul shook his head. He could no longer simply sit and let his colleague talk around the subject. 'What he means is that after all these years, the false judgements, the hoaxes from even our own people, how can we be sure that what this man Stephenson has found is the evidence?' He looked at the others for support. The man on his right, a taller, slimmer man with half-rimmed glasses, nodded his agreement. Paul looked straight at him, and he felt obliged to elaborate.

'What Paul says is valid, Benjamin. We have given you our unstinting support. When you have called we have responded. But this ... *evidence* does not seem to be conclusive. It is a mere fragment, from what we know of it. How can we be sure, and more importantly how will the world be convinced? Yes, we have influence, but only to ensure that the Word is heard. We cannot convince nations with a mere scrap of paper.'

The fourth man, Isaac, the journalist amongst them who had quite unexpectedly become a highly successful media tycoon and vice-governor of the ubiquitous BBC, decided that it was his opportunity to express his concerns at the recent turn of events.

'The incident in Milan was ... regrettable. My sources are already linking it to Cardinal Cornelli's work on the Scrolls. I have managed to suppress it, but I don't know for how long.' He looked back at the others. 'I have no doubt, though, my friends, that we can, and will prevail.'

They nodded somewhat reluctantly, but Isaac had raised something they had all thought but did not want to face. The possibility of linking them to the increasingly violent methods that they all privately believed Benjamin capable of employing seemed a greater possibility, and, although they had all been prepared at one time in their formative years to employ such tactics if they had been asked to, time and success had blunted their appetite for such measures. The Shomrei Emet had never been spoken about at any of their meetings, but over the years they had all concluded that they were indeed part of a much larger and far-reaching organisation than they dared believe, one within which they were trapped, and from which they could not extract themselves.

They all turned to Benjamin, each concerned that this unprecedented questioning of his authority, albeit obliquely, would bring an unwanted reaction. But Benjamin merely sat back in his chair and gave them a wry smile.

'You small little men!' he exclaimed. 'Have I not taught you enough of patience that each of you should doubt my thoroughness?' He shook his head slowly. 'Why do you think we have not yet moved on Mr Stephenson? Do you think I have shown weakness ... or did it occur to you that there is a reason?' He slowly looked at each of them in turn, taking care to ensure that they each saw the passion in his eyes that would leave them in no doubt of their individual role in his greater plan.

Eventually he stood up and straightened himself, gently resting his knuckles on the table. The anger within him was barely under control, but he knew that now was not the time to scare these mere pawns, accomplices with whom he had little option but to persevere until they had served their purpose. He would have to be patient himself. The final hour was approaching and soon he would be free of them, of all of them across the world. The intricate web that he had woven would ensure that, once it came, the glory would be his.

Chapter 13

Benjamin left the four men stuck to their seats and swiftly made for his office across the corridor. They would play their part when the time came, he was sure of that. He opened the door and entered the large, well-lit but windowless room, strode to the oak-panelled wall to his left and waved his hand across a small silver panel set at waist height. The door bolted locked with an audible click. He moved to the middle of the room where a large crescent-shaped desk sat on top of a raised platform half a metre above the surrounding floor level.

He paused for a moment, his hands grasping the back of his leather-clad chair. His mind wandered back briefly over random but nevertheless defining moments of his life. He could see the resignation and fear in his father's eyes as he bade a hasty goodbye to his only son, the sound of gunfire and urgent cries from Jewish men, women and children as they were rounded up by the Nazis to be shipped out to face near-certain death in the concentration camps. The journey out of Germany – brokered by a family friend who had been only too willing to profit from the desperation of a wealthy Jew – had seemed to last an eternity. Young Benjamin had been old enough to realise that the promises of an adult, even one known to him since birth, were not to be relied upon. But, true to his word, the friend had delivered him to the safekeeping of the Dominican brothers in their monastery high in the French Alps.

He thought again about his father. To Benjamin he was

like a god. His mother, having died giving birth to Benjamin, had created an intense bond between father and son. Benjamin had only ever wanted to be like his father – strong, assured, respected and, above all, truthful. He had only these pure thoughts and recollections, intensified by the nature of their separation. For years after the war had ended, he waited for his father to come for him, to return them both to the land of his birth, to the only place he really knew. Eventually, of course, he had conceded that he would never see him again, but he refused to believe that his father, such a clever, strong man, could not have escaped his captors and avoided death, and was now living a necessarily covert life somewhere where his accounting skills would be appreciated and rewarded.

He pictured his father's face as he held his young son tightly in both arms, the frantic yet gentle eyes trying desperately to calm the hysterical boy.

'Remember three things, my son. Be truthful to yourself, read the Scriptures and never show your fear.' He had always thought that these were words that could have been spoken by a thousand fathers to a thousand sons, but never in such circumstances, and never with the devastating effect they had on the young Benjamin. His father then leaned over and whispered to him as he pushed a small envelope into his son's coat pocket. 'Guard this carefully and let no one see it. One day you will understand its meaning.'

He winced slightly as he pictured the family friend desperately urging them to be on their way. As he was prised, crying uncontrollably, from his father's grasp, he recalled, as he had done a million times since, his father's parting words: *Remember, my son, a man is measured by the wake he leaves, not by the direction in which he swims.*

* * *

140

'Henry's in Scriptures – row 14 at the back,' said the receptionist, hardly looking up at Nick.

'Thank you,' answered Nick, not feeling inclined to draw attention to himself by extending the comment. He found row 14 and moved quietly down the narrow book-lined passage. He could see Henry perched on a small footstool, folded up over a book, his knees tucked under his chin. He still looked tall.

As Nick approached, Henry leapt to his feet, pointing at Nick. 'The Scrolls!' he said, as if reminding Nick why he had ever been in the place.

Nick nodded. 'You remember,' he said, consciously forcing a smile. It was remote, of course, to say the least, but could Henry have made a connection with the news of Cardinal Cornelli?

Nick's thoughts were quickly interrupted. 'You got me thinking,' said Henry, a serious frown of enthusiasm bursting across his thin face. 'I hadn't read up on them for some time and I've been getting back up to speed.' He held up a book in front of Nick to prove the point.

'Good ... good.' It was all Nick could think of. He took Henry's arm and led him away from the stool. 'Look, can we have another chat about them? I've got another couple of questions that the books I looked at the other day have thrown up.' Henry's face beamed as Nick led him back along the passage toward the reading room.

'Sure, why don't you come into the office? I'm due a tea break anyway. It's nice and private there, and we can talk.'

Nick smiled. 'Perfect.'

The office turned out to be no more than a large cupboard and seemed to be doubling as a book hospital. There were ripped and coverless books everywhere – on the room's single desk, on the floor, on the bookshelves that covered all four walls, and on one of the two rather battered- looking chairs sitting in the middle of the room. Henry removed the pile of books from one seat and offered the other to Nick. He sat on the edge of his seat and looked at Nick intently. 'So, what can I do for you?' he asked, sounding to Nick like an enthusiastic junior doctor.

'Well, Henry,' Nick began, trying hard to sound as though this was simply a general enquiry for knowledge from someone who knew little. It wasn't far from the truth. 'The thing is, I'm perplexed. All these scrolls, or thousands of bits, as I now realise they are, were all found together in one place at the same time. Now they're all in the hands of one of two groups of academics...' Nick paused. He was waiting for Henry to jump in. He did.

'Well ... not quite,' Henry said slowly, like a great detective about to reveal the missing piece of evidence. 'You see, the Bedouins who found them tried to sell them initially, and no one really took any interest. There was a lot of confusion in the region at the time, what with the war ending and so on. No one really knew what they were.'

'So could some of them have been removed before the authorities got there?' asked Nick.

'God, yes!' stated Henry, as though the fact was obvious. 'The Bedouins were traders! Businessmen! Some of them held on to them and then flogged the stuff later when it was realised they were valuable.'

'How valuable?' asked Nick.

'I'm not sure,' replied Henry, as though the question was somewhat irrelevant. 'How do you value something like that?'

'Well, presumably there would be private collectors who would pay a lot of money for something like that?'

'I suppose so, but once the authorities realised what they were, they put the word out that they were willing to buy any unaccounted for.'

Nick thought for a moment. 'How could they tell what was unaccounted for?' he asked. 'Did they have a ... an index of some sort?'

Henry looked at him; it was his turn to think. 'No, not as far as I know.' He looked thoughtful, as though he was about to fail a customer with a question on *his* chosen subject. 'There was only a space of a few months between the cave being discovered and the authorities taking complete control of them and their contents.'

Nick looked at him intently. 'A few months, are you sure?'

'Yes,' replied Henry.

'In 1947?' Nick added.

'Yes,' said Henry, a smile appearing on his face. 'You should know the year by now!' he added, nudging Nick with his elbow and feeling once again that his superior knowledge had been established.

Nick shrugged his shoulders. He decided to chance his arm. He leaned forward in his chair and rested his elbows on his knees. Henry instinctively did likewise. Nick started to whisper. 'Look. Henry, what if someone had got to the caves earlier – a child perhaps, or a traveller – who stumbled across them and removed a handful of them before the Bedouins ever found them?'

Henry looked at Nick intently, the expression on his face indicating he was absorbing the suggestion but considered it highly unlikely.

Nick continued, realising that he was going to have to spell it out for his new-found friend.

'If these scrolls were hidden away as ... an investment, shall we say, by an unscrupulous collector, wouldn't they be worth an awful lot of money in today's market?'

Henry sat up a little and scratched the back of his head. 'Well, I suppose so,' he said, clearly unconvinced. He shook his head. 'It's pretty doubtful though that anyone

143

finding them could have kept them quiet, or wouldn't have returned to the place for some more. Finding them must have been like entering Aladdin's cave!' He laughed to himself.

Nick grinned. 'Well, I'm sure *you* might think so, Henry!'

Nick decided that, although Henry knew a lot about the Scrolls, he wasn't the sharpest person he'd ever met. He had to take a chance with someone who could find out more information without being overly suspicious, or being able to piece the whole puzzle together. He thought back to Cardinal Cornelli's last words, and the report in the morning paper. Henry was his only chance.

'What is the Emet Scroll?' he asked, as casually as he could.

Henry looked at him with a blank expression. 'I don't know. *Emet* is the Hebrew word for "truth" but I've never heard of a "Truth Scroll". What is it?'

Nick grinned. 'I was hoping *you* would know, Henry. I think it may be one of the Dead Sea Scrolls. What do you think?'

Henry sat up straight, a deep, thoughtful look on his face. He shook his head slowly. 'I don't recognise it,' he said. 'If it is, it must be one of the least researched. Why do you ask?' Nick leaned even further toward him, almost bent over completely to exaggerate the importance of what he was about to say. He looked back out of the door, as if checking that no one could hear him and he beckoned Henry toward him. Henry enthusiastically obliged.

'Let's just say I have an interest in that particular scroll.'

Henry looked at Nick with another blank expression and nodded his head slowly. He paused for a moment or two, then gradually a grin appeared on his face.

He raised his finger and pointed at Nick. 'Wait a minute,' he said as if a penny had suddenly dropped. 'You know a collector who has a scroll and he wants to know if it's an original, don't you?' Henry sat up straight again, pleased with himself, and still nodding his head.

Nick pretended to check the door again, to make sure no one was listening. 'Shhh,' he said quietly. 'My ... friend doesn't know if it's real or not, but he does know that it was found before 1947 and it's called the Emet Scroll. I'm trying to find out discreetly, on his behalf, whether he's got the real thing or not, but you'll understand my ... reluctance to be too open about it.'

Henry nodded reassuringly, to signify that he understood the importance of being discreet.

'Well,' he said, 'it wasn't just the books of the Old Testament that were found. There were extracts from parchments that were referred to as things like the War Scroll, but I've definitely never heard of the Truth Scroll.' He seemed to think about it for a moment. 'Seems a peculiar name for a scroll. I mean, they're all supposed to be truthful when you think about it.' He chuckled. 'Are you sure that was the word...'

Nick looked at him. He thought of Cardinal Cornelli. He would never forget the word. He had no idea if it referred to the title of a scroll or not, but in view of his total lack of understanding of what was going on, it seemed an idea worth pursuing.

'Yes. It is the word,' he stated.

Henry shook his head and rubbed his long, pointed chin. Suddenly he clicked his fingers. 'I know. I had some papers sent from the University of Jerusalem a couple of years back which identified the various different passages and books which they had been able to identify among all the fragments.' He sprung to his feet. 'Give me two minutes and I'll go and get them. They're in the reference section.'

Before Nick could say anything Henry had shot out of the door and was heading rapidly back along the narrow passageway. Nick sat back in his seat. He thought again about Cardinal Cornelli. He was sure about the word, but thought that perhaps the Cardinal had not used it in a literal sense. Perhaps there was another scroll with a different title. In any case, what was it, and why was it so important? Nick knew he had taken a risk in telling Henry as much as he had, but on the other hand he needed help quickly, and there was little that Henry could do with the information anyway.

Several minutes passed as Nick sat in the cramped little room looking around at the hundreds of books lying motionless and silent, yet bursting with knowledge and information. He looked at his watch and thought of the Holborn site. He would have to make a site visit and eventually face the music with Mr Forster. Henry was taking too long to find what he was looking for. Nick decided to find him.

The long passage from the room was enclosed by row after row and shelf after shelf of books of every size, colour and shape. He reached the end of the passage and moved out into the reading area. He looked around, trying to spot Henry's mop of curly hair. The library seemed to be completely empty. There was no sign of him, so Nick moved across through an empty row of desks, then turned to his left and walked toward the reference section. He stopped at the neatly aligned rows of wooden index files that stretched ahead of him for what seemed like miles, row upon row of tiny brass handles set into the beautifully carved cabinet.

He looked around, but there was still no sign of Henry, nor, he noticed, anyone else. He slowly started walking along the length of the cabinet, glancing left and right down the narrow aisles packed with books, files and papers on either side. He reached the fifth row and suddenly heard what sounded like a muffled cry followed by a thud

146

coming from somewhere ahead on his right-hand side. He stood still for a moment listening for any further noises, but looking ahead noticed the bookcase two rows in front of where he stood shake slightly.

He strode quickly forward and turned the corner into the aisle. The first thing he noticed were Henry's sizeable brown shoes and cord trousers protruding out from underneath a man dressed all in black. As Nick drew closer he could see a knee was pressed against Henry's chest and a large hand apparently grabbing at Henry's throat. As Henry tried to struggle free, Nick instinctively leaped forward and grabbed at the man's hair and pulled back his head with considerable force. As he fell backwards onto the floor a syringe flew out of the man's hand and landed against one of the bookshelves. Nick was so shocked he couldn't move and his legs felt like they were glued to the spot. In that fraction of a second the man grabbed Nick's right leg and pulled it towards him, sending Nick sprawling backwards across the tiled floor.

The man rolled over and grabbed the syringe. He got up onto his knees. Nick regained his senses and leaped back onto his feet, stepping back as he saw the man kneeling in the aisle, his outstretched arm pointing the syringe menacingly at him. Both stared at each other, neither making the slightest movement, other than that caused by their heavy breathing. Eventually the man slowly raised his left hand and pointed for Nick to back off. Nick looked over the man's shoulder at Henry, who was still lying on his back, moaning. He could see that a heavy tape had been placed across his mouth, and his arms appeared to be folded behind his back as though tied in some way.

The man slowly crouched up on one leg. Nick placed both hands at his sides, palms up. 'Now,' he said nervously. 'Don't do anything silly.' Nick realised that for all intents and purposes the man was trapped in the aisle. The far end had no exit and, although Nick was only a step or two from the open end, he was not yet inclined to turn and run. His only thought was to make sure that neither he nor Henry received whatever concoction the syringe contained.

The man extended his left hand further out in front of him and slowly turned round to look at Henry. Nick noticed that the man was slowly bending down, and his right hand suddenly shot back towards Henry, the needle of the syringe pointing directly at Henry's leg. Nick looked in horror at the movement, and without thinking took two rapid steps forward and kicked out his right leg, catching the man on his outstretched arm and sending him flying backwards towards Henry. As he fell, the man raised his right arm out to the side and let go of the syringe, trying to break his fall by grabbing at the shelves of books on his right.

This time Nick didn't hesitate. As the man landed backward on top of Henry, Nick threw himself at him, rolling him to the side and pinning him to the ground. Instinctively he lashed out at the man's face, catching him square on the jaw, momentarily concussing him. Nick scrambled full on top of him, and rolling him over onto his side pushed his right arm underneath his back before pinning him down. He knelt on the man's stomach and placed his right arm under his chin and hard against his throat.

'OK, you bastard, who are you?' he said in a voice that expressed all the anger and pent-up frustration that had built up within him over the last few days. The man stared up at him with a glazed look and grunted. 'What do you want?' Nick continued, 'Why have you been following me and why have you attacked this man? ... Who *are* you?' The questions flooded out of Nick. He had so many and now that he had actually managed to trap one of the mysterious men in black he was not about to let go until he had all the answers.

The man's eyes began to focus on Nick. He gave a curious smile, like someone who was finally conceding defeat after a long hard struggle. Nick thought back to the underground in Milan. He waited for a few seconds and took some deep breaths to regain his composure and sort out his thoughts. He eased off his arm, which he suddenly realised was almost blocking the man's windpipe. 'Who *are* you? I want an answer now!' he said more slowly,

The man looked up at him. 'You can kill me if you want, but another will take my place,' he answered calmly. Nick looked at him in disbelief. Who was this man, and the others who seemed so unafraid of pain? Nick raised his right arm and clenched his fist to make it obvious that he intended to punch him in the face again. He watched the man's reaction closely. He did not flinch, but kept his focus firmly on Nick's eyes.

Nick decided that the man was calling his bluff. He was a trained killer and Nick was out of his depth, but he had to try to scare the man into believing that he, too, could kill, or at least inflict some serious pain if necessary. Nick clenched his teeth together and brought the full force of his right hand down onto the man's face, closing his eyes at the last moment in anticipation not only of seeing pain in the man's face, but also feeling the expected pain in his own hand.

When he opened his eyes he realised that both had occurred. Blood started to trickle from the man's nose, and his face was grimacing from the blow, his eyelids momentarily shut tightly and the muscle in his left cheek twitching uncontrollably. He uttered no sound.

Nick sat up slowly, shocked at what he had forced himself to do. He looked over at Henry whose eyes were now open, but was clearly still dazed.

Nick decided he had to carry through the threat. He placed his right hand around the man's throat and leaned over him once more.

'Now, shall we try again?' he said, in a voice he did his best to make sound convincingly menacing. The man opened his eyes and stared once again at Nick. 'I am ready to die,' he answered and forcibly brought his lips together as if signalling that he intended to say no more. Nick was momentarily lost as to what to do next. He glanced around him and caught sight of the needle next to the man's throat and slowly reached down with his left hand to grab hold of the syringe. The man did not move. Nick slowly, carefully, pulled it towards his hand until he was able to grab it. He sat up quickly back onto the man's chest and held the needle directly above his face.

'Perhaps this will help you talk,' Nick said, squeezing the syringe gently, sending a small spurt of liquid out onto the man's reddened cheek. He looked at the man's face, which nonetheless remained expressionless, his eyes still firmly fixed on Nick's. Nick reached out and grabbed the man's right arm, rolling up his sleeve to the elbow. There was no struggle from the man whose body now seemed to be totally relaxed.

Nick moved across the man's chest and leaned with the full force of his knee on the man's upper left arm. He lowered the needle until it was touching the bare forearm. He looked back at the man's face, which remained totally impassive. Nick decided to have one last go. 'This is your last chance to talk,' he said, pushing the syringe against the forearm as hard as he could without breaking the surface of the skin.

The man's lips parted slowly and he continued to look straight into Nick's eyes. 'Goodbye, Mr Stephenson,' he said calmly and slowly, before closing his eyes.

Nick was stunned. Here was a man quite prepared to

die for whatever it was he wanted or believed in, but there was no way he was going to tell Nick what is was. At least Nick knew it *was* him that the man was interested in, but he couldn't understand what his interest would be in Henry, and why he ... they ... had not attacked *him*.

Slowly, Nick eased the syringe away from the man's arm and reaching up placed it on a shelf above him. He looked at the face of the young man and shook his head. He had threatened him in a way he never knew he was capable of doing, and he was not inclined to try anything else to make him talk, or indeed hurt him.

Nick thought for a few moments and concluded that there was no option now but to go to the police and tell them as much as he could. He knew it would sound ridiculous and that he would be risking his own future. There seemed little alternative. He slowly raised his knees from the man's chest and stood up, constantly watching for any sudden movement. 'Get up!' he said to the man, still trying to sound in control of the situation.

The man kept his gaze firmly fixed on Nick's eyes as he gradually rose to his feet and stood upright in front of him, straightening his body up in an almost defiant gesture, arms firmly straightened at his side. Nick wasn't sure what to do next. As he pondered his next move Henry let out a muffled grown at the man's feet. Nick looked down at him, and in the split second while his guard was down the man lunged past Nick, causing him to stumble against the bookshelf and end up on one knee in the narrow passageway.

Henry lifted his torso off the ground as far as he could, muffling exaggerated expletives at the man's escape. Nick decided not to give chase. He was suddenly very glad to have rid himself of the attacker.

Henry continued to mumble through the tape and rolled over onto his side, revealing what Nick had suspected.

His wrists had been taped together behind his back. Nick pulled the tape off Henry's mouth and rolled him onto his side to release his hands. He helped him slowly get onto his feet, Henry's entire body seemingly trembling under his helping hand.

'Are you OK?' he asked, staring directly into Henry's eyes.

'I don't know,' answered Henry, blinking hard, as if he was checking he wasn't asleep and merely dreaming the nightmare.

'Come on, let's get you back to your office. I'll see if we can get you a drink.' Henry started walking slowly along the aisle, Nick still holding his arm to steady him. They reached the empty librarian's desk in the middle of the great room when Henry suddenly stopped and turned to Nick.

'Did you see the stud in his ear?'

Nick looked back at Henry and shook his head.

'The Qumran Brotherhood. It was their sign ... their identity,' Henry added with a look of disbelief. 'A triangle, the sign of the three elements of life – Earth, Man and God – laid on top of the eternal circle – the Sun.' He took a long breath. 'What's going on?' He stood up as straight as he could and pulled his arm away from Nick's clasp, now looking at him suspiciously, his eyes darting back and forward between Nick's, as if he was trying to see beyond them and into his head. He backed away slightly, a look of fear now taking over. 'Who are you anyway?' he asked Nick, as if a huge gulf had suddenly opened up between them.

Nick didn't know where to start. But he had his connection. Somehow he wasn't altogether surprised, but things were perhaps now beginning to come together; connections were being made. The trouble was, having more of the pieces didn't actually make the picture any clearer.

Nick glanced around him. There were now a few people

standing as still as statues facing the endless bookshelves. The place was still as quiet and peaceful as any library would be anywhere, as if nothing had happened. Nick decided that he had no time to waste trying to placate his frightened companion. He grabbed Henry's arm and started marching him back toward the storeroom. 'Look, I'll explain everything. The truth is I'm not sure myself, but you have to trust me.'

He led Henry into the room, forcibly pushed him down into a chair, kicked the door stopper away and firmly closed the door behind them. He walked over to the water chiller in the corner of the room and poured a full measure into a plastic cup. He handed it to Henry who nodded slightly and held the cup in both shaking hands, sipping a small amount carefully as if he was terrified to spill a drop.

Nick grabbed the other chair and pulled it across the floor close to Henry. He sat on the edge and leaned forward, staring intently into Henry's eyes to make sure he gained his full attention.

Henry stared back at Nick, his eyes heavy and the slight movement in his torso betraying the fact that he was clearly still in a state of shock. After a few moments, Nick decided Henry was regaining his faculties and was once again capable of having a meaningful conversation.

'Are you OK?' he asked, gently tapping Henry on the side of his knee.

Henry nodded his head, but the expression on his face didn't change.

'Look, Henry,' said Nick in a softer tone, realising he had to work at gaining his trust once again. 'I know this must feel like a bad dream, but it's one I've been living for the past five days. I know you don't understand any of this, but I think you might be able to help me end it.'

Henry looked back at Nick with a puzzled expression on his face. 'End what?' he asked, a deep frown appearing across his pale face. 'This has got something to do with your ... Truth Scroll, hasn't it? I'm only a low-paid assistant librarian, you know. I don't want any trouble.'

Nick looked back at him. 'Yes, Henry, I believe it has,' he answered, trying to sound sincere and as honest as possible to make the confused librarian feel more at ease. But he realised he had to strike now, gain as much information as he could before Henry had too much time to think. He could not afford to have him clam up completely.

'You said you recognised the man's earring', Nick pursued, hoping to illicit more information from his stunned companion.

Henry screwed up his eyes, as though trying to picture the attacker.

'Yes,' he finally said, firmly. 'The Qumran Brotherhood. It was their sign, their ... membership badge.' He straightened up in his seat. He started to shake his head, a nervous grin appearing on his face. 'But we're talking about something that existed over two thousand years ago. The Qumran Brotherhood doesn't exist any more. It's ... gone. Like the Roman army or ... King Arthur. It's like any other ... legend.'

Nick interrupted him, thinking back to *The Times* article. 'Have you ever heard of the Shomrei Emet?'

Henry screwed up his eyes again as if searching some great catalogue in his mind, flicking through the index until he found the relevant card. Eventually he nodded his head. 'Yes. It's a Jewish terrorist group. Nobody really knows what they're about, or what exactly they stand for, but they've been more active in recent years. Acts of sabotage and attacks against prominent Roman Catholics, scholars ... you know, theologians, who don't share their beliefs. Pretty random acts though. I don't think the authorities have ever worked out any real motive'.

'What do they believe in?' Nick asked.

Henry shook his head slightly. 'Well I'm not really sure. They're linked to other orthodox Jewish groups, but most of *them* disown "The Guardians of the Truth"...'

Nick interrupted Henry again, his eyes and mouth wide open. ' "The Guardians of the Truth"? Is that what Shomrei Emet means?'

'Yes,' said Henry. 'Typically obscure name really. They always seem to pick names that...' He stopped suddenly and stared at Nick.

'No! You don't think this is linked to your friend's scroll do you? You think that man was one of them, don't you?'

Nick looked straight back at Henry. It was a hell of a coincidence, but of course, he thought, that may be all it was. His mind was racing now. He tried to make a link between all the elements, the incidents of the last few days. What did a Jewish terrorist group want with him, or, more exactly, with people he seemed to come into contact with? The scroll certainly seemed to be the key, but there was something missing. Something didn't add up about the way they had been acting. He had not been attacked directly. Why not?

He sat back in his seat slightly. 'Assuming my friend did have one of the Dead Sea Scrolls,' he hypothesised, 'why would they be keen to get their hands on it?'

Henry looked at Nick with a blank expression and shrugged his shoulders. 'I don't know', he eventually offered.

Nick had thought about this before, but now it seemed to take on a fresher impetus. He decided to try out a couple of other hypotheses with Henry. 'What if they were merely being used by some rich collector who wanted to add a genuine Dead Sea Scroll to his collection ... at any cost? It seems to me it would be an ideal front to protect his anonymity.'

An expression of doubt appeared over Henry's face. 'I suppose it's possible,' he said. 'But it seems unlikely to me that such a group would let themselves be used in that way. I did study one or two of the more renowned Middle Eastern terrorist outfits, and they don't tend to be driven by money ... or philanthropy. Ideology's their thing.' He shook his head. 'No,' he continued, 'if they want what your friend has then they must see some other value in it.'

Nick looked at Henry. He had, of course, thought of the same possibility, but in some way had hoped that Henry would see the sense in his first possibility. Greed always seemed the easiest motive to comprehend. 'OK, let's try this. Assuming there is a connection between the group and the scroll that my friend has – which may, or may not, be called the Truth Scroll – why would they be so keen to get their hands on it? If it isn't money, then, as you say, it must be purely to have it in their possession. Surely the scroll itself can't be that valuable?'

Henry looked at Nick and shrugged his shoulders. 'At the end of the day, it would be down to what the scroll says.'

'Yes', said Nick. 'But if it was stolen from the original fragments found in 1947, then surely that would have been reported. And I don't imagine that those involved in cataloguing the scrolls would hire some terrorist group to recover it, do you?'

Nick could see that Henry's mind was again working in overdrive.

Henry wagged his finger toward Nick. 'That's why you think this scroll may have been found *before* 1947, isn't it?'

Nick gave a wry smile. He knew he had led Henry to

the conclusion, but a conclusion it was. If he was right, and this wasn't about money, then whatever was written in the scroll must be worth dying for ... literally. At least it was to some.

'Oh, one other thing, Henry. I seem to remember reading that the Scrolls were handed over to a bunch of Catholic priests and scholars.'.

'Yes,' said Henry. 'The Ecole biblique.'

'The Ecole biblique?' repeated Nick slowly.

'Yip. The Ecole biblique et archéologique française de Jerusalem, to be precise. It's an institution run by Dominican monks with backing from the French Government. It wasn't until a couple of years after they were found that the Scrolls' potential importance began to be realised and there was a sort of power struggle to see who would get control of them.'

Nick interrupted. 'But if these writings are supposed to be the foundation of Judaism, why is it the Catholic Church has control of them?'

'Ah!' said Henry. 'The great conspiracy theory!'

Nick's eyebrows jumped. 'What conspiracy?'

'Well, you see one of the theories on why so little has been released suggests that the Scrolls threaten the whole basis of Christianity, and for that reason the Roman Catholic Church is suppressing information about them – about what they actually say.'

'How could the Scrolls do that?' asked Nick.

'It's been suggested', continued Henry, 'that some of the statements and phrases attributed to Jesus in the New Testament have been found written in the Scrolls.'

Nick looked at Henry with a blank expression.

'Look, don't you see? If some of Jesus' teachings were written in the Scrolls a hundred years before his birth, then he may only have been repeating things already written by the Qumran Brotherhood. He might even have

157

been one of them! There's very little known about him before the age of thirty. Some writers have suggested that he was only repeating stories and prophecies that had been recorded in the Scrolls by someone who is referred to as "The Teacher". Jesus might have been little more than a brilliant PR man for the Brotherhood.'

Nick ran his fingers through his hair. 'This is unbelievable, Henry,' he said, a sarcastic grin breaking across his face. 'Do you really believe that sort of stuff?'

Henry threw an innocent-looking glance back at Nick and shrugged his shoulders. 'You asked me the question. There are all sorts of theories, but that's not really surprising given the lack of information that's come out about the Scrolls. The biggest mystery remains the fact that so little is still known about them after all this time.'

Nick thought about it. An organisation indirectly controlled by the Catholic Church in possession of what seemed to be the very foundation of the Jewish religion, and yet so little of it made known. But then again, he thought, it seemed a bit like adding two and two, and getting fourteen. The whole thing seemed to be getting more ridiculous by the day. He shook his head. He decided he had got as much from Henry as he was likely to need. He decided that the option of going to the police had somewhat evaporated now that the 'captive' had escaped. He thought of Robert ... and Rachel.

'One other thing, Henry. What would an eagle insignia have to do with this ... if it was found on something associated with the scroll?'

Henry shrugged his shoulders. 'The eagle has been a symbol used by many tribes and even individuals throughout the ages. I suppose the obvious connection would be with the Nazis. They used the symbol of the eagle in the same way as the Romans over two thousand years before them as they went to war. It is a sign of strength.'

Nick thought about it for a moment. It seemed obvious that the connection had to be with the German expedition that had discovered the scroll.

'Look, I have to get back to my office, Henry. I'll straighten this out in the next day or so'.

Henry looked at him in disbelief. 'What do you mean? You can't just walk away! Aren't we going to phone the police? I've just been attacked! Here, in my own library!' His face was now fully animated, if somewhat drawn-looking. 'Anyway', he added, 'if it is your friend's scroll they are after, why attack me?'

Nick had, of course, wondered the same thing. The Cardinal, Henry, the break-ins at his apartment and the site. He realised that he had to put Henry off taking this any further.

'I'm sure it must have been mistaken identity. They're after me, Henry, not you. I'm the one who knows where the scroll is.' He looked intently at Henry and patted him again on the knee. 'I promise I'll stay away from here. I know they won't be back, Henry'.

Henry didn't look convinced.

'Look, here's my card. If you want to speak to me you can reach me at my office or on my mobile.' Nick stood up, removed a business card from his wallet and handed it to Henry, who stared at it for a few moments, a look of hopeless disbelief on his face. Nick turned and walked to the door. He looked back to Henry. 'Thanks, by the way. You've been very helpful. If I ever think of rejoining a library, I'll come here. I never realised they were such exciting places these days!'

Henry smiled ... briefly.

Chapter 14

Benjamin sat at the large crescent-shaped desk and took a deep breath. He stretched out his long arm and touched the glass top with his right forefinger. Immediately, the whole central section of the desk lit up like an aircraft control panel. A series of unmarked lights flashed repeatedly in the middle of the display, and a digital touchpad keyboard illuminated directly in front of him. Two small display screens flickered at the far end of the desk, the busy cursors eagerly awaiting his instruction. A polite-sounding mechanical voice, recognising his fingerprint pattern, welcomed him. He looked up at the wall directly ahead as he touched the glass above one of the lights. Two of the oak panels in the wall slowly peeled away revealing a bank of television screens, a large widescreen one in the middle flanked by another three on either side. All six of the smaller TVs were silently broadcasting different channels from around the world. He quickly scanned them and then gave an instruction to an invisible assistant.

'Review of news. Last eighteen hours.'

A mechanical voice responded quietly. 'Topic please.'

'Cardinal Gianfranco Cornelli, Milan.'

After only a few seconds the voice returned: 'One late-evening news item on the life of Cardinal Cornelli. RAI.'

'Play,' he commanded.

Benjamin relaxed back into his seat and watched the ten-minute piece on the night-time news review. After the initial coverage of the Cardinal's death, no one had yet picked up on the story as anything other than a tragic accident. Two members of the public had already been injured during the repairs to the Duomo, resulting in a ban on anyone accessing the roof area. This, of course, had not applied to the resident clergy and the precarious temporary footways had clearly been less than adequate to give safe passage to the ageing Cardinal. No suspicious circumstances were being reported. His associates had done their job.

He leaned forward again in the seat and spoke. 'Washington ... Martin Weinberger, National Security Agency ... full encryption.'

The voice repeated the command. Within twenty seconds Benjamin was connected to the second highest-ranking official in the US Security Administration, in Langley, Virginia. The small, plump, bespectacled face of Martin Weinberger appeared on the screen. 'Hello, Benjamin. Do you have news for me already?' His tone was pleasant if somewhat to the point. 'Everything is prepared at this end.'

'Not yet, Martin. I want to be assured that the entire network is in place and ready. The United States will be the first to challenge, and you must be prepared for every eventuality. I am trusting you with a great responsibility.'

Weinberger frowned. 'I have known you for a long time, Benjamin. I have never let you down. I will not let you down at the time of our final deliverance. I have over 400 agents, all locally handpicked – the best we have. They were dispersed yesterday to their targets as we discussed. No team knows about the others. Maximum security. We will have the control we need, when we need it, but I can only hold them in place so long. I have designated a training exercise, but suspicions will be raised amongst my subordinates if this starts to drag on...'

Benjamin interrupted. 'It will not "drag on" any longer

than it has to, of that you can be assured.' His tone was commander to subordinate, but in the back of his mind he knew that the situation was becoming more urgent. He would need to draw out the precious evidence quickly, but for now he was still convinced that his patient strategy would give the best result.

'I want you to inform the media about the operation. Channel it through the normal route.'

'What? You want me to ... leak the operation to the press? Why?' Weinberger sounded incredulous at Benjamin's request. 'This will merely expose our hand. It is not yet time.'

'Time is moving on as you said yourself. We must start to prepare the way. Do it! I will call you when it is time to move.' Benjamin tapped the top of the desk and the wall screen immediately went blank.

He sat back in his chair again, closed his eyes and took a long deep breath. After all these years the final piece of the jigsaw was almost in his grasp. He had never doubted that it was there and that one day, in his lifetime, it would emerge, although there were many of his accomplices, apparent believers, who had wavered. Many indeed had come and gone, their silence either bought or in most cases 'arranged' when they could no longer be trusted. Too many red herrings had made him cautious, but also patient.

Benjamin's mind started to wander, and he chose to let it do so for a few moments. He was able to match his physical presence with an intellect that had set him apart from his peers from an early age. He spoke six languages fluently and could pass as competent in another three. He had studied at three of the world's finest seats of learning on three different continents, leaving each with distinctions in a vast range of subject matter from politics to fine art. It was a grounding he had carefully calculated would provide him with the measured insight he knew he would need to carry out his father's dying wish. He had an unsurpassed knowledge of the cultures, the psyches, of a dozen nations. Leadership had come naturally to Benjamin Goldstein and through the sheer power of his own personality and self-inspired determination he had overcome, or perhaps blanked out, the terror and fear of his childhood trauma.

He thought back to his time at the monastery, the coldness and brutality meted out by the Catholic brothers to himself and the other little Jewish orphan boys whose families could afford to smuggle them out of a hostile Germany to a hidden refuge in the mountains. And yet he had learned so much from them. Their passion for Scripture – the reason, he had later surmised, for his father's decision to plead sanctuary for the young Benjamin in the Catholic hideaway in the first place, a decision that God, or fate, had already decreed.

It was eight years after arriving at the place of his incarceration before he had eventually understood his father's cryptic note, thrust into his pocket as a parting gift. The code for a secret bank account in Switzerland into which his father had managed to deposit his entire savings, close to one million dollars, before the Nazis managed to get their hands on it or, more likely, tried to have him pass it over to them in return for the false promise of anonymity. His father knew bribery would have been futile.

But of more value to the young Benjamin was a message, hastily scribbled by his father, in which he urged his son, in the likely event of his death, to seek out an old friend. It was in the spring of 1954 that he finally tracked him down, a rabbi who had escaped the wrath of the SS by being smuggled out of the country by a Jewish sympathiser who had learned the true horror of Auschwitz. Rabbi

Stein had been a mentor to his father, rich in knowledge of ancient Scripture. He was a frail old man by the time Benjamin met him, ensconced in a retirement home in Salzburg, his body weak but his mind as alert as ever it had been. He saw in Benjamin, the son of his old friend, the chance to pass on the quest that he had started but had long accepted was beyond his capability. He spoke of the scrolls unearthed by the Bedouins, of how German Intelligence had discovered their source, and had attempted to plunder the caves at Qumran for their own purposes. He told of the rumours he had heard of the incredible content of some of the scrolls, authentic beyond reproach, content that would throw into doubt the fundamental basis of one of the biggest religions in the world, and potentially destabilise entire continents. His father had been immersed in the search for these scrolls and had been instrumental in ensuring that those that had been recovered had remained hidden from the Nazis.

The old man had captivated Benjamin. His unwavering belief that the proof existed that would once and for all free the Jewish people from centuries of tyranny and blame became engraved in his mind, his life at a stroke given purpose, and his father's death in a bizarre way made meaningful. He knew what he must do. He had made his way to Switzerland and taken possession of the safe deposit box.

Its contents had stunned him, and at that moment given meaning to his life, both in terms of what he had endured and, more importantly, what he must do. It still felt as though it was only yesterday that he had first set eyes upon it.

Within twenty years he had built up one of the biggest commercial empires on the planet. *Time* magazine described his interests as being the most diverse of any entrepreneur that had ever lived – '...from noodles to missiles...' was its simple summary of his global interests. Yet he was effectively a recluse, shying away from public notice, declining interviews through his army of advisors and assistants. His face did not grace any broadsheet, and his dealings had become more covert as his empire grew. It was influence he craved rather than commercial success. It was merely a means to an end. His strength of personality and knowledge of different parts of the world had allowed him to venture into commercial markets that others in the West could or would not approach.

His strategy was simple and ultimately staggeringly effective. In Europe and North America, where the uncertain and constraining hand of democracy restricted his ability to forge quick alliances, he had befriended and supported opposition leaders in several countries, sometimes personally, or, where sensitivities demanded, anonymously through one of his many companies or trusted associates. He preyed on the politicians' weaknesses, their complete devotion to power, whether through the democratic process or otherwise. And one by one, over time, those he backed, pampered, cajoled, generally came to rule, lead or control their countries. If they failed, he would move on to another, more likely candidate. Rarely did he target existing leaders. They were, he believed, too corrupt already, and in the pockets of too many others, to be useful. No, the power and influence he had to wield required that he had control over the raw product. Men with ambition, who would do whatever it took...

Benjamin sat back down at the large desk. He had much work to do. He took a deep breath and in his mind pictured his father. What had once been an intense need for him to achieve recompense for the loss of the only person he had ever loved, and had been forced to lose, had become something else. It was God's work he was to fulfil.

Chapter 15

Nick jumped into the Morgan and pulled up the roof. The summer sun was no friend, and he did not feel like being exposed to the streets around him. He had been as shaken as Henry at the attack by the unknown assailant in the library, but had managed to keep himself together, if for no other reason than for the sake of the innocent librarian. He had at least owed that to Henry, but his strength was fast ebbing from his whole body as he sat in the room with the terrified young man.

He picked up the mobile and called Keri. 'I suppose you've got some messages for me?' he asked sarcastically, knowing his voice would sound almost like a stranger's to his confused and probably concerned secretary.

'Nick!' she answered, her voice sounding more relieved than surprised. 'Where are you? Everybody seems to be looking for you. When did you get back from Milan?'

'Oh, it was pretty late last night. I had some things to do this morning. Has Forster phoned?'

'Phoned! He's been in twice this morning already. He's threatening all sorts of things. Says if you don't speak to him this morning he's going to take over the site and close down the firm.' Keri gave a little laugh. 'I don't think he's happy, Nick!'

He laughed, knowing that Keri was too shrewd not to be worried. She simply knew it was out of her control and understanding. But she trusted him.

'Oh, and Joe's been on a couple of times,' she added. 'Forster's been down to the site and tried to issue instructions.

Joe's refused, and Forster told him he was fired. I think you'd better speak to him quickly'.

'OK,' Nick replied. 'What about Robert? Any news?'

'Rachel phoned. He's coming out of intensive care this morning. He's going to be fine, but Rachel says he's talking about retiring early. She wants you to phone her.'

It didn't come as a surprise. He was sure Rachel would have had something to do with that decision. 'Right. I want you to send a fax immediately to Forster. Tell him I am issuing an instruction this morning to order the steel, and that I will speak to him later. Then phone Joe and tell him that I've sorted things out, and that I will come down to the site later this afternoon.'

'OK, Nick. Do you want me to tell Joe about the steelwork?'

'No. Don't mention it at all. I'll sort that out later too. But you can tell him to start removing the embankment, and that I'm sure he won't find any more little surprises!' Nick added, smiling to himself. 'I'll speak to you again later. I'm switching this thing off.'

Keri got the message. At least she wouldn't be bothered by Mr Forster again today, and Nick knew what he was doing. 'All right, Nick... Oh, I nearly forgot', she added apologetically. 'There's a priest here to see you. A Father Howe. He's from an organisation called the...' There was the sound of papers being shuffled as Keri searched through her notes. 'Sorry, Nick. He's from somewhere called the Ecole biblique. He said you would know what it's about.' Keri sounded doubtful. 'Do you? Or do you want me to tell him you're not available? I know you're busy on something.'

Nick froze on the other end of the line, staring blankly ahead into the London traffic. His mind began to race again and he thought back to Milan. It was too big a coincidence for a priest to appear suddenly the day after the Milan incident. On the other hand, it could be nothing to do with Milan, although it was bound to be somehow related to the scroll. He had no option.

'Hello? …. Nick, are you still there?'

'Yes … I'm here,' he stuttered, trying not to sound concerned. 'Tell you what, Keri, I'll nip into the office and see him on my way to the hospital. I should be there in ten minutes.'

'Oh, all right,' answered Keri. She could tell that something was not quite right and reckoned that perhaps Nick didn't know exactly what it was about. All the same, it wasn't like him to see someone without an appointment.

Benjamin tapped the glass top of his desk and the screens on the wall opposite burst into life.

'Get me Moshe Rosenfeld,' he stated calmly.

'Immediately,' answered the metallic voice.

A few moments later the large central screen was filled with the face of the Israeli Prime Minister.

'Benjamin, it has been some time since we spoke. Are you well? How is our hunt going?' The Prime Minister's voice sounded relaxed, almost dismissive.

He continued: 'My people tell me there has been a bit of activity at your end recently. Another goose chase as you Brits call it?' He laughed.

Benjamin felt the anger well up from within him.

'Have you forgotten to whom you are speaking?' he asked menacingly, rising slightly forward in his seat. 'Do not mock me!' Benjamin's fists tightened. "You are closer than you think to oblivion if you do not do what I say.'

The Prime Minister's whole demeanour changed. He was visibly shocked at Benjamin's tone. No one had spoken to him like this for a long time, but it suddenly all came flooding back to him, the reason he was in power, and had been for the last ten years. Benjamin Goldstein. He could say nothing.

Benjamin continued. 'We have found it. We will soon have it in our possession, and you will ensure that what needs to be done is undertaken exactly as I say. Do you understand?'

The Prime Minister swallowed hard, his confident demeanour now reduced to a feeble nod. His fear of Benjamin and his followers would ensure his compliance with Benjamin's demands, whatever they may be. Even with the power of the revered Mosad at his disposal, he knew they could get to him. At one time on becoming leader, he had contemplated using his power to root out the 'fundamentalists' only to discover that even Mosad had not been immune from infiltration. Benjamin's grip on his people was total.

'I will be … *am* ready to do whatever is needed,' he responded.

'Good.' Benjamin sat back in his seat and altered his tone. He surmised that the Prime Minister, this intellectually inferior former accountant whom Benjamin had picked nearly twenty-five years ago as a future leader of the most threatened state on earth, had no idea of the impact the information that Benjamin would shortly release to the world was likely to have on his country.

He would prepare him as far as he needed to, but the reality was that Benjamin foresaw the end of the State of Israel. There would be no need for it. The Prime Minister's task would be to ensure it happened.

Nick swung the car around at the first opportunity he had, and used all of his local knowledge to identify the quickest route back toward the office. He was there in twelve minutes. He strode through the front door and waved his arm at an ever-smiling Maggie, walking quickly through the open-plan office and up to Keri's desk. 'Hold all my calls. I'm not here,' he said before she had a chance to speak.

'Fine, Nick,' she said, knowing not to even try discussing anything else. 'He's in your office.'

Nick looked at his door and took a deep breath. He calmly walked forward and opened it, not knowing what to expect on the other side. He stepped into the room and saw the priest staring closely at one of his drawings hanging on the wall. Nick closed the door behind him, causing the priest to turn quickly. He was a small, white-haired man who looked to Nick as though he was in his late sixties or early seventies. He had a kind-looking face, and he smiled at Nick in such a way that Nick immediately felt that he was not under threat, even if he knew he would have to be on his guard.

The priest clasped his hands together. 'Ah, Mr Stephenson. Thank you for seeing me. I know you must be a very busy man. I am Father Howe.'

Nick gave a half-hearted smile back at him. 'Well, actually, Father, I am rather busy today...'

'Oh I'm sorry,' interrupted the priest. 'I won't keep you. I was just hoping that you may be able to help me with something that my organisation has ... misplaced.'

Nick walked toward his desk, consciously trying not to look over at the priest. 'Really? I can't see how I would be able to help you with that, Father. What *exactly* has your organisation misplaced?'

The priest followed Nick's movements closely. 'Something very valuable. Something that we would dearly like to have returned.'

Nick sat down at his desk and shuffled a few of his papers around. After a few moments he eventually looked up at the priest. 'Look. I can't imagine anything which I might have that belongs to your organisation. What's it called ... the Ecole ... something? I think you must have the wrong person, Father.' He leaned forward and picked the mail out of his in-tray, very deliberately placing it in front of him on the desk.

The priest gave another little smile. 'Come, come, Mr Stephenson. We all underestimate the number of other people our own lives touch, whether we realise it or not.' He moved closer towards Nick's desk. 'I had another friend who also had an interest in retrieving my ... our possession. Unfortunately he died in a tragic accident yesterday. Most unpleasant. His young assistant was very upset.'

Nick tried not to react to the priest's statement, continuing to avoid eye contact, but felt his grip tighten involuntarily on the letter he was holding in his hands, his heart beat beginning to race. He said nothing.

'Never mind,' said the priest, 'accidents will happen, as the authorities are almost certain to conclude.'

Nick finally looked up at the priest's face, sensing that there was no immediate threat from the uninvited visitor. 'This possession you've lost, what exactly is it? And why do you want it back so much?'

The priest looked back at him, his face now more serious, but his manner still relaxed. 'I think you know the answer to the first part. As to the second, let's just say it has great sentimental value. It is not its monetary worth that concerns us, although I am sure we may be prepared to reward you for ... keeping it safe.'

Nick thought back to the conversation with Henry. Nick had already concluded that it was what it said that gave the scroll its value, not the parchment itself. The problem he had now was knowing whom to trust. He had to work that out before he could hand it over to anyone. Nick decided he had nothing to lose in trying to get a reaction from the priest. He sat back and looked straight into his eyes. 'OK, who do you represent, Father – the Shomrei Emet?'

The priest smiled. 'Does it look to you like I would be one of them? I am a Catholic priest and a scholar. I have worked for the past ten years with an organisation called the Ecole biblique. I don't imagine you have ever heard of us, but we are purely interested in theology, and the study of religious scripture.'

Nick did not let on. He thought again about his conversation with Henry, and how he had scoffed at his 'conspiracy theory'. For all he knew, both groups could be one and the same. Certainly, the priest at least knew who they were. Nick stood up. 'Well, Father, I assure you I have nothing at the moment which would interest your organisation.' He walked toward the priest and put out his hand as though encouraging him to move toward the door.

Father Howe smiled weakly and nodded, a look of disappointment on his face. He turned and walked away slowly. When he reached the door he stopped and looked at Nick. 'Be careful, Mr Stephenson. It is often very difficult to tell good from bad. The *truth* is not always what it seems.' He took a card out of his jacket pocket and handed it to Nick. 'Please, call me if you wish to talk further.'

Nick took the card without looking at it. 'I will, Father.'

He opened the door and Father Howe left, smiling at Keri as he passed her desk and made for the exit. Nick closed the door and leaned back against it. When was this all going to end? he thought. He looked at the card. It had the priest's name on it and the address of the Ecole biblique in Paris scored out, and another, handwritten, in London added. Nick knew the building. It was in Hanover Square, and Nick had been involved in refurbishing part of an upper floor with a previous commission. He turned the card over. Handwritten on the back was an inscription:

'The Truth *will out eventually.' Cardinal Cornelli to Vatican Congress 1981*

Nick swallowed hard and then allowed himself a little smile. Clearly, the priest had expected to leave empty-handed, but he had begun to win Nick's trust. If nothing else, it was the most subtle blackmail note he had ever heard of. He stuck the card in his pocket and opened the door.

'Have you sent the fax to Forster yet?' he asked Keri as he passed her desk on the way out, trying to look as composed as he could.

'Done, Nick,' she replied, holding a large pile of unanswered mail in her hand.

'Good. It's time I got on with my job. I'll be at the site.'

She shrugged her shoulders and dropped them back into the 'pending' tray as he breezed past her. He's going to have a busy weekend, she thought to herself and shook her head.

The silence of Benjamin's thoughts was broken abruptly by the speaker lodged in the left side of the head cushion in his leather chair, a device that afforded a great deal of privacy for messages while others were in the room. His eyes remained closed. The two nervous men sitting ten feet away, and six feet apart, heard nothing, their gaze fixed on the leader in front of them, one unconsciously rubbing his silver lapel badge.

'We have confirmation,' said the deep, almost mechanical

voice. 'They failed to prevent the Cardinal imparting knowledge. Import ... unknown. Howe has made contact.' The voice cut off. No response was expected.

Benjamin sighed and slowly exhaled. He opened his eyes, the two men instinctively straightening in their seats as he did so. 'It seems the Hummingbird was able to sing, gentlemen.' He watched their reactions closely, observing the growing sharpness of their movements, the dilation of their pupils, the panic building in their minds as they struggled to respond to the tortuously controlled, almost calm, unspoken threat.

The men darted looks at one another for a few seconds. One swallowed hard and tried to compose himself, consciously trying to check his words before saying them. 'There was very little time that they had together... We reacted as quickly as we could.' He looked at his colleague for help. The man looked terrified and said nothing. The first man looked back at Benjamin and continued. 'I doubt he could have said anything that was important...' He was stopped in mid-sentence by Benjamin smashing his right fist on the table, and jumping to his feet behind the desk.

'This was Cardinal Gianfranco Francisco Xavier Cornelli, one of the most important and articulate men of Rome! Nothing he said was unimportant, do you understand?' He was leaning over the table, his fists tightly gripped, carrying the full weight of his upper body, the veins in his neck protruding grotesquely through red skin. 'You failed! You are pathetic! I will not tolerate weakness ... anywhere! It is your pity that you did not have the same sense of responsibility as your colleague. He was prepared to give the ultimate commitment.' He reached toward the front of the desk and touched the glass screen. 'Get out of my sight!' he ordered, looking straight into the eyes of the now cowering speaker. 'You sit there!' he continued, his eyes switching to the other, silent man.

The one who had spoken stood up slowly, his mouth opening as if to make one last plea, but nothing came out. Behind him the door made a muffled clicking noise, then opened silently. Behind it a shadow swayed gently. As the man left the room, slowly as if afraid of what lay beyond the room, the door closed silently behind him, the other man continued to stare straight ahead at his angry leader.

Benjamin sat back down and took a long hard breath. He could not tolerate excuses ... or weakness. 'What do you have to say?' he asked the remaining man, as he clasped his hands in front of him, his voice now restored to a more controlled pitch

'We have failed you ... and the cause, Benjamin. We deserve our fate.' The man lowered his head, clenching his fists tightly as he did so to stop his hands shaking

Benjamin sat back in his seat. 'Indeed you have,' he said slowly, pausing to let the man consider the fate to which he might have exposed himself by his admission. At length he continued: 'But, better the man who admits his faults, his weaknesses and chooses ... begs to redeem himself. Do you not agree, Arial?'

The man looked up quickly, his eyes opening widely at the words. 'Anything, master. I would do anything to show my commitment. Just tell me.'

The door opened again slowly. Arial took a sharp intake of breath and turned his head in fear. A tall man, dressed soberly in a plain black suit and immaculately polished shoes, strode into the room and walked straight to the large desk. He stretched out his hands and, without saying a word, placed a small silver brooch on the desk in front of Benjamin. No words were spoken, but Arial felt himself ready to explode, clearly aware of the previous owner's identity, and now even more terrified for his own safety. The man turned and left, his gaze fixed stubbornly on the door as Arial tried desperately to identify the man's intentions from his unnaturally bright-blue eyes, following his every move. The door closed quietly behind him. Arial looked back at Benjamin.

'You will have the opportunity very soon to show your commitment, my friend,' said Benjamin quietly, his gaze fixed on the silver bobble he was now rubbing gently between his thumb and index finger. 'But first, I think it is high time we had a word with Mr Stephenson. I want you to get him for me.'

Chapter 16

In the distance Nick thought he could hear a siren. It was getting louder. He tried to look around, but everywhere seemed foggy. Where could he run? The noise grew louder still. It was becoming clearer. A bell, not a siren.

He jumped up in bed, his eyes suddenly wide open. A dream. He relaxed for a second before he heard the bell again. It was the telephone. He stared at it for a moment, his mind frantically untangling dream from reality. Had he really been in Milan? The man in the library ... Jewish extremist groups ... Father Howe. What had his life become? It certainly *felt* like a bad dream.

It was all too real. He glanced at the biscuit tin sitting partly hidden behind the kettle on the marble worktop where he had left it last night. *I should have put it back in the cupboard*, he thought to himself. He chastised himself. To hell with it! I should have stuck it in the garbage, that's what I should have done! Involuntarily he shook his head. He had spent over an hour the previous night trying as he might to grasp what secret the parchment might hold, what it said and why it seemed so important to an ever-growing group of people. Whatever it was, he did not feel he could suddenly hand it over to someone else without knowing the answers first. Besides, he was now almost out of time. He had only two days left before he would be forced to make a decision that could close the company for good.

The phone rang again. Nick ran his hand through his hair and stared at the threatening object. The dial on the hands-free showed the time in luminous green. Seven o'clock in the morning. Who would call him at this time of the morning? He immediately remembered the previous Saturday. His head sank into his chest. *Here we go again*, he thought.

Another ring. Whoever it was clearly had no intention of hanging up until he answered. *OK*, he thought, *I might as well get it over with quickly*. He leaned over and picked up the handset, swooping on it and grabbing it to his ear with a flourish.

'Yeah?' It was all that he could muster.

'Nick ... Nick ... it's me. Have you got your TV on?' Rachel's voice sounded frantic, but he felt his whole body relax with relief. He lay back down on the bed and put the palm of his hand up to his forehead, flicking away some of the perspiration. In the turmoil he had put Rachel to the back of his mind.

'Rachel, its seven o'clock in the morning. I've had a terrible week. Why would I have the television on? You know I hardly ever...' She interrupted him.

'Quick! Quick! Switch it on! It's about the scroll! They're talking about your scroll!'

Nick reached over to the bedside table and picked up the remote control. He felt surprise more than concern. 'It's not *my* scroll, Rachel,' he rebuked her, trying somehow to distance himself from the thing and everything it seemed to have caused. 'Did they announce that I had found one?' he added sarcastically. 'Which channel?' he asked as he aimed the remote at the TV, not seeking an answer to his question.

'One ... BBC One. It said they had an exclusive,' Rachel blurted out, her voice now sounding half excited, half scared. Nick pressed the number on the remote. The TV seemed to take an age to flicker into life. Finally the face of the newsreader appeared on the screen:

... and is said to contain a series of startling revelations that will have serious implications for religious scholars and even challenge some of the fundamental beliefs of Christianity. In an exclusive report for the BBC, over to our Religious Affairs correspondent, Paul Blanchfield...

Nick stared at the screen, the phone still anchored to his left ear. 'Are you watching it?' asked Rachel, her voice now sounding intense.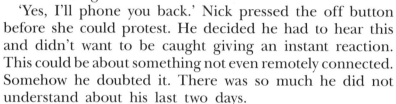

'Yes, I'll phone you back.' Nick pressed the off button before she could protest. He decided he had to hear this and didn't want to be caught giving an instant reaction. This could be about something not even remotely connected. Somehow he doubted it. There was so much he did not understand about his last two days.

Thank you, John...

The Religious Affairs correspondent was a familiar enough looking face, but Nick realised he had never really listened before to a word the man had said in the past, other than the occasional story about the death of an archbishop or a paedophile priest. It must be a story the BBC are taking seriously, though, he thought to himself:

... Yes, the BBC has been given an exclusive briefing by a senior religious academic who has confirmed the discovery of a manuscript, stretching back to the time of Jesus, which academics from many faiths have long believed may exist but, until now, has been little more than rumour and the subject of heated debate in Christian theologian circles.

Nick turned up the volume control, worried he would miss a word of the report unfolding before him:

In the past twelve hours, I have been given unprecedented access to a treasure trove of documents written over the past two thousand years, some of which come from the famous Dead Sea Scrolls collection...'

Nick straightened up. 'Treasure trove'... 'collection' ... It sounded more like an advert for a new magazine series than a piece of investigative journalism – 'Buy the first edition and get the second free ... along with your very own Dead Sea Scroll to keep...'

... telling a convincing story of the existence of a ... master scroll that puts in context, explains and ... effectively overrides all others known to form the basis of the Bible we know today.

Nick wondered just how long it had taken the journalist to speak a sentence that seemed at a stroke, to wipe out two thousand years of religious belief.

It is this scroll, the so-called 'master scroll', which, it is claimed, has now been discovered ... and some of its contents are likely to rock the very foundations of the Christian community and seriously challenge the authority of the Church throughout the world...

The correspondent paused briefly for effect.

Back to you John in the studio

Nick threw his hands open in disbelief. *Is that it?* he thought. There was no doubt it was sensational stuff, but lacking just a bit in substance.

Thank you, Paul. Did you have access to this 'master' scroll?

'Exactly!' Nick said out loud, a smirk on his face.

Well, John, the reporter smugly replied, the question clearly anticipated, *my source has indicated that the contents of the scroll will be released to the public within the next few days, but that its contents are so potentially explosive that those who have it in their possession are genuinely concerned about the impact it may have on the Western world...*

He tailed off for effect, his head now slightly crooked over to one side:

This is Paul Blanchfield for Breakfast News *somewhere in Central London.*

This last part of the report set Nick's mind racing. What are they waiting for? Why not release whatever 'they' have – whoever 'they' are – now, and get it over with? He didn't like the conclusion it led him to. The phone rang.

'Well ... didn't I tell you it was about...'

Nick interrupted her. 'Rachel, the report said nothing. No detail. No facts ... nothing.'

'What do you mean, "nothing"?' she queried, her tone stating incredulity at his comment. 'It's obvious. It must be the scroll. How did they get it? Do you still have it?'

'They haven't...' Nick stopped and glanced again at the biscuit tin. He jumped out of bed and walked swiftly over to the kitchen, his feet feeling cold on the Italian ceramic tiles, even in the continuing heat of the London summer. He picked up the tin and pulled off the lid. It was still there.

'Hello? ... Nick? ... What's wrong?'

'Nothing ... Just checking.'

'Checking what?'

Nick decided he needed to be more careful with the tin. He walked over to the kitchen and buried it deep in the cupboard again with the other biscuits and tins of Morris's cat food.

'Look, I know you want this to be something ... well, something it's hopefully not, Rachel, but I need to sort this out.' He knew she would not be easily put off unless he gave her some indication of his intentions. 'Someone came to see me yesterday. A priest. He was from the Ecole biblique. He ... suggested I may want to speak to him about what I found ... about the scroll.'

'He knows you have it?'

'No ... well, yes. He didn't specifically mention it, but he knows I have ... something.'

'How?'

Nick thought for a few moments. There seemed to be a lot of people who suddenly knew about it, but surely this BBC story couldn't be connected?

'I'm not sure, but I think I will go and see him. He left me his card.'

'I want to come!' It was the bouncy child like voice again. 'Wait there!'

'No!' Nick literally heard her drop the phone on the floor as she cut the communication. He put his own phone down and lay back on the bed. How was he going to sort this out? He thought about Robert. How could a man he had trusted all his adult life, whom he regarded as a second father, and whose judgement he had trusted beyond reason, be so stupid to deal with a charlatan like Forster? Then again, if the lease deal transpired, at least Robert's financial worries, his pension, his future would look a whole lot more comfortable. He *had* to sort this mess out ... on his own.

* * *

At his control desk, Benjamin let out a heavy sigh, sat back in his chair and tapped the glass panel on the table top in front of him. The news pictures disappeared, and the large oak panels retreated silently across the wall to hide the plasma screens. His mind momentarily flashed him a picture of his father again. He swore he could see a smile on his face.

At long, long last, the end had begun.

Chapter 17

The two figures did not stand out from all the others gathered at Speakers Corner in Hyde Park. Tourists, office workers on their way to the Tube station, pretty young sun worshippers, and a handful of policemen apparently going about their duty, stood, lay or sat on the odd bench, soaking up the unique atmosphere of the place. The more enjoyable warmth of the late afternoon offered a relaxing, contented end to another busy day in the capital. Already, the news of the biblical mystery had inspired those who would otherwise have limited sharing their great insights to abandon their clerks' desks and taxis to proclaim how they had been right all along. The orators spread around the parched lawns spoke with rekindled passion, inspired by the seemingly unlimited interpretations and possibilities that the unfolding story of the scroll had opened for them.

'Best free entertainment in London,' remarked Isaac, the Deputy Governor of the BBC.

'Yes, and it would seem there is a new show in town,' answered Benjamin, with the merest hint of a smile that quickly disappeared. He started to walk along the gravel path. 'The report was handled well. I trust you have a tight leash on these reporters of yours.'

'Oh, I can hold them back long enough. Your briefing was thorough, and after all these years it is good to make use of our library of documents. I had almost forgotten how intricately we had woven the web!'

Benjamin nodded. 'Good, but we do not need any

further intrusion. The whole world is now chasing the story. We must keep control of it. It is the key. By tonight every corner of our little planet will know of the scroll. He looked contentedly at the scene around him. 'Communication', he continued, 'is *the* weapon of mass distraction, Isaac.' He threw his arms wide open. 'The opium of the masses!' He watched as the throng of people moved slowly from speaker to speaker, ears cocked and intently listening, eyes fixed and bright. 'Look at them, my friend. Their minds are suddenly wide open, and at their sharpest!'

As he took in the scene around him, Benjamin thought of his carefully built empire. He had anticipated the explosion in mass communications, the Internet, mobile phones, even cheap travel between countries, and understood their ever-rising power. The hardware had been put in place by the clever electronic wizards and geeks, many working for companies he himself controlled, but more importantly it was others like himself who were seizing control of the software – the press, television stations, global websites and all forms of media. That was where the real power lay. *Beyond the control of individual governments.* Through a multitude of offshore and sheltered companies, his Truth Foundation had gained control of large media corporations across the globe, often fronted by flamboyant and instantly recognisable individuals who were skilful in deflecting any lead back to their true master.

Isaac interrupted his thoughts. 'You have prepared everything to perfection, Benjamin. I know this is the moment that you planned for me. Some of the others may have forgotten. I have not. The journalists will be led as ever. When *I* handed over the briefing papers, it was with an insistence on the anonymity of the source. They appreciate that this will have been expected by someone providing information to a deputy governor of the BBC.' He straightened up slightly, as if to emphasise the importance of his position. 'Anyway', he continued, 'Blanchfield has been sent on a wild goose chase to Morocco as you suggested.'

Benjamin placed his hand on Isaac's shoulder. He had never had a close friend. His life's work would not allow it. He had never felt the craving or the desire for a woman's love, or for the bond of another man's friendship. It had made him stronger to put this down to his sense of destiny. But Isaac had been the closest he had come to a confidant. He had no doubt that Isaac's belief in what they were about to reveal was all that really mattered to him.

'I chose well,' Benjamin announced, as he tapped his companion gently on the shoulder, smiled and bowed his head slightly. It was the closest he had come to showing emotion to the man.

He turned and started walking along the gravel path. 'Your contacts in the press here have also served you well.'

'Ha! They are like hyenas! A little crumb here, a titbit there. They leap on any morsel they can have! Blanchfield told me that twelve journalists quietly booked themselves onto the same flight he is on, all of them using ridiculous pseudonyms! They are all stumbling through the Sahara as we speak!'

'Do not be fooled,' interrupted Benjamin, his face once again serious, his manner stern. 'These ... hyenas *will* pick up the scent sooner or later. By then it will be too late. Our footsteps must be covered up. You have your instructions. Be sure to carry them out.'

'I will, Benjamin. You have my word.'

Benjamin nodded. He stopped and looked at a man standing on an upturned beer crate less than twenty yards away, an old, battered cardboard placard propped up against it. The words 'The Truth' had faded, barely legible in large handwritten letters that spelled out the speaker's simple message. Benjamin guessed that he was about the same age as the speaker, but he was stooped, his demeanour that of a man driven by the passion of his belief, but with the body of a broken man. Benjamin recognised him. He had seen him, and listened to his words, at the same spot on and off over the past twenty years or so that he had frequented this place. There were times when he had envied the man the freedom to shout aloud, to share with anyone who would listen. They had the same goal, the same desire, but they had chosen very different paths.

This evening the man's eyes shone brightly. News of the scroll had filled him with hope. There was a heady feeling of expectation in the words he preached, his voice hanging in the air, louder, steadier than Benjamin could recall hearing before.

'The Truth' indeed, he thought to himself, *and it is closer than you think, my old friend.*

Chapter 18

Nick parked the Morgan in its usual spot in a small private courtyard adjacent to the first apartment block in the waterfront development. Like many London schemes built in the 1990s, Admiral Quay felt like a fortress, with signs marked 'Private' and 'No Trespassing' throughout the tightly secured site. The waterfront itself was blocked off from the public by ornately imposing wrought-iron gates at either end of the granite-paved promenade. Although meant to reassure residents, the effect of the security measures was to give a sense of siege, the fear that if all the gates and cameras and signs weren't there, the place would be overrun by swarms of unwanted peasants, intent on ... well, walking along the waterfront, as Nick had once amusingly concluded.

He pressed the key fob and the lights flickered twice to confirm the alarm was set. The green Audi parked three spaces away went unnoticed. At least there was a small shop to service the closed community, a newsagent's that acted almost like an informal concierge service, arranging everything from dry cleaning to holding onto apartment keys when tradesmen or deliveries were due. As he passed the newsagent's Nick's eyes briefly caught the banner headlines on the advertising board sitting outside:

Markets in Chaos!
Scroll Story Blamed!

Scroll. The word his world seemed to be revolving around.

What was *that* all about? He opened the door and entered the shop.

'Evening, Mr Stephenson,' the newsagent proffered blithely, his eyebrows raised in expectation.

'Evening, Gerald... Eh, do you have a paper, please?' Nick stumbled out the words, his mind still contemplating the meaning of the headline.

'Lot's, Sir! Any particular one?' the jolly man replied.

Nick refocused his concentration. 'Sorry ... yes. The headline outside. Which paper?'

'Ah, you've heard then.'

'Heard what? I haven't heard anything. That's why I want...'

'Unbelievable, ain't it?' the newsagent interrupted as he leaned over and picked up a copy of the *Evening Standard* Late Edition. 'I don't understand these ... markets anyway. It's all paper money, ain't it?' He handed Nick the newspaper with a broad smile.

'Been on TV all night as well,' he added casually as he placed Nick's coins in the till and glanced at the screen of the small portable TV to the side of the counter. 'Headline news.' He shook his head. 'Must be a hell of a story in that old ... scroll thing!'

Nick decided not to enter into any further discussion. He took the paper, smiled and left quickly. Outside he scanned the headlines. The whole front page was covering the story. The main headline read: 'Scroll speculation sends markets tumbling.' The other two lesser headlines further down the page were equally direct. 'Bank of England urges calm' and 'Church dismisses claims.' He folded the paper over and headed for the apartment, his mind working overtime. He was desperate to read the articles, switch on News 24 and find out more, but all the time his mind tried to dismiss the possibility of any connection with the brittle parchment found on his little building site in the middle of London. How *could* there be any connection?

Once inside the apartment, Nick threw off his jacket and leapt for the remote control. He sat down on the leather chair and opened the paper as the TV clicked into action. Morris purred loudly as he suddenly appeared at Nick's feet. 'Hey, pal. Are you hungry?' He went to the kitchen and opened the cupboard, pulling out a tin of food for the starving cat. He looked beyond the other cans and bottles to the biscuit tin. He picked it out and looked at it, wondering whether this was the cause of the growing panic that seemed to be enveloping the world for reasons he could not fathom.

Morris purred, rubbing his head and back against Nick's leg. 'OK! Patience, friend!' He put down the biscuit tin on the work surface and pulled out a tin opener from a drawer. Morris wasted no time in polishing off the tuna and vegetable dinner he had been patiently awaiting.

Nick sat down again and started to read the main article:

World stock markets were sent into freefall today, following apparent panic selling of stocks as a result of a BBC report this morning on the discovery of a religious scroll, rumoured to challenge the basis of Christianity.

Although dismissed immediately by the Church of England and the Roman Catholic Church as 'absolute nonsense' the London Stock Market saw an immediate marking down of stocks when trading opened at 8.30 this morning. The apparent stampede to sell appeared to have been triggered by an anonymous analysts' briefing circulating from what insiders called 'a highly credible source', which implied that the scroll was likely to be genuine, had been known about for some time, and had the potential to create political instability across the Western world.

Nick couldn't believe what he was reading. What could be so important and influential that it could cause such panic? He read on.

Unsubstantiated reports suggested that the initial turn in the market was created by a small group of offshore fund managers representing substantial Jewish and American–Jewish funds who withdrew huge amounts of equity from British, American, French, and Italian stocks.

The Bank of England urged calm in the markets despite the 850 point drop in the FTSE 100 index, the largest ever single-day drop on the London Exchange. It wiped a staggering £500 billion off company values. The Bank refused, however, to rule out the bank taking unilateral action to raise interest rates. This in itself shook the markets, and did nothing to steady the City's jitters.

Nick had been so immersed in the paper that he had forgotten about the TV busily chattering away in the background. But a familiar-sounding voice suddenly caught his attention:

Well, as you know, the Ecole biblique has been the sole Trustee of the Dead Sea Scrolls for the last fifty years, and these rumours ... and let's be clear, it is all they are ... these rumours have certainly not emanated from our institution. We have no record of any parchment or scroll which substantiates any of these ... these wild claims.

The reporter, however, was not about to let his interviewee kill off the story of the century:

But isn't it true, Canon Howe, that many of these scrolls have still not been released by the Ecole biblique, even after all this time in your control? Do you accept that

191

there are some who would suggest that you have been hiding something, and that this scroll has perhaps come from an insider who believes it is time to release what you have discovered?'

Canon Howe smiled, clearly not wishing to rise to the bait:

Many of the scrolls we received were in very poor and fragile condition when they were found. As well as translating them, which in itself is a sometimes difficult and painstaking task, we have been anxious not to damage them, and to make sure they do not deteriorate for future generations.

The reporter addressed him again:

So are you confirming that this is not a Dead Sea Scroll?

Canon Howe paused for a moment, the friendly, reassuring face making way for an intense, concentrated look as though he was trying hard to choose his words carefully. He spoke slowly, deliberately and directly at the reporter:

I am saying that we have no record of a scroll or any other document that covers the issues which the report I have seen suggests this scroll purports to.

Nick had to think about the statement, repeating it over again in his mind. What does that mean? It was hardly a clear denunciation of its existence, or the hysterical reaction to its contents. But then again, Canon Howe did know about Nick's scroll...

His thoughts were interrupted by the telephone ringing. 'Hello, Nick here.'

'Ah, Mr Stephenson. I'm sorry to disturb you. It's Gerald from the newsagent's ... downstairs.'

'Oh hello, Gerald. What can I do for you?' Nick asked, still half listening to the reporter who had apparently been as confused by the Canon's answer as everyone else, and was now summing up his report.

'Well, you've left your wallet in the shop.'

'My wallet?' Nick answered, still only giving the conversation passing interest.

'I think it must have fallen out of your pocket as you were leaving... It was on the floor. Another customer spotted it and handed it in.' Gerald's voice changed down an octave as he chastised his careless customer. 'You've been very lucky, Sir.'

Nick sat up, his attention now fully on Gerald's words. 'You can say that again! I'll come right down and pick it up.'

Nick grabbed his keys and the newspaper, and headed for the door. He could read the rest of the articles in the elevator. He wanted to waste no time in learning more about the story. He called the lift and started to read the lead story from where he had left off:

The move by the fund managers was copied by investment houses around the globe. Analysts have suggested that the way in which the markets reacted to news of this find means its contents are already known, and that it will be shown to be not only genuine, but has the potential impact of destabilising governments across the Western world...

The elevator doors opened smoothly in front of him, and Nick entered, pressed for the ground floor and carried on reading:

Some commentators have gone as far as to suggest that

some unknown force is behind this mornings dealings, manipulating the market for its own ends, although what that may be, and who would have the power to initiate such an audacious attack on the world's stock markets is beyond speculation.'

The elevator door opened again and Nick stepped out into the entrance hallway. He tucked the paper under his left arm and walked through the door out onto the pavement. As he turned to his left toward the newsagents, he caught the merest movement of a figure, now behind him and moving rapidly. As he started to turn, a sudden pain hit him, and his world went black.

Chapter 19

Nick's eyes flickered open, then closed again rapidly, the intense bright light administering a sharp pain through to his head and temples like a laser. He was spinning, groggy, yet alert at the same time, his mouth seemingly uncontrollable, uttering words he couldn't hear properly. He wanted to rub his eyes, but he couldn't lift his arms. What was wrong with him?

There was a voice. Nick struggled to identify it. He couldn't. He tried opening his eyes again, the merest squint, but it was still too painful. Where was he? The light disappeared, and he realised a dark figure was now standing in front of him, blocking the light source, but only allowing him to see the man's outline.

'What is your name?' the voice asked in a strangely calm, reassuring way. Nick felt as though his mind was churning. He wanted to say it, but something was blocking the connection between his mind and his mouth. The figure moved slightly and the light pierced his temples again. He winced and moaned loudly.

'Can you give me your name please' the voice asked again, quietly.

'I'm ... Nick Stephenson.' He was relieved to have said it, even if he did feel as though he was mumbling.

'Thank you, Mr Stephenson. We are hoping you can help us with a little problem.' Nick felt as though he was in a dream. He felt like a piece of elastic, loose and light, and his mind was floating, conscious of his surroundings, but not frightened. He felt strangely at peace. The man

195

came closer and bent over towards Nick. 'You have come into possession of a rather unusual ... artefact, haven't you? What is it, Nick?'

Nick felt his face break into an involuntary smile. 'Biscuit tin...' he quipped through the smile.

The man stood up and stepped back. He turned round and looked at his colleague. 'What's he talking about? Are you sure this will work?' It was a deeper, and less friendly-sounding voice. Nick didn't like its sound. He could now make out two figures. The first had been joined by a taller and fuller figure, Nick thought, given the shape of his profile.

'Who's that?' he asked.

'A friend, Nick', replied the first voice.

Nick felt himself relax. 'I don't like his tone.'

The two men looked at one another. The first spoke in a quiet voice that Nick couldn't make out. 'Sometimes it takes a while to work. Everyone has a different resistance to the serum.'

'Well, let's get on with it. I do not have all night.' The taller man stepped back again and looked at his watch. The first man turned back to Nick.

'Nick, what is it that has come into your possession in the last few days? Something that has been causing you a lot of ... concern.'

'It's a ... scroll thing. A piece of old ... garbage!' He grinned as he pictured it in his mind, thinking about the havoc a mere piece of paper could cause.

'You need help with it, Nick, don't you?'

'Yes, I need help with it,' Nick replied, his thoughts turning back to the scroll and the predicament he found himself in.

'Do you want to tell us about it?' the voice enquired.

Nick felt his stomach churn. There were flashes in his mind of the last few days. He groaned and mumbled as he thought about Cardinal Cornelli, Richard and the library.

'Where did you find the scroll?' the voice asked, this time slightly louder.

'At the bloody site!' spluttered Nick. 'Why the hell couldn't it have stayed there ... no use to anyone ... only trouble...' Nick felt the figure move closer to him.

'Is that the scroll you took to Dr Weisman?'

Nick pulled back slightly and frowned. 'He knows something... Don't trust him... Looked like he knew what it was, but wouldn't tell me. I gave him a piece, you know.'

'Was it the same scroll you found on the site that you gave Dr Weisman, Nick?'

Nick thought about the question, but couldn't quite comprehend it. He tried to straighten up, as if this would somehow help him hear better. He noticed the man move back as the taller one stepped forward and pushed the first firmly to the side. He bent towards Nick, his face still blacked out by the strength of the light behind.

'This is too slow,' said the man. 'Give him another shot.'

Nick felt his arm being pulled away from his side, but there was nothing he could do. A hot flowing sensation swept through his arm, across his chest and ran down through the rest of his body.

The drugs kicked in harder on Nick's racing mind. He suddenly seemed to be flying backwards through time, floating in a sea of black with images from his past bouncing off the space around him. He was not in control of what he was seeing, but at the same time he felt a freedom that seemed to be unblocking thoughts he had been suppressing for years. His parents, long lost in the car crash when he was twelve years old. The years of anger that followed, and then guilt as he took it out on his surrogate mother and father, mentally draining them for five years before he eventually ran from home in Manchester and found refuge with a group of squatters in South London.

He was still floating when he saw the social worker who befriended him and persuaded him that his talent for drawing could be better used than simply decorating the bare walls of the squat. It was he who had talked him into enrolling at the architecture course at London College, finding him a job in a Greek restaurant in Canning Town to earn enough money to share a flat with three other students from his course. It had saved his life.

Nick's emotions at what he was seeing started to clear. He realised there was no fear in him now. The barriers that he had built up to stop him trusting anyone in those years had been slowly withering away without him truly realising it.

Robert came into his mind, the caring fatherly figure who had the ability to lead him, but at the same time leave him to find his own path, to release his own talent, his personality in time. Nick realised he had comfort with himself.

Rachel shot into his mind. He smiled involuntarily.

The voice cut into his thoughts. 'He's back! Hurry up with this.'

The other voice spoke. 'Where are you, Mr Stephenson?'

Nick tensed again and the images accelerated into a blur. He could feel himself tighten as though he was flying through a meteor storm. Something wasn't right. The defence mechanism he had felt during his teenage years was back. But this time he knew it was needed. His strength of will had to protect him from whatever the voice wanted from him. He would not bend.

'We will get to ... the truth, Nick. It's only a matter of time. Now tell us, do you have any idea what it is you found?'

Nick thought hard. He could not seem to resist giving an answer, but he knew that he could not truly understand himself what he was dealing with. 'Whatever it is, it's something others want to have.'

'Who are these...others?'

'I don't know. Some group called the Shop ... Shor... no, wait, the ... Shomrei...' The word tailed off. 'Could be them.' He thought back again to Milan. He couldn't seem to get the Cardinal out of his mind. 'Poor Cardinal Cornelli,' he added.

The figure moved closer to Nick's face. Nick tried hard to focus on the face that was now only a few feet from his, but it seemed blurred. Why couldn't he see this man?

'Did you give Dr Weisman the same scroll you found on the site?' the man asked, his voice firmer, his question slower.

'Yes ... yes!' Nick laughed out loud at the absurdity of the question. 'I've only got one of the things!'

'Do you think there is another one?'

'Another one?' repeated Nick, laughing sarcastically. 'It sounds as if there are dozens ... no hundreds, maybe even thousands of them!' His smile subsided quickly. 'I just wish I'd never ended up with one...'

The figure stood up and Nick involuntarily shut his eyes as the light hit him again. The two figures moved away a few steps into the darkness

'He thinks it's genuine.' Benjamin took out the black leather gloves from the pocket of his jacket and carefully put them on, one finger at a time. 'Someone went to a great deal of effort to have this copy produced and found on his building site.' He glanced back at Nick. 'Fate can deal us some pretty extraordinary cards sometimes. Other times it merely messes us about for no apparent reason.'

He clasped his hands in front of him and turned back to his accomplice. 'He knows nothing about the *real* scroll, that's evident. He doesn't know he's got a fake, and without the original we are not ready.' Benjamin put a hand on the man's shoulder. 'On the other hand, he is still the only connection we have. Mr Stephenson *will* lead us to it, of that I am sure.' As he walked toward the side entrance door he glanced over at Arial who had been standing silently at the back of the room. 'Keep a tail on him,' he stated firmly.

Nick's head continued to spin. His eyes remained tightly shut, and his mind was jumping from one picture to another as he relived the last few days. Suddenly, he felt the sleeve of his shirt being rolled up, but there was nothing he could do to stop it. A faint but sharp pain shot up his arm, then he felt a warm glow rush through his veins. He smiled to himself as he closed down his mind and fell into a deep sleep.

'Take him back to his apartment. He'll sleep it off overnight and won't remember a thing.' The man opened his medical bag, replaced the syringe in a plastic holder and sealed it. Arial nodded and clicked his fingers.

Out of the darkness behind him his two accomplices walked forward and lifted Nick up and into the back seat of the black sedan that was still sitting at the end of the warehouse. 'Just another drunk businessman having to be brought home by caring colleagues.' Arial laughed along with his accomplices, as he pictured Nick's neighbours.

Pity about the hangover, though, he thought to himself and sniggered.

Chapter 20

Nick sprang up with a start. Another nightmare. His eyes were open wide, but he felt he was looking through a haze. Although the heat wave continued unabated, he felt cold on his bare torso. His mouth was incredibly dry, a strange metallic taste in his saliva, and why was his head thumping with what felt like the mother of all hangovers?

He tried to remember the night before. The strike on the back of his head. He lifted his right arm to feel the bump he knew would be there, but even his arm felt painful. Very painful. He looked at his forearm, which was throbbing. A pinprick with the telltale signs of early bruising, a small yellow-brown patch no bigger than a postage stamp, was obvious through the light body hair. What on earth had happened to him, and, of more concern, why could he not remember? He ran his hand through his hair.

Jumping up onto the bed beside him, Morris purred hungrily. Nick looked around the room. Nothing looked out of place. He made a move to get out of bed, but gave up almost immediately as the movement caused the sensation of giant pincers squeezing each of his temples. What had caused him to feel this bad? He lay back down on the bed, his head spinning. He tried again to relive the evening before, trying desperately to retrace his movements. He recalled the visit to see Henry and the car journey home. The rest seemed a blur.

He rolled over and slowly slipped out of the bed, trying to move as little as possible from the neck upwards. He stood up gingerly, realising for the first time that he was still wearing his khaki-coloured chinos. Glancing at the chair in the corner of the room he noticed his shirt and jacket neatly folded over the arms, and his shoes sitting underneath, perfectly arranged together.

He walked slowly over to the kitchen and ran the cold water tap. He leaned on the top of the work surface as his head started spinning again. He reached out and filled his hand with water, throwing some onto his face, and then running his hand through his hair. He touched the bump on his head and winced. He threw more water on his face and made a slow, sweeping circle with his head, feeling a slight improvement each time. His mind suddenly shot back to the car park outside the apartment. He could see the cobbled pavement below him as he started to fall. The picture disappeared as quickly as it had come. He realised someone had struck him from behind with a very hard implement.

Nick took a glass from the cupboard and poured himself a drink from the tap. He downed three glassfuls, one after another, desperately trying to rid himself of his thirst. There was still an unpleasant taste in his mouth. He thought of the scroll. Opening the cupboard, he pushed aside Morris's supplies and there it was. He took out the tin and opened the lid. He emptied the contents out onto his hand. Once again, he opened out the first few inches, his eyes scanning the words that looked as unintelligible as ever. Another flashback. He felt the implement strike on the back of his neck. This time, as he looked down at the cobbles, he saw a newspaper tumbling to his side. The scroll! He tried to remember the headlines. His mind went blank.

He shook his head and placed the scroll gently back in the tin. He returned it to the back of the cupboard and took out a tin for Morris. He opened it and turned round to place it onto the floor beside the patiently waiting Morris. His eyes caught the newspaper sticking through the letterbox. He walked over to the door and extracted the copy of *The Times*. As he did so, his foot struck something lying on the floor. It was a black leather wallet. He immediately thought back to the newsagents. He recalled the telephone call from Gerald, but he couldn't seem to remember anything beyond it. He bent down and picked up the wallet. As he did so he realised straight away that it wasn't his. He flicked the button catch open. There was nothing inside. He ran his fingers through his hair. What was going on?

Nick walked back to the kitchen and placed the wallet and the newspaper on the kitchen surface. He filled the kettle, deciding that he needed coffee. A strong one. He pulled a croissant from the bread tin, realising that he was in desperate need of provisions. The last week had been so bizarre and he yearned for a return to his normal routine. Architects definitely weren't supposed to have this sort of trouble. As the kettle boiled, he glanced at the paper. The headline hit him immediately.

World Waits for Moment of Truth

He opened it out and laid it on the worktop. Scanning the first paragraph, Nick started to remember the story from last night.

After a day of turmoil on the world's markets, there is growing pressure on governments on both side of the Atlantic to take action to prevent a repeat of yesterday's hysteria surrounding reports of an imminent release of a religious scroll that is said to be potentially catastrophic for the Christian Church.

Nick shook his head. Had the world gone mad? How could there suddenly be such a devastating impact by something that no one had apparently seen? He still could not believe this could in any way be associated with the piece of parchment stuck in the biscuit tin at the back of his cupboard. How could it?

He glanced down the page. Three other headings covered different aspects of the same story. One in particular caught his eye:

US Denies Operation Connection

The US Department of Home Security denied that the commencement of an exercise, codenamed 'Operation Peacemaker' was in any way connected to the apparent imminent disclosure of the so-called 'Master Scroll'. In a pan-US operation, the country's leading rabbis and Jewish scholars have been given 24-hour security cover by a team of CIA agents.

Officially the Pentagon refused to confirm or deny even the existence of the operation, but sources within the CIA indicated that it was merely a training exercise, planned months ago, and that the timing was purely coincidental.

Nick put down the paper. *Some coincidence!* he thought. But why would the US Government want to protect leading Jews? If this was connected with the scroll, and clearly *The Times* had reason to think it was, why would the Government not share it? He looked at Morris and grinned. This was becoming a conspiracy theorist's dream! Even he was falling for it. And as to even *thinking* that his scroll could have anything to do with it...

He glanced at the rest of the front page. Halfway down the page a name caught his eye. Canon Howe. He looked at the start of the paragraph:

The credibility of the 'Master Scroll' theory was boosted by comments made in an interview with recognised religious scholar, Canon James Howe, who, for the past 30 years, has been involved in the painstaking task of translating, recording and preserving the famous Dead Sea Scrolls.

Speaking to a gathering of the world's press, Canon Howe confirmed that it was feasible that a religious writing of some sort could exist that had not been known about by academics or religious scholars. He pointed out that it had taken almost 2000 years to find the Dead Sea Scrolls, and that we should not be surprised to learn that others exist. He even suggested that some private collectors or even innocent members of the public could have in their possession important historic documents, the contents of which they were completely oblivious to.

Nick froze at the words. They were aimed at him. He was sure of it. Canon Howe was trying to speak to him, convince him of his credibility, his integrity. Surely *he* didn't think there was a connection? Nick knew he was in a corner and he needed help to sort this. If he wasn't keen on going to the police, maybe the priest would be the best option. Yet how did he know about Nick's scroll in the first place?

Nick shook his head. The pain was incessant. He made the coffee, but it only seemed to make the metallic taste in his mouth even worse. His head reminded him that there were still a few loose ends. He looked at the puncture mark on his arm. This was getting out of control. Whether connected or not, he had to rid himself of the scroll, once and for all. But to whom could he hand it over, and on what terms? For the first time, he felt like a pawn in some macabre game, and he was determined to control the next move. He would open up the game ... on *his* terms.

Chapter 21

'Rachel, it's me.'

'Hi, Nick. Feeling better this morning, are we?' Rachel's voice was warm and inviting. He paused for a moment, not sure that he wanted to put any more worry onto her delicate shoulders. Then again, he would need at least one person to help him, and he knew he could trust her.

'Well, actually ... something's happened ... last night. I'm not sure exactly what.' He had tried to pick his words carefully, but somehow he wasn't sure she would be anything other than alarmed.

'Meaning?' Her voice sounded as concerned as he had feared.

'I'm OK. But I think I may have been ... well drugged with something. Someone knocked me out last night when I returned to the flat.'

'That's it, Nick. You have to go to the police. This is out of control, and I don't want you getting ... hurt.' Her voice was beginning to tremble.

'You're right, Rachel. It's time to put an end to this.' Unconsciously he again started to think back over some of the incidents in the past few days. An image shot into his mind. A shadow. A light at the back of a blacked-out figure. It was blurred. He heard himself speaking... *I found it on the site...*

'Nick, are you still there?'

'Yes, I'm sorry. I just had a thought jump into my head.' He realised he was reliving a piece of last night's missing memory. Why was he saying that? Who was he talking to?

'Rachel ... how's Robert?' He wasn't sure why his mind had suddenly thought of his partner.

'He's fine. Improving by the day, but they've kept him in until his blood pressure stabilises. He's mentioned you a couple of times, Nick. If you get the chance...'

'I know, Rachel. I'm sorry. Everything is just so ... mixed up at the moment. I will go and see him. I promise.' He didn't like sounding so self-centred. Although he had always enjoyed having complete control over his own time, his own agenda, Robert was like family, and the last few days had shown him just how much he needed other people. He smiled to himself. 'The old bugger probably needs some cheering up anyway! You don't know what they could be pumping into him.'

Nick hadn't thought about that. He looked down at his arm, suddenly concerned that he had been given a shot that may have lasting consequences. He rubbed the pin mark, and hoped that the pain was only temporary.

'Look, I've just read an article on this scroll thing in *The Times*. Canon Howe's quoted in it. I was thinking of going to see him, and I wondered if you ... wanted to come.'

Rachel's voice sounded concerned. 'Are you sure that's a good idea? What's wrong with the police?'

'Rachel, I have no idea what it is I have, but I don't see what the police will be able to do with it. Think about it. What do I tell them? That I might have accidentally found the story of the century on a building site, which has had black-clad terrorists attacking everyone around me...'

Rachel interrupted. 'They've attacked you as well now, Nick'

He thought about her words for a moment. Her point was valid. They seemed to have waited to do so, and he didn't understand why. But now that they had ... a thought jumped into his head. 'Truth serum?' he blurted out.

'What did you say?' asked Rachel, who had half caught his utterance.

Nick was still thinking. Could that possibly be what had happened to him? Had he been given something to make him talk? But why? What did he know? What might he have said?

'Nick?'

'Sorry, Rachel. I was just trying to think about...'

'You said something about a ... *serum*? What are you talking about?'

Nick was worried about Rachel's possible reaction to his sudden turn of thought 'No, no. I said ... *to see him*. I want to go and see him. Canon Howe. Look, if you're too busy...'

'No! I'm good. Of course I want to come. I don't want you out of my sight. I don't know what you'll get up to. Seems to me you need someone to keep an eye on you anyway!' Her voice had perked up, and her voice expressed more excitement than concern. 'Give me an hour and I'll be there. And stay out of trouble in the meantime, will you?'

'Promise', answered Nick, his mind picturing Rachel with one hand resting firmly on her hip, the other waving an outstretched index finger, like a mother scolding a child.

Nick hesitated for a second as he picked up the receiver. He was determined to get to the bottom of the mystery and do it on his terms. He had wasted a week of his time on protecting a building for a client he despised, and it was time to get his business, and private life, back on track. There was the silver lining in Rachel, of course, but even that needed to be kept on hold for the moment.

He looked again at the card. He assumed the priest would be in London and not in Paris. Certainly the TV and press interviews had taken place in London, but Henry had indicated that the main work of the Ecole biblique was done in Paris.

He rang the number. A polite-sounding young man answered at the second ring. 'Yes? How may I help you?'

'Is that the Ecole biblique?'

There was a momentary silence. 'Whom do you require?'

Nick took a breath. 'I'd like to speak with Canon Howe, please.'

'Are you from the press?' the voice answered in a more distant fashion.

'No . . . no.' The response, although natural, Nick realised, in the light of recent events, was not what he expected. It suddenly occurred to him that he might not get through. He continued. 'I met the Canon a few days ago and he gave me this number to call if I wanted to get in touch with him.'

'But you're not from the press?' the young man added, clearly convinced that this was merely a ruse to get another interview.

Nick's growing concern was evident in his voice. 'No, as I said, I am not with the press. Look. Give him my name and if he does not wish to speak to me that's fine. It's Nick Stephenson.'

'And which organisation are you from?'

'I'm not with an organisation! Will you just give him my name . . . please? Trust me. I will hang up immediately if he doesn't want to speak to me.'

The voice on the other end sounded more convinced. 'I will ask the Canon now, Mr Stephenson. He is very busy, as I am sure you realise. Hold on, please.' Nick waited for only a few moments before he heard a click on the line then a different voice.

'Mr Stephenson. I hoped you would call.' It was Canon Howe.

'I wasn't sure I was going to get through to you. You have a pretty stubborn telephonist.'

'Ah, Charles. Yes, he ... protects me well. He has had to learn fast these last few days, I am afraid. Things have been rather difficult, as you may have seen.'

'Yes, you seem to be cropping up all over the place.' Nick didn't really feel comfortable holding a conversation on the phone. He wanted to come to the point, but the Canon interrupted his thoughts.

'Do you want to come and see me?'

Nick was slightly taken aback by the directness of the question, but it was welcome. 'Yes, I would. How did you know that I would call?'

'I didn't, but now that you have, it could only be for one reason.' The priest's voice was as calm and reassured as ever. Nick doubted whether the priest had ever been out of control or caught unawares. He seemed unflappable, yet blunt and to the point. 'Will you bring it with you?' he added. Nick's mind stumbled for an answer. He had made the approach, it was he who wanted to control things, but in the space of a few moments the priest had put him on the back foot once again. He couldn't hesitate. There was little point now in pretence or shadow boxing.

'I will bring it, Canon. But I would like to come straight away, and I would also like to bring a friend, a colleague, if you have no objection.'

'Not at all, Mr Stephenson. I agree we should not delay. I have until three o'clock, and then I must fly to Paris. I will be waiting for you. Oh, and one more thing. When you come to the building, please ask for the Literal Research Centre. We guard our privacy, and do not like to advertise our presence. I'm sure you can understand that.'

Nick shrugged his shoulders. 'Fine. I'll ask for you at that office then.'

'Thank you, Mr Stephenson. I will be waiting for you.'

210

Chapter 22

When Nick reached the ground floor of the apartment block he cautiously looked around the car park before emerging into the sunlight. As he did so, Rachel's Mercedes drew up and stopped in a parking bay ten yards from the door. She waved and smiled as she got out the car and skipped over to him as though she had no care in the world.

Convinced there was no one around, Nick handed Rachel his car keys and the biscuit tin, which he had placed in a plastic bag. 'You go on, I just want to pick something up from the newsagents. Give me a minute.'

Rachel did as she was asked, and Nick entered the shop. Before he could say anything, Gerald waved to him from behind the counter. 'Morning, Mr Stephenson. Hope you got the wallet. I couldn't wait much longer last night... Had to get away for the twins. Storytime from Dad, and all that. Always my turn on...'

Nick put up his hand to stop him. 'Yes, I got it, thank you. Silly thing to do. I was wondering, though, who found it. Don't suppose they left a name or anything?' He tried to sound as casual as possible.

Gerald nodded. 'Ah, for a reward you mean. Very good idea. Encourages honesty that does. I always believe in...'

Nick interrupted him again. 'Yes. Did they leave a name, or can you remember what they looked like? I assume they were from the complex?'

Gerald looked at Nick with a quizzical look. 'Well ... I don't know all the residents, and we do get visitors from time to time. Sometimes visiting a resident … or delivery men, you know the sort.'

'But no name left then?' Nick enquired again.

'No. He just handed over your wallet and said he had noticed you dropping it. Said he didn't have time to give it back to you himself, but that I should perhaps call you in case you needed it before you went out.'

Nick was now puzzled. 'He said I might be going out?'

'Yes. I think he said something like "Mr Stephenson will be needing this later, I imagine." That's why I called you straight away.'

'Did you look in the wallet', asked Nick.

'Oh no! I didn't like to. Anyway, no need to. Your friend must have checked…' Gerald straightened up, suddenly aware of his possible mistake. 'It *was* your wallet, wasn't it?'

Nick had learned all he needed. 'Yes … yes, Gerald. Thank you again. I'm sorry I didn't get down for it. Took a call, and it went right out of my head.' He headed for the door, waving the empty wallet at the newsagent as he went. 'Excellent service as ever!' he added, trying to put him at ease.

'Nick, are you going to share it with me?' Rachel asked, her eyes intensely fixed on his face.

'Share what?' asked Nick, suddenly aware that he had been lost in his own thoughts for some time. He had been trying to picture the building in Hanover Square. A few years ago he had received a commission from a media company to help them fit out their offices. Nothing grand or too expensive, but they wanted an architect to help sell their brand through a cleverly designed internal layout. Nick had enjoyed working with them and had been proud of the results. Little did he suspect then that he would be revisiting the building in such bizarre circumstances.

'Whatever it is you're thinking about.' Rachel looked back at the road ahead. 'It would be nice to have a normal conversation for a change.'

Nick looked over at her. She looked for all the world like someone who had no worries or cares, her perfect pale skin radiant with only the merest hint of blusher on her cheeks. Her hair cascaded freely, almost wildly, over her shoulders as ever, yet looked completely natural and, yes, beautiful. He smiled, leaned over and patted her on the knee. 'You're right. Let's talk about football.'

'Oh, you are either serious or obtuse!'

'Obtuse? Me? You said you wanted a normal discussion. Football *is* my normal discussion.' He laughed as she prodded him in the side. 'I just don't seem to be talking a lot about it at the moment.' He looked back at her smiling face. 'God, I miss it!' he added, mockingly.

'Nick! Why can't we just talk about ... well, I don't know.' She puffed up her cheeks as though she was about to explode. 'Food. Yes, what about food. She put her hands between her legs and angled her body to look at him. 'Can we go out for a meal later? Please? There's this really good new Thai restaurant in Covent Garden that everyone's been raving about.'

Nick looked over at her and forced a smile. Rachel saw straight through it. 'You're up to something, aren't you? You're busy tonight, aren't you? Is it the scroll?'

Nick shook his head and continued the smile. He wanted to say yes to her suggestion of a meal, more than she probably realised, but he had other things on his mind. 'Look, Rachel, I don't know what I'm doing tonight. It depends, I suppose, on what happens when we meet Canon Howe.' He checked the road in front, then leaned over to her and put his hand back on her thigh, stroking it affectionately, and then letting his hand settle on top of her hands. 'I promise you, Rachel, when this is sorted, I'll take you for as many meals as you can last with me! You won't need to ask again.'

Rachel smiled back at him and held his hand. 'I'm not pushing, Nick. I know you need to have an answer to all of this, and I want to help. Let me help.'

'You are, I promise.' Nick answered, aware of the role he wanted her to play. 'Just trust me with this visit. There are a couple of things I need to do that you may not understand, but bear with me.'

Rachel looked puzzled and intrigued. She thought about asking questions, but decided that it was exactly this trust that Nick was talking about. 'Just tell me what to do,' she replied.

Nick parked the car and they both walked to the offices of the Ecole biblique in Hanover Square, the bag containing the biscuit tin tightly gripped in his right hand. The building was multi-let, one shared by a number of companies who made use of common services such as reception, security and cleaning. As they approached, Nick slowed down and took Rachel by the hand.

'I want to check something out first. Let's walk past the offices so that I can take a look. He moved to the inside of the footpath as they approached the glass-fronted entranceway, a large revolving door in the centre, framed on both sides by two glass panels and separate entrance doors. They walked slowly past, Nick absorbing as much of the internal layout as he could. A large glass-topped wooden reception desk, stood in the centre of the reception hallway. Two bespectacled receptionists sat behind the desk, one with her head down, the other busily checking a book in front of her in which a man dressed in a black pinstriped suit was writing something. A visitors' book. Nick nodded to himself. Good.

To the right of the desk a commissionaire stood dressed in the smart black outfit of the Corps of Commissionaires, the shiny black sash across his chest depicting the importance of his station, his hands clasped in front of him as if trying to force a welcoming stance. Although discreet, the Ecole clearly took security seriously along with all the other occupants of the building. As they approached the end of the run of glass panels, Nick watched as the receptionist tore away a strip from the book in front of her and placed it in a plastic pocket before handing it to the visitor in front of her. The man straightened out a piece of cord attached to the wallet, and placed it over his head, leaving it dangling on his chest. The receptionist smiled and pointed to her right, past the commissionaire who had been carefully watching the movements of the other visitors and workers in the entrance foyer. Beyond him, Nick could see three elevator doors against the back wall.

'Well?' asked Rachel. 'Did you get what you wanted out of that?'

'I did indeed,' answered Nick. 'They have a visitors' book.'

Rachel looked at him. 'Is that it? Not much of a surprise there then really,' she couldn't help commenting, but as soon as she had said it and Nick looked at her, she knew it was the wrong thing to say. She put up her hand. 'Sorry ... sorry.' She closed her mouth in an exaggerated fashion.

Nick shot her an annoyed look, but decided they had no time to waste. 'Just do as I say, and follow my lead. I won't say it again. Now, let's go in.'

As they approached the front door of the building, Nick grabbed Rachel's arm and pulled her slightly toward him. 'I'll explain later, but when you sign in I want you to use the name Leslie.'

Rachel looked at him. 'What?' She started to grin. 'Rachel Leslie?'

'No. Leslie Smith,' answered Nick.

'This isn't one of those funny hotels, is it?' she quipped, a smile on her face as they approached the door.

Nick wasn't laughing. 'Trust me, Rachel. Please, just do as I say. I'll explain later.' He pushed the revolving door to start it off, and then motioned for Rachel to enter. As soon as he was inside, he scanned the entrance hallway again. Two CCTV cameras were obvious, one directly behind the reception desk that was straight ahead of them, the other high on the wall to their right, mounted on a small metal platform. It was scanning the room in slow movements. The commissionaire clocked their entrance immediately, his eyes alert, but his manner relaxed and efficient, both hands still clasped in front of him. They walked up to the reception desk and Nick smiled at the receptionist.

'Good morning, how can I help you, Sir, Madam.'

'I'm here to see Canon Howe of the Literal Research Centre,' answered Nick in a calm voice.

The receptionist eyed them suspiciously. 'Are you both here to see the Canon?'

Rachel moved to Nick's side. 'Yes, thank you,' she answered.

'And your names please?' enquired the receptionist.

'Mr Stephenson and Miss Smith,' answered Nick, trying hard to sound natural, and desperately trying not to catch Rachel's eyes.

The receptionist pointed at the visitors' book. 'Would you sign in, please'? She picked up the telephone and pressed four numbers on the keypad. After a few seconds she spoke into the mouthpiece. 'A Mr Stephenson and a Miss Smith for Canon Howe.'

Nick quickly scanned the security book while she spoke. It was a standard type he had filled in on numerous visits to other offices. A single sheet on top had a carbon copy below, allowing an imprint onto the bottom sheet when

216

the top one was written on. Nick wrote his name in capitals on the first section of the sheet, and Canon Howe's where asked to state whom he was visiting. Another section requested his time of arrival. Nick glanced up at the receptionist. She was still concentrating on the phone, awaiting a response. He handed the bag to Rachel and looked at her directly to catch her eye, and then very deliberately moved his eyes down to the sheet. She understood and watched his movements. He carefully lifted the top sheet away from the bottom one and wrote the time on the bottom one – 11.35 a.m. – while leaving the top one blank. Placing the top sheet down on the book again, he signed his name in the final section. He stepped aside and motioned to Rachel to repeat the exercise. She handed the bag with the tin inside back to him.

The receptionist looked up at Nick as she replaced the handset on the desk. 'Canon Howe is expecting you. You can go straight down to the basement. It can only be accessed from the far-left elevator.' Her eyes moved to Rachel's, just as she was finishing the Canon's name. Nick realised he needed to attract the receptionist's attention. He smiled and leaned his right arm on the desk.

'Very hot for this time of year, isn't it? I imagine it has been pretty uncomfortable working in here.'

The receptionist gave a somewhat forced smile. 'Well, the revolving door gives us some air circulation, so we don't complain,' she proffered.

Nick guessed that she was unlikely to complain even without a revolving door. He couldn't see a conversation lasting too long. He glanced at the book, and could see that Rachel had followed his lead and written their arrival time only on the bottom sheet. So far so good. Rachel put the pen down, and the receptionist stretched out her arm and turned the book toward her. Nick decided he had to distract her just to be sure.

'Well, I suppose it could be worse. At least you'll be finished by ... five o'clock?' He shrugged his shoulders to illicit a response.

'Actually we finish at 5.30, Mr Stephenson,' she answered, her eyes darting a severe look at Nick as she tore the first strip from the book and placed it unceremoniously in the plastic pocket. She handed it to Nick. 'Please wear this at all times in the building. You may be asked to show it at any time if you remove it for any reason.' She looked back at the book, and started to tear off Rachel's strip.

'So, if I am here after 5.30, do I just leave this at reception?' Nick asked, dangling the identity wallet in front of him.

The receptionist looked back up at him. 'If you do happen to be here that long, the commissionaire will take it from you. We have 24-hour security, Sir.' Nick felt duly chastised.

She handed the second plastic wallet to Rachel who slipped the cord over her head. 'If you make your way to the basement someone will meet you there.'

Nick smiled at the receptionist and placed the cord over his head. He put his hand on Rachel's arm and led her towards the elevator lobby.

As he passed the commissionaire Nick checked he was out of earshot of the receptionist. He smiled and nodded, flashing the plastic bag at him. 'First day. Can't wait to get started!'

The commissionaire smiled back. 'Well, have a good day then, Sir, and ... welcome.' He touched his cap and nodded toward Rachel who nodded back. They walked toward the elevators.

'What are you up to?' Rachel whispered, as Nick pressed the button on the wall.

'I told you before...', Nick answered, pleased that the

first part of his plan appeared to have succeeded, '... trust me.'

The elevator door opened and they stepped inside, Nick turning back briefly to look at the commissionaire. He was watching them as the door slid closed in front of them.

They reached the basement and the elevator door opened again. Canon Howe raised his arms from his sides to greet his visitors

'Mr Stephenson. Good to see you again.' He looked at Rachel. 'And you have brought a beautiful friend with you, I see.' He glanced at her badge. 'I am very pleased to meet you, Miss Leslie Smith.' Rachel smiled back at the Canon, impressed by his warmth and courteous manner. She decided to let Nick do the talking, though.

'Thank you for seeing us at such short notice, Canon. I know you have been very busy.' He started following Canon Howe who was now moving along the short corridor.

'I saw your interview on television last night. I suppose this must all have come as a bit of a surprise to you, this press interest I mean,' Nick added while busily scanning the surroundings. He could only see one door, ahead of them on the left-hand side. The rest of the corridor seemed to comprise of bare, cream-painted walls, and a plain white ceiling. There were no other doors or an obvious means of escape, which Nick found curious.

'I am the spokesman for the organisation in all things relating directly to the Scrolls. I cannot say it is my chosen role, but the press are insatiable. Once you have lifted your head above the parapet, they all want a piece of it.' He looked back at the two of them and smiled as he continued to lead them along the brightly lit passage. 'It is important that we are heard in the right way, and at least I can ensure that anything attributed to us is fact. It is only I who speaks on behalf of the organisation.'

Nick was even more convinced about the man's complete self-control and belief. 'Oh, and it does allow me the privilege of meeting some interesting people,' he added, flashing a glance at Rachel.

'Oh, really? And who might that be, Canon?' she asked, her curiosity aroused.

'Well, this morning, Miss Smith, I gave a private briefing to the Queen, and only twenty minutes ago I had tea with Steven Spielberg.'

'Steven Spielberg? Why would you meet him?' asked Nick, the naming of the two individuals in the same sentence seemingly incomprehensible to Nick.

'He has long been fascinated by the Scrolls. To him they are a magical story waiting to be told to the world, and, even better for a master of special effects, it is a *true* story. This latest ... rumour, has merely rekindled his interest.' The Canon slowed down as he approached a door halfway along the corridor. Nick moved up to his side. To the left of the door at shoulder height was a small metal box, a touchpad with numbers and a digital display above.

As the Canon moved his hand out toward the box, he blocked Nick's view of the pad. Nick swung quickly in front of him and spoke loudly, ensuring he would distract the priest. 'But why would he be interested in that? Surely he hasn't lost his brilliant imagination?'

The Canon looked a little startled at the loudness of Nick's intervention. He pulled his arm back to his side, allowing Nick time to move to the other side of the door, giving him a full view of the touchpad. 'If there is one thing a great director knows, it is that he must make the audience *believe*, Mr Stephenson. That is why green men from Mars and giant ants have had their day. Special effects are so real that they have destroyed themselves. What people want now are *stories* that they can believe in. And what greater story than who we are, and why we are here!'

For the first time Nick heard passion in the Canon's voice. He wasn't sure he understood his meaning, but it was clear that the Canon was a man with many sides. 'I'm sorry, Canon. I didn't mean to question your work. It's just a surprise to hear that you would be ... mixing with filmmakers, that's all.' Nick smiled as warmly as he could, while at the same time watching the priest's every move.

Canon Howe smiled back at him. 'We are not all what we may seem. I enjoy a good film, even a good science-fiction one like the rest of us...' As he spoke, he lifted his right hand up to the pad, partially obscuring Nick's view. Nick moved a little closer, while trying hard not to make it obvious that he was watching closely. Two, five ... blanked! ... two. He missed the third digit! Damn! He tried to picture the priest's hand movement again in his head. He couldn't make out the position. '...and in any case,' Canon Howe continued as the door opened, 'there is a great deal we can learn from which films it is that people are watching, not just the films themselves.'

The room was long and brightly lit, even though the two small windows on the opposite wall, which Nick guessed faced out onto a basement lightwell, had been blacked out with what appeared to be silver foil. A low hum filled the room with a background sound, and the air felt dry and chilled. Nick realised an elaborate air-conditioning system had been installed and that they had entered a very controlled environment. A large white-topped table, seven or eight metres long, dominated the centre of the room. Part of it was lit from below creating a light box. Along a side wall, a series of large wooden chests with heavy strapping and what appeared to be elaborate silver locking mechanisms, were standing side by side. The wall at the far end had a number of normal-looking office desks, two of which were occupied by men who had now stopped reading the papers that were set out in front of them, and were curiously watching the small party which had just arrived through the door. Visitors were clearly not a daily occurrence.

'Who are your colleagues?' Nick asked.

'They are linguistic experts from Oxford University. They have been working here with me for a number of years. Brilliant scholars. Only trouble is they keep university hours. Disappear at four o'clock and won't be back until ten tomorrow. I suppose it is very monotonous for them though, so I can understand ... and we keep it very quiet ... for security reasons.'

Canon Howe motioned for Nick and Rachel to move further into the room. They walked slowly along the side of the table until they came to a section on which a number of papers were lying. A single piece of parchment about the size of an A4 sheet was spread out on the table, the corners held by silver catches clipped onto the table itself, a powerful table light shining directly from above.

'This, Mr Stephenson, is one of the Dead Sea Scrolls.' He had said it in such a casual way, but Nick felt genuinely struck by the sense of being in a place where the past was being brought back to life. He could see and feel the intensity with which the scrolls were being examined, and the care with which the delicate parchments were being treated. There was only a single sheet exposed under the light and Nick could see that the material had a waxy, almost leather-like look to it.

'Is this ... page particularly important?' Nick asked.

The Canon smiled. 'They are all important. But to answer your question, no, not particularly. This is only one of thousands of pages we are examining, but it all takes time, I am afraid.'

'So why are these particular scrolls here, and not in Paris? Isn't that where most of the work is being done?' replied Nick.

The Canon raised his eyebrows. 'I see you are not completely without knowledge of our organisation. Yes, most of them are indeed in Paris. The scrolls were written in a number of different languages, different dialects even, and we have some experts here in London who have the necessary linguistic skills and are best to work on them.' He looked down at the parchment below him, with the look of a father over a sick child. 'Fortunately, there are some which are in better condition than the rest, and not as sensitive to our modern world. I ... we have only a few here, but we have some of the best people in the world working on them.' They looked along at the two others who had now continued their work, bent silently over their desks, motionless.

'Now,' said the priest, looking back at Nick and rubbing his hands together gently. 'You have something to show me.'

Rachel handed the bag to Nick who removed the biscuit tin and placed it on the table next to the scroll sheet.

The priest looked at the tin and smiled at Rachel. 'A very appropriate receptacle. I am fond of the odd biscuit myself.' Rachel smiled back.

He undid the lid and let the scroll slip out onto his hand. He placed the scroll on the table and started to unroll it. Once he had exposed around twelve inches, he placed what looked like a heavy metal ruler across the scroll to keep it in place, while holding the other end down with his left hand. He bent over the scroll and started to examine the writing. Nick watched closely at the expression on the man's face, eager to spot any sign of recognition, or any other reaction. After a few moments trailing the words with his right index finger, the priest's eyes started darting around the rest of the manuscript, as if he was looking for something.

Nick looked at Rachel whose gaze was also transfixed by the priest's face. 'Have you spotted something, Canon?' he asked eventually.

The priest stood up slowly. 'Where did this come from?' he asked, a puzzled look on his face.

Nick was surprised by the question. Although they had never discussed how the priest knew about the scroll, Nick had assumed that he had gained a certain amount of knowledge and had been prepared to play whatever game Canon Howe wanted to if it let Nick get to the bottom of it all. He looked straight into the priest's eyes and crossed his arms. 'Tell me what you *do* know, Canon.'

'I know that this is not genuine, Mr Stephenson.'

'I already know that,' Nick answered, disappointed by the reply.

'But I also know that it is a very important find,' the priest continued. 'It may not be the real thing, but the contents are possibly genuine.'

Nick felt confused. 'How do you know this? What does it say?'

Canon Howe paused, choosing his words carefully. 'There are references here to things that are mentioned in other scrolls we have found. But they are written in a different way from those we have.'

'Could this be anything to do with the scroll in the paper ... the Master Scroll?' asked Rachel bluntly.

'Not this particular parchment, no. If you had the original version, who knows? There are many ancient documents from the time of the Dead Sea Scrolls that appear to be missing, as far as we can tell. One of our biggest and most difficult tasks is cross-referencing what we have. There are gaps in our knowledge, even contradictions. It is important that we gather as much information on the whereabouts of all these scriptures as we can. Only once we have all the writings from that time will our work be finished. Then, and only then, will the full picture be revealed.'

Nick thought about the words. 'Does that mean you are holding all this back because you're not sure what these scriptures all mean?'

The priest hesitated. 'Not quite, but you're on the right lines.'

'So you're worried about what might come out?' pressed Nick.

The priest straightened up, and the calm grin that Nick was beginning to recognise appeared on his face. 'We are dealing with an industry here, Mr Stephenson. There are unscrupulous collectors who would pay a great deal of money for the genuine article, and there are those who are only too eager to supply them, if they can get their hands on them. Unfortunately we need to be in the marketplace to complete our work.'

'So you're telling us that you buy and sell these scrolls like everyone else?'

'We have no option but to satisfy a demand if it means we can ... acquire those parchments that we have not been able to document.'

Nick looked at the priest with incredulity, but thought back to Henry's comments in the library. He decided to challenge the priest head on. 'Are you telling us that you've *sold* some of the Dead Sea Scrolls?'

'We have parted with some that we have already documented and which we are satisfied are of little consequence, yes, but only where our gain has far outweighed the loss. Expedience, Mr Stephenson, is essential for the momentum we need. We have been aware for a number of months now of an unknown buyer who has paid vast sums of money for those scrolls we have put

in circulation, and those we have never seen. We don'
know who or why, but these latest … rumours were
something we expected could occur.'

'Someone is building their own picture,' Nick proffered
'and it may not look like yours when it is complete!' He
glanced at his watch.

'Very astute, Mr Stephenson. That is what led us to
you. It appears you have stumbled across something which
may have great value.' The priest looked down again a
the scroll and shook his head slowly. 'Then again, it could
be a complete hoax. Without the original version, if there
is one, it is worthless.' The priest looked puzzled again

Rachel moved forward and touched the edge of the
page lying spread-eagled on the table. 'Can you translate
our scroll?' she asked.

'In time, Miss Smith. It will need time. I would like to
keep it here, but more importantly, we need to identify
where the original is.'

Nick thought about the likelihood of their being an
original. His mind briefly thought of Robert. 'That won'
be possible,' he said firmly.

'What won't?' answered the priest, surprised at Nick's
tone.

'Keeping it here. I can't leave it here,' replied Nick.

'But I thought you wanted to find out more about it
To find out if it was meaningful. We may be able to
determine where the original is.'

'I have the answer I need, Canon. This may not be
real, and it may be interesting to you, but until I can
answer all the questions *I* have, it stays with me.' He
leaned over the table, removed the metal ruler and rolled
up the parchment.

Rachel looked at Nick in surprise as he placed the
scroll back in the tin. 'Why not leave it here, Nick. A
least you would find out if it has any value.' She looked

around the room. 'They have all the equipment here to translate it. Don't you want to know what it says?'

Nick looked at her sternly. He almost said her name before remembering that he couldn't. 'I am not interested in that. Come on, we're going. Thank you for showing us your ... facility, Canon.' He turned to walk away.

'Is it money you are after?' the Canon asked quietly.

'I beg your pardon?' replied Nick.

'Money,' repeated the Canon. 'What is it you want? This scroll can be of no interest to you. It is not genuine. It cannot interfere with your work, and surely you would be better off without it. Has it not caused you enough grief, Mr Stephenson?'

Rachel pleaded. 'He's right, Nick. All it has done is bring you trouble. You would be better off without it.'

Nick started walking towards the door. 'You're both right.' He opened the door as Rachel reached his side. 'But it's still coming with me.'

'Very well, but you know where to reach me when you have had enough of it' the priest answered his tone now more direct than Nick had heard before. 'I will be waiting. Be careful'

The door closed behind them and Nick strode back along the corridor, just as a man in a black security jacket came out of the elevator. 'What are you doing?' asked Rachel as she skipped along to catch him up. 'He was trying to help you.'

Nick didn't look over at her. 'Didn't I tell you to trust me? I know what I'm doing, Rachel. We don't know him from ... Adam, and at the moment I am not in the mood to trust anyone.' He looked at his watch – 12.32.

The security man put his hand up in front of them as they approached. As his mouth opened to speak, Canon Howe interjected. 'It's OK, my guests are just leaving. But I would like a word, please.'

The man lowered his hands and stepped to one side. 'Certainly, Canon.'

Nick and Rachel stepped inside the elevator as the man made his way along the short corridor. The door closed. 'Give me your tag.' Nick pointed to the security pass hanging around Rachel's neck. She did as asked, and decided not to ask questions. Nick took his off and stuck both in his pocket. 'Stay close to me, and when I make for the door, keep up.' She nodded her understanding of his request.

The door opened on the ground floor, and, as he hoped, the reception area was much busier than before. Secretaries and business-suited office workers were making for an early lunch, the chit-chat of office gossip already in full swing as they headed toward the security barrier that separated the lobby from the entrance area. 'Stay close,' he whispered. The commissionaire was busily moving his head from side to side, occasionally smiling or nodding to one of the throng. Nick spotted three men who were clearly workers from an upper floor as they noisily exited an elevator. He swung over behind them and lowered his head. Rachel copied his movements as they headed for the door. They were joined from both sides by others, and the human wave moved closer to the barrier. Neither looked up, afraid of catching the commissionaire's eyes. The barrier was suddenly upon them, and Nick pushed through and hurriedly headed for the exit. They were out in the street.

Rachel looked up at Nick and smiled. 'I have no idea what you are doing, but at least it's not dull!' He smiled back at her relieved that they had not been caught. His plan was still intact.

In his office, high above London's streets, Benjamin allowed himself a restrained smile. The CCTV footage of Hanover

Square that was illicitly fed to his PC stared back at him from the bank of screens on the opposite wall. The two figures had just emerged from an office building and were busily making off in the direction of the nearby taxi rank. 'You are an interesting adversary, Mr Stephenson,' he quietly muttered to himself, 'but what are you going to do next, I wonder?'

He leaned over the desk and touched the glass top. Immediately the screens went blank.

Chapter 23

Nick entered the library and headed straight for the main reception desk. Even from nearly thirty yards away he could make out the unmistakable outline of Henry, sitting in his woolly cardigan behind the desk, his shoulders hunched over a book, a mug of coffee resting in his right hand. He smiled to himself as he anticipated the reaction from the young librarian.

'Hello Henry,' Nick whispered as he reached the desk.

'Ah!' came the startled reply as Henry recognised the voice immediately, some coffee spilling over the side of the cup. 'Oh no. What do you want? Can't you leave me alone?' His voice wasn't loud, but it caused a number of visitors nearby to turn and shoot disapproving glances at the two men.

'Charming!' replied Nick quietly. 'I thought it was part of your job to encourage people to visit the library?'

'Yes … the ones who want to read books!' Henry responded, pushing aside his own book and standing up to meet Nick's face directly. 'I don't know why you're here … and I don't want to know either.'

Nick feigned a hurt look. 'I thought you might want an update on our little project,' Nick volunteered.

'Our… What are you talking about? We don't have a … project!' Henry looked bemused. 'I don't ever want to see you again. You're trouble!'

Nick persisted. 'Look, Henry, things have got, well … a lot more interesting.' He looked about the room in an exaggerated fashion, then leaned closer again. 'You were right! Have you seen the news recently?'

Henry stood up and stepped away from Nick slightly. He shook his head slowly. 'Please tell me it has nothing to do with you?'

Nick stood back, smiled and said nothing. Henry's shoulders sunk. 'Oh no. I knew it was. I just knew it!'

Nick leaned forward again. 'What do you think?'

'What do I think? I think you're nuts, that's what I think!' He looked around the room. 'Do you know how many idiots we've had in here in the last two days wanting to read about the *magic* or *mythological* scrolls? Are you the one planning to have a press conference and tell the world you're an expert on the Scrolls and somehow give them evidence that will ... will turn the world upside down? If you are, could you make it quick, please!' Henry closed the book in front of him and pushed away the coffee cup.

'No, of course not' replied Nick. 'I don't know what this scroll says, but *someone* thinks they do.' He looked closer at Henry and his voice quietened. 'Have you heard of a Canon Howe?'

Henry thought for a moment. He knew that he really didn't want this conversation to go on any longer, but he couldn't help himself when challenged with a question. He repeated the name to himself and started to mentally flick through the card-index system in his brain. 'Ecole biblique. He's their press spokesman... Been on TV this week, if I recall, talking about this nonsense.'

'What makes you think its nonsense?'

'Of course it's nonsense!' replied Henry, grinning. 'You don't believe it, do you?'

'After what you told me? You said yourself that not all these scrolls were accounted for. What if one, just one, had something so damning, so different from all the others that it could throw doubt on everything?'

'Like what?' asked Henry shaking his head.

231

'I don't know,' replied Nick, 'a premise so different that it could only be true?'

Henry chuckled. 'I have no idea what you're talking about ... and neither do you!' He picked up a handful of books and walked away from the desk in the opposite direction. Nick followed him.

'But *what if*, Henry?' Nick responded, trying to draw Henry into at least thinking about a proposition that he guessed must be of some interest, if not excitement, for someone like the geeky librarian.

Henry stopped. 'You're serious?'

'Yes,' Nick responded, the look on his face confirming his view.

Henry started to walk again along the central aisle. He hated himself for even continuing to think about the subject. 'Well, I suppose this ... scroll ... would have to somehow overrule others, like a ... a *Master* Scroll.' He lifted both arms out to his side and shook his head. 'Oh come on, we're going down the same route here!'

'But is there no other way of looking at it?' asked Nick.

'I don't see how,' replied Henry as he turned into a side aisle, walked along in front of a shelf and then started to place a book on the top row. 'If such a thing existed it would need to either invalidate the others ... or somehow pull all the others together in some new way.'

Nick thought about Henry's words, and then froze. *Then, and only then, the full picture will be revealed.* The priest's words. After visiting Canon Howe, Nick had doubted he was searching in the right direction, but now, perhaps, he realised he may be right after all.

He grabbed Henry's arm and spun him around. 'You're brilliant, Henry! I think you may have the solution.' He decided it was time to share with Henry why he had come. 'Have you ever been to the Ecole biblique?'

Henry looked startled and once again wore that frightened

look Nick had seen before. 'I've never been to Paris, never mind the Institute.'

'No, the office in London.'

'They have an office in London?' replied Henry, a look of surprise on his face. 'I didn't know that.'

'Yes, in Hanover Square, although they use the name "Literal Research Centre" for security reasons. I was there earlier. It's where I met Canon Howe.' Nick took a breath. 'I want you to come with me to see something there.'

Henry giggled nervously. 'Why would I want to do that?'

Nick let go of his arm. He knew he would need Henry, and he had to persuade him that it was worth taking yet another risk in his quiet, humdrum life.

'Henry, I know I've brought a lot of hassle to your life in the past week, but I believe that this stuff in the press is somehow linked to the scroll I have. I can't explain how or why, but I truly believe that.' He looked at Henry's face. At least he still had his attention. 'You have a talent, Henry, one I don't. You know about these things. You've studied this subject, and quite frankly, well...' – he knew he was laying it on a bit thick – '...I need your help, and you are the only one who *can* help me. I promise if you do this for me, I will never come here again. You have my word.'

Henry looked at Nick but said nothing. He realised that he had thought about the last few days many times, and as the hours had gone on his thoughts had faded from the pain and fear to something closer to excitement. If nothing else, his encounters with Nick had made him feel more alive than he had for a long time. At least, the monotony of his life had been thrown aside for a few moments. He relaxed his shoulders. 'What would I have to do?' he asked hesitantly.

Nick couldn't believe it. He hadn't really expected Henry to capitulate so easily, although he hadn't explained his proposal. *One step at a time*, he thought.

'I just want you to look at some papers, and tell me what they mean, that's all.'

Henry looked surprised. 'Is that all? Where are they?'

'They're at the Ecole ... the Research Centre'

Henry thought for a moment. 'Why couldn't you bring them with you?'

'Ah. Well, they probably wouldn't let me.'

Henry looked confused. He thought some more and then tried to back away. 'You don't mean you want to ... steal them?'

'No, no. Of course not!' Nick knew he had to choose his words carefully. 'I only want us to find them and look through them, that's all.'

'Find them? What do you mean? Do you know which papers you want me to look at?'

'We will sort that once we get in.'

'Get in? What do you...' Henry stopped. Maybe this wasn't such a good idea after all. 'You want us to break in, don't you?'

Nick hesitated 'Not ... exactly.'

'What does that mean?' retorted Henry, his voice now at a higher pitch.

Nick pulled the two security tags out of his pocket. 'I have passes.' He handed one to Henry, who examined it.

'Leslie Smith? Who's Leslie Smith?' asked Henry.

'That's you,' replied Nick.

'Isn't this the way you spell the girl's name?' asked Henry.

'Is it? I can never remember which one is spelled which,' replied Nick, shrugging his shoulders. He smiled at Henry who was lost for words. 'Anyway, no one will look at it. They never do. We're not talking about a high-security establishment here.' He looked at his watch. 4.35. 'The only trouble is we have less than an hour to get there. Can you get off now?'

234

Henry shook his head. 'I have a bad feeling about this. It sounds very illegal.'

'It'll be fine. Trust me. I've already been there and it will be a piece of cake. Over in no time...' Nick pushed him back down the aisle towards the main desk. 'What time are you due to finish?'

'Five o'clock.'

'OK. That should just give us enough time. Oh, and could I borrow some books on the Dead Sea Scrolls, please?'

Chapter 24

Benjamin sat quietly on the blood-red chesterfield, his head slowly scanning around the oak-lined room, absorbing the unmistakable aura of power exuded from the handsome portraits of past residents of this office in the Palace of Westminster.

'The Home Secretary will see you now, Mr Goldstein.' The pretty secretary smiled as she gestured for him to move towards the panelled door that was barely discernible from the walls either side.

'Thank you, Miss Stevens,' replied Benjamin as he picked up his briefcase and walked over to the entrance. There was no need to show him the way in.

'Benjamin, how are you?' asked the Home Secretary, as he rose from his desk to greet his visitor.

'I am well, Paul. I trust things are also well with you?'

Paul came straight to the point. 'I have everything in hand. The Bill is being prepared as we speak, just as you wanted. It will give us ... the Government, the emergency powers we seek. By this time next week, the Home Secretary will be as powerful as the Prime Minister!' He smiled contentedly.

'Why will it take so long?' snapped Benjamin. 'You will need the power before then.'

Paul looked crestfallen. 'Benjamin, I am forcing through an extraordinary measure! These powers have only ever been used in a time of war. I cannot simply grant them to myself. They take time, even in this place.' He straightened up. 'It took me a great deal of time and effort to persuade the Prime Minister that the Government would need these measures. He is...'

'...a fool!' interrupted Benjamin. 'That's what he is! After six years in power he has lost the people's trust. They are ready for change. It is the perfect time. He is in a weak position, and you *will* seize the opportunity.'

'I am ready,' replied Paul, his voice betraying his disapproval of Benjamin's tone. 'When I have these powers, I will show what I am capable of.'

'Good,' replied Benjamin, satisfied that his subservient accomplice had been suitably reminded of the importance of his role. He softened his tone. 'You have used the file?'

'Yes. It was invaluable, and not a little shocking, I have to say. The promised suppression of my colleagues' ...*indiscretions* has worked with those you identified. The others will fall in behind my leadership. I have promised strong portfolios to those in the Cabinet who will support us, and I have handpicked those junior ministers who will also join my Cabinet once the Prime Minister has ... resigned.' He grinned. 'I don't know where you obtained your information, but it certainly hit the spot, as they say!'

Benjamin smiled. 'Good. I think you *are* ready. You will receive favourable coverage from our sycophantic press, of that I can assure you. They are already beginning to taste blood and they will enjoy nothing more than believing they have brought down a Prime Minister.' He opened his briefcase and handed Paul a red folder. 'I have arranged a series of photo shoots for you, and there are some press statements I would like you to release at the appropriate time.' He looked straight into Paul's eyes and spoke slowly for effect. 'In one month from now, you will be the Prime Minister.'

* * *

Nick and Henry stood beside the door as the building's rush hour started. Nick glanced at his watch ... 5.31. The receptionists were still hovering around the desk. The office workers were streaming out like lemmings and the commissionaire was now frantically trying to keep an eye on the moving mass, his back against the wall on the left side of the entrance hall. One of the receptionists waved to the other and joined the throng. Nick knew they had to time their move as accurately as possible. He took out the two security tags, and scrolled the time on both empty sections. He turned to Henry. 'Now remember, as soon as we're inside, get that security tag over your head and follow me. Don't say anything. I'll do the talking.'

Henry nodded his understanding of the instruction and reached into his pocket to place the tag firmly at the bottom. He shifted the five books in his arms to his left arm. They were heavy.

Finally, the second receptionist turned out the desk light, stood up and waved to the commissionaire. She made for the revolving door and, as soon as she was through, Nick gestured to Henry and they quickly entered through the same door, just managing to catch it as it spun effortlessly to accommodate the exiting mass. As soon as they were inside, they pulled the tags over their heads and headed for the barrier. As they reached it, the flow of people seemed to increase. Nick put his hand up as if trying to stop them. The commissionaire spotted the two people who were now beginning to cause havoc and raised his arms quickly to stop more from coming through from the lift lobby. He shouted over at Nick and Henry as he made his way through the crowd toward them. 'Stop there please.'

Nick smiled at the commissionaire. 'I didn't realise it got so busy at this time. I'll need to remember this tomorrow!'

238

The commissionaire looked at Nick. 'Can I see your ID please?' Nick lifted up the tag, as did Henry. The commissionaire read Nick's carefully. The time had been entered as 5.30 p.m.

'Just bringing a few things to let me get started early. Hell of a first day.'

The commissionaire looked at Nick carefully, and then relaxed. 'Oh yes. I remember earlier. Just got in on time though, Sir. You can't get into the building with a visitor pass after 5.30. Quicker you get a staff badge the better.' He looked at Henry. 'Who's this, Sir?'

'Oh, this is my assistant, Leslie. Brought a few books to help me get started,' Nick responded. The commissionaire looked at Henry's tag and then closely at his face. He started to open his mouth when a voice shouted from the other side of the barrier. 'Come on, Archie, we want out of here!' Another few voices added their support to the proposition. The commissionaire looked at the throng now gathered on the other side of the barrier, and then signalled to the crowd of office workers to let the two through. He could do without this hassle at the end of another hot day.

'Thank you,' Nick said, throwing a quick wave toward the swamped commissionaire, as they walked through into the lift lobby. Nick glanced at Henry and caught sight of a sweat bead running down his face. He winked at his young accomplice. They slowly made their way past the sea of bodies toward the elevators. They waited for the far-left elevator to empty, then stepped quickly inside. Nick pressed the basement button. As the lift door closed they both let out a sigh of relief.

'So far so good,' Nick said. 'Now all we have to do is get through the security pad and we're in.'

Henry looked at him. 'Security pad? What does that mean?' he asked.

Nick frowned, then turned to look at him directly. 'There's a box on the side of the door, a security pad with numbers on it. We have to enter a four-digit number to open the door.'

'And you have the number. Tell me you have the number.' Nick could see the sweat on Henry's face becoming more pronounced by the second.

'Relax ... I have three of them. I only missed the third one, but it can only be one of ten ... including zero. We'll just try them all.' He smiled at Henry who seemed to be visibly wilting, the books under his arm now seeming to be weighing him down.

Henry shook his head. 'Did it not occur to you that there would be an automatic cut-off if you tried more than once and got it wrong?'

Nick hadn't thought about that specifically, but he had hoped he would have come up with an answer before now. He somehow hoped that seeing the door again would help him think of a solution.

'And another thing,' asked Henry, clearly now regretting having agreed to Nick's crazy idea. 'How do you know this room will be empty?'

Nick smiled. At least he could answer that one. 'Canon Howe is flying to Paris as we speak, and his two colleagues will be on their way back to Oxford. They keep short hours.'

The elevator door opened, and they walked out into the short corridor. It was still brightly lit and, to Nick's relief, empty. They hurried along to the door and Nick stared at the pad, Henry right behind him, sweating profusely.

'It's not going to open just by looking at it, you know,' remarked Henry, not knowing whether he should be scared or glad they couldn't actually break in. At least they were still the right side of the law, he surmised. 'What are the numbers you have?' he asked.

'Twenty-five, something, two,' answered Nick. 'I can't see a pattern in that, but there must be some logic to it.'

'It could be his bank pin number for all we know,' replied Henry unhelpfully as he started to throw around the numbers in his head.

'I'm sure we can crack this. I think his hand was near the top of...' Nick's voice tailed off as he heard the lift make a pinging sound. The door was about to open! 'Quick, get behind me, Henry, and don't do anything!' Henry moved aside and let Nick move back down the corridor toward the elevator. The lift door opened, and the security man Nick had passed earlier in the day emerged. The man looked up and was startled at the sight that met him. Before he could speak Nick stretched his arms out in front of him. 'Thank goodness you're here. I was just saying to my colleague that...'

But the security man had quickly regained his composure and had now placed his right hand on the baton hanging at his side.

'Move against the wall please, Sir, until I check your ID.' He looked past Nick to where Henry was staring at the pad. 'Sir,' he added in a loud commanding voice, 'please don't move.'

Henry's face remained fixed on the pad. 'Sir!' said the man in an even louder voice 'Please...'

'Just one moment,' replied Henry as he moved his hand up to the pad. The security man moved swiftly down the corridor, past Nick toward Henry, who was now pressing the pad. Nick held his breath as the man started to pull the baton from its holster.

Henry looked around, as the door made a sudden hissing noise as it opened. 'I'm sorry, my good man,' said Henry. 'Didn't want to break my concentration. Never very good at remembering numbers.'

The security man stopped in his tracks and placed the baton back in its holster. 'Could I see your ID please?' he asked Henry, determined to check out the two strangers. Henry held up the tag toward him and smiled.

Nick regained his composure, still amazed at Henry having opened the door. He cleared his throat and ran his hand through his hair. 'Thank you, Leslie. I was just about to tell the officer here that I had hoped Canon Howe had informed him of my intention to return, and that I would be here until probably after six o'clock.' He looked at the security man. 'You did get the message?'

The security man looked at Nick and then at his tag. 'As a matter of fact I didn't.' He looked back at Henry. His body language told Nick that the situation was now under control. One way or another, they had convinced him that they were legitimate visitors to the office. The man looked confused. 'The old man's getting on a bit. Seems to forget things all the time. I'm sure he didn't tell me...'

'Well, we won't tell if you don't,' said Nick, interrupting, deciding that the quicker the encounter ended, the better. He casually walked past into the dark room. 'Come on, Leslie, we have some work to do.' Henry smiled at the guard and followed Nick into the room, closing the door behind them. The security man thought for a moment, then walked slowly back to the elevator. He would check on them at six o'clock.

Inside the dark room, Henry and Nick pressed themselves up against the wall, their breathing noticeably heavier. Eventually Nick spoke. 'Find the light. We don't have much time.' They both lifted their arms and trailed them along the wall, searching for the switch. Henry found it and the lights came on brightly.

'How the hell did you do that?' asked Nick, shaking his head.

Henry smiled nervously. 'It was easy, actually, once I thought about it.' He looked at Nick teasingly.

'Well? Tell me! What was the third digit?'

'One,' said Henry. He waited to see if Nick would get it. He didn't.

'Two, five, one, two. There's still no pattern to that. Come on, tell me. What does it mean?'

'What's a priest's favourite birthday?' answered Henry, enjoying the feeling of superiority as long as he could.

Nick looked at him, still none the wiser. 'A priest's favourite birthday? Henry, we don't have time for riddles. Just tell...' The penny dropped. 'Christmas! Henry, you're brilliant.'

'I know. Just don't tell everyone, will you?' Henry answered, the sweat now disappearing from his face as the air conditioning took its affect. 'At least it's nice and cool in here,' he added as he looked around. 'Now, what exactly are we looking for?'

The light on Benjamin's console flashed red. 'Yes?', he asked speaking softly, his eyes still trained on the screen ahead, his brain digesting every movement in the share prices of the world's leading companies as they continued to scroll across the screen in bright red and green letters and numbers.

'Stephenson is in the office again, and he has the librarian with him,' the voice stated, the tone clearly implying an unexpected event.

Benjamin thought for a moment. It was indeed a surprise, but immediately his mind was contemplating permutations for possible outcomes. His target was proving a surprising adversary after all, but with every unexpected movement came opportunity. It had proved his success in the past. Control the game, and always prosper from the unexpected.

He spoke calmly. 'I understand. Keep him in your sights. Make no move and report back to me when he has left the building.' The voice confirmed the command and Benjamin tapped the desktop. The scrolling figures returned, but Benjamin's thoughts were drifting. He was more sure than ever that Nick was the key to finding the scroll he had long been searching for. Nick Stephenson was winning Benjamin's respect.

Chapter 25

In Tel Aviv, Moshe Rosenfeld nervously fingered the red, wax-sealed envelope. It was only the second one he had ever received. The first had told him of his imminent elevation to leader of his party, his country and his beloved people. The excitement with which he had reacted had been multiplied by the anticipation the glossed red envelope had created. The fact that a hand-written, personally delivered letter from Benjamin, the seal ensuring absolute secrecy from prying eyes, had delivered such news made it all the more precious.

This second letter, coming as it did less than twenty-four hours after his conversation with Benjamin, filled him with fear. The fact that Benjamin had forsaken normal sources of communication – Internet, telephone and even his favoured giant screen, which allowed him to look into the eyes of his conspirators, told Moshe everything he needed to know about the importance of this communication. There would be no chance of interception.

He wanted to put the envelope down, stick it in his drawer for a few hours, to gather his thoughts, but the emissary standing directly in front of him impassively was under instructions to watch him open the letter. As before, Moshe would return the envelope, with the broken seal and the letter, signed on each page, replaced inside, to the emissary, who would in turn hand-deliver it back to Benjamin.

The Prime Minister smiled nervously at the man, dressed all in black, and took a deep breath. He broke the seal and tore open the envelope. The golden crest of the Truth Foundation stood proudly at the top of each of the three pages. Moshe read the letter carefully, his eyes tracing back over several of the sentences to make sure he had taken in every detail, every nuance of the plan. He knew that everything Benjamin did, or asked, was for a reason. Nothing would be superfluous, unimportant, no matter how trivial it might appear. When he had finished, he would write down a note, an aide-memoire, but for these few moments as he read the words, the world seemed to stop spinning.

When he had finished, his face was ashen, his hands scarcely able to hold onto the three sheets of crisp white paper. He looked at the emissary. He was standing absolutely still, as he had done the whole time, his eyes fixed on the carpet below his feet. Moshe signed each page, trying desperately to stop his hand shaking as he did so. He just wanted the letter and the emissary out of his room. He needed his own space, time to think.

When he had gone, Moshe sat down at his desk and opened the top drawer. He pulled out a bundle of blank sheets of paper and began to scribble notes. He felt his eyes well up, but he fought back the tears. There would be no chance of him writing the instructions verbatim. The notes would be in his own handwriting. There would be no trace of Benjamin.

'So, what exactly are we looking for?' Henry asked, as they looked at the large wooden trunks in front of them, the heavy straps around their middle held tightly where each end entered a metal cylinder on top of each box. There was no obvious way of releasing the straps. There were no joints or buckles on the surface, and no buttons or markers, other than a series of shallow dimples, set out in three rows of four, which ran across the cylinder, each one painted in a different colour. Henry placed the books on one of the desks, as the two men looked at the trunks curiously.

'I'm not sure to be perfectly honest, Henry,' answered Nick. 'I'm out of my depth here, and I'm hoping something will click with you. This is all mumbo-jumbo to me, but something's not right with all of this, and I'm hoping you might spot what it is.'

Henry looked at him, his eyebrows raised in a look of bewilderment rather than disbelief. 'You have no idea what we are looking for?' he said, though it was really a statement of fact rather than a question.

'Correct,' answered Nick, deciding that giving Henry a completely open canvas, and the opportunity to create his own decisions might be the best approach and, in the circumstances, the only approach to thinking through the next move. Time, however, was not something they had in great supply, especially not after the encounter with the security guard.

Henry gazed at the dimples. There was something vaguely familiar about the pattern of colours. He wanted to think it through before he spoke, but Nick could see that he was trying to make sense of them. 'Have you seen these before?' asked Nick, hopefully. Henry decided to give up on them for the moment. He wasn't going to be able to think about them with Nick breathing down his neck. He would let his mind think it over.

'No, although there is something familiar about them,' he proffered, shrugging his shoulders and trying to sound as if it was an insignificant fact. 'Is this all there is to look at?' he added.

Nick had decided that there was unlikely to be any interest in the small number of parchment and scroll extracts which were neatly set out on the large table in the centre of the room. What he was after was more likely hidden in the trunks, or perhaps in the desks of the two workers, or the third, larger desk that he took to be Canon Howe's. He walked over to the larger desk and tried to pull open the top drawer of the bank of three. Not to his surprise, it was locked. He looked at the table and caught site of the long metal ruler. He picked it up and, returning to the desk, pushed it between the underside of the desktop and the first drawer. He picked up a stapler that was sitting on top of the desk and hit it hard against the end of the ruler. After four or five blows, each one harder than the last, the drawer started to split from the barrel of the lock. With one more, hefty blow, the drawer burst open. He placed the ruler and stapler on top of the desk and smiled at Henry who was standing rooted to the spot, past caring that they were now well and truly of the criminal fraternity.

'Guess finding the key was out of the question then,' said Henry, resigned to his eventual fate.

Nick ignored the comment and quickly pulled out the papers from the drawer. He split the pile in two, handing one lot to Henry. 'Here, have a look through these.'

'What am I looking for?' asked Henry again.

'Anything incriminating ... or give us evidence about this scroll.' He looked up at Henry who was simply staring down at the pile in front of him. 'I don't know, Henry,' he added. 'Something tells me that the Canon may have information here that might help, even if he doesn't realise it himself.' He touched Henry on the arm, as if trying to gain his confidence. 'You're more likely to understand this stuff than I am. Please, have a look.'

Henry sighed. He wished he could have been in here under different circumstances. He glanced around the room. He noticed the pieces of parchment spread out on the table, the sheets around the walls that had photocopies of other extracts with notes pinned along side. This was a potential treasure trove for someone with an interest in the subject, yet here he was, now a common criminal rifling through papers of a highly respected academic to find ... what, he didn't know. He looked at Nick. 'You must have some idea of what you're looking for?'

Nick smiled. 'I wish I did. All I know is that this is about the only place I can think of that might hold a key. I'm sure Canon Howe knows more than he's letting on to. He told me the Ecole has been negotiating sales with dealers. If there is someone out there controlling these Scrolls, it seems unlikely that the Canon doesn't know who it is.' He started looking through the papers. Henry did the same.

After a few minutes of flicking through invoices and press cuttings from the last few days, Henry stopped. 'This is interesting,' he commented slowly.

'What is?' asked Nick, looking up expectantly.

'Well, it's a list of names.' He showed the typed sheet to Nick.

'Is it?' asked Nick, not recognising any of them.

'Yes, and they are all Jewish as far as I can see.' He shook them again in front of Nick. 'Look again.'

Nick cast his eyes down the list. There was no heading on the sheet and no other information, just a list of forty or so names. Most of them certainly sounded like Jewish names to Nick, but that could just be coincidence. He turned to Henry. 'How do you know they're all Jewish?'

'I can't be definite, but there are quite a few here I recognise.'

Nick was impressed. 'How come?' he asked.

'Because I'm Jewish,' replied Henry, looking straight into Nick's eyes.

Nick felt rather stupid. The thought hadn't occurred to him. Then again, Henry hadn't mentioned it.

'These names at the top are all leading rabbis in England. My father has a directory at home with various contact names. The others below are less familiar. Some are media people, and there are one or two actors. Actually, now that I look at it again, I have heard of most of them.' The two looked at one another.

'What do you think it means?' asked Nick. 'Would this list ... sorry, *does* this list mean anything to a Jew as opposed to the general public?' He looked at the names again. 'I've only heard of one or two, and they're the ones on TV or in films.'

Henry shook his head slowly. 'I don't know. But I suppose what I do find strange is why Canon Howe would have such a list.'

They decided to continue their search. Nick opened the second and third drawers and distributed the contents between them. They gathered together the various press cuttings and Nick started sifting through them. Most were recent, with news of the Master Scroll from publications spread around the world. A small plastic envelope was almost hidden away in among the cuttings. Nick opened it. Inside were a number of extracts from what appeared to be more like newsletters than quality newspapers. Nick cast his eyes quickly through them and then suddenly looked up at Henry. He had spotted the thread. They all made reference to the Shomrei Emet.

He stopped Henry reading his bundle. 'Look at this,' he said slowly. 'Why would he have a load of cuttings on them?' He pointed to the name.

Henry looked up at Nick, a look of equal concern etched on his face. 'I don't know, but I don't like it.'

The search had taken an unexpected turn. They gathered their thoughts as Nick continued flicking through the envelope.

'Well,' said Henry, finally. 'I suppose he could simply

be tracking their movements. Let's remember it is prominent Catholics that have been attacked by these terrorists. He could simply be afraid or concerned.' It sounded plausible.

Nick continued looking through the various clippings. He looked at the next cutting. He froze and felt a chill go down his spine. It was *The Times* report on Cardinal Cornelli's death. At the bottom of the page, written by hand with a black felt-tip pen, was one word.

'*Stephenson.*'

Nick took in a long breath and felt his throat tighten. He thought back to his first meeting with Canon Howe at his office. He had referred to Cardinal Cornelli indirectly. Here was proof, however, that the Canon knew about Nick's direct involvement. Yet he had clearly chosen not to turn him into the authorities or confront him directly. *Why not?* he thought to himself. He briefly considered showing the extract to Henry, but decided against it.

He was about to put it in his pocket when Henry tapped him on the shoulder. 'You'd better take a look at this.'

Nick took the piece of paper from Henry's hand and sat down on the chair behind the desk. It was a fax. There was no identifying company, and no return telephone or fax number. Even the normal receipt identification giving a time of receipt at the top of the page was missing. Nevertheless, they both knew it was a fax. Nick started to read it:

Project Messiah commenced. Subject yet to yield crop but time limited. Must move to force conclusion immediately. SE ready and protection to doves in place. May God be with us all. B.

Nick looked at Henry. 'Now, we could read an awful lot into this. It could be ... well old for a start. It was in among these other cuttings, and they're all from the last few days. I think this is recent.' He shrugged his shoulders slightly. 'It could of course simply be another item the good Canon has managed to "acquire" through whatever sources he has.'

Nick thought about it. Yes, that was plausible. Why not? 'OK. Let's assume for the moment that you're right.' He looked closely at Henry. 'What does it mean?'

They both thought about it. Nick looked at his watch ... 5.58. He remembered the guard. The last thing they needed was to be caught red-handed. He would deal with the consequences of his action tomorrow when the Canon found the damage. He needed time to think about the fax, and the other bits of information they had gathered.

He put the fax in his pocket. 'Come on, Henry. We've chanced our arm long enough here. Let's get out while we can. This can wait.'

Henry was about to protest, his mind busily contemplating the meaning of the coded message, and then remembered their predicament. He nodded and they both headed for the door to make their escape.

Chapter 26

Benjamin tapped the desk, and the face of the man on the screen, barely visible by the night light, flickered into view. 'Stephenson has returned to his apartment. He has no documents with him.'

'What about the librarian?'

'Likewise. They came out empty-handed. The security man let them pass, as agreed. He insisted on a routine search, and they took only the books they had brought in.'

Benjamin considered the report. He had to assume the two 'burglars' had found something that would lead them in the right direction and hopefully not send them off on a wild goose chase. He was fast running out of time, and he was hoping that Nick's apparent ingenuity would speed things up for him. If not, then he would be taking the biggest gamble of his life.

'OK. Stay with him. I don't want him out of your sight.'

'What about the librarian?' asked the voice.

'Leave him. Stephenson won't let him do anything on his own.' He reached down and tapped the desk several times. The picture disappeared only to be replaced with another one showing an empty study. After a few moments a plump, balding face appeared on the screen, the man fiddling frantically with his glasses.

'Ah, Dr Weisman. Good of you to join me. I'm moving Project Messiah forward. I think we may be ready earlier. How much time do we need?'

On the other end of the link Weisman took a deep

breath. He had made the arrangements as precise and as robust as he could, given the last few days. To contemplate bringing it forward at this late stage was a risk. He did not feel he could guarantee that all his contacts would have had time to implement his instructions. Then again, he was not about to tell Benjamin that it could not be done. 'Well, Benjamin, I think it could be achievable in say ... thirty-six hours, but I...'

'Good. Let's say 6 p.m. tomorrow evening. I will inform the network. We must ensure that everyone is ready to move at that time.'

'I ... will do my best, but there are so many...'

Benjamin interrupted. 'Your best will suffice, because your best will ensure that we do not fail. Am I not correct, Doctor?' The tone was threatening, but restrained.

'Yes ... yes. Of course. It will be done.'

Weisman's image was summarily cut off.

Benjamin's calm exterior did not betray his sense of frustration and anxiety at his reliance on others. He had made them what they were, and now it was time for them to pay him back. But he had to use time like a weapon. *Do not give them time to think, time to ponder the enormity of what is about to be revealed.*

Nick hardly slept, his mind bouncing around all the facts and snippets of seemingly interconnected yet random information that now seemed to clutter his brain. He kept coming back to one conclusion. The scroll he had was not genuine, but it was something that others wanted and was of some significance. Whether it *was* the so-called Master Scroll, he couldn't decide. It seemed too incredible, but then again so had the last few days. He had finally worked his way back to the known starting point of the scroll, and something was amiss. Whether it was Robert's recollection of how he came by it, or something else, he wasn't sure. As he lay wide awake in his bed, he decided on his next move. He would visit Robert as soon as the sun came up.

Chapter 27

Nick ran up the stairs to level three of the hospital. He stopped briefly and looked back down to the bottom of the stairwell. There was no sign of anyone following, but he was still convinced they were there, somewhere. He pushed open the ward door and stepped into the corridor. He looked in both directions before heading right towards the private room to which he had insisted Robert was moved. As he reached the room, the first face he saw was Rachel's.

'Hey, handsome,' she said, her face beaming at the sight of Nick smiling back at her. 'How are you today?'

Nick forced a smile back, although he realised in the same instant he was glad to see her. 'Hi, gorgeous. Never mind me. Is Robert OK?' he asked, rubbing his hands down her arms.

Her smile faded slightly. 'He's fine. I've been worried about you. I thought you might have called.'

Nick smiled back. 'Too busy taking in the sights!' The last thing he wanted was Rachel worrying any more than she had already over the past few days.

She stared at him, searching for a telltale look. He stared back. 'I'm fine! It's sorted ... almost.' He laughed.

'I hope you're telling the truth,' replied Rachel. She instinctively teased him. 'Anything come of the secret spy trip to the mysterious Father's lair?' she asked, her nervousness weakly hidden behind the humour.

'Nah. I decided he couldn't help us any more than we could help him,' he lied, trying to sound as though he had moved on with his life. 'Besides, if the thing had been that important to him, I'm sure he would never have let me leave.'

Rachel looked at him, surprised. 'You mean us?' she stated, looking concerned again. The thought hadn't really occurred to either of them until that moment. Nick decided it was best to change the subject. He walked past her side.

'Come on, I want to see Robert' said Nick, taking her hand and leading her into the ward.

Robert was sitting up in bed, at least half the tubes and pads and the banks of monitoring equipment now gone.

'Nick! How are you? We've been worried' said Robert, looking pale, but, Nick felt, also looking as if a great weight had been taken off his shoulders.

Nick darted a look at Rachel who shrugged her shoulders and gave him a guilty look.

'I'm fine, Robert. I don't know why you were worried about me. It seems Mr Forster has found another tenant for his building. He's pushing me like mad to get on with the site. I'll be sorting out the steelwork today.'

Rachel squeezed Nick's hand. 'That's wonderful. So it *is* all sorted then.' She glanced at Robert, who was looking relieved rather than happy. He hadn't forgotten the lies and deceit he had been forced to enter into over the last week, and at the end of it all he had Nick to thank for sorting things out. He knew he should have trusted him in the first place.

Nick sat on the edge of the bed. He put his hand up as if to stop his partner from expressing any thanks.

'Well, it's not quite over yet,' he added, realising that he might have to coax the information out of Robert without sending him into a relapse.

Rachel's smile wilted immediately. 'What does that mean?' she asked.

Nick took a deep breath, his eyes falling on both of them alternatively. 'Look. We know that Robert here planted the ... scroll in the embankment, and we all know it was a fake. So there's no question of us having to call in the Council or delay the work any further, particularly now that Forster's got his pre-let and Robert's money is safe.'

'Sounds like it's over to me', said Rachel, giving Nick a stern look, and almost pleading for Nick to stop his conversation right there.

Nick, however, continued. 'The only problem is that what I have is a copy, isn't it, Robert?' He looked at his partner, who was nodding his head.

'Yes. It's a copy of the one my father gave me for my tenth birthday. I told you that.'

'No, you didn't, Robert. You may have thought you did, but we didn't get to finish our conversation. Where is the original ... the one your father gave you?'

Robert sank back slightly on the bed. He realised he had been economical with the truth, but not deliberately. Anyway, he couldn't see why this fact made things any different. 'Is this relevant, Nick?' he asked.

Nick fixed his eyes on his partner. 'Yes, Robert,' he answered briefly, as if to emphasise the point.

Robert let out a long sigh. 'It's with an old friend in Kent, John Brown.' He glanced at Rachel who had a look of disbelief on her face. 'He has a reputation for good forgeries, apparently,' he added with a guilty look.

Rachel stared at Nick. She didn't know what to say – or at least where to start. Nick leaned forward toward Robert. 'Do you remember your father telling you anything about the scroll when he gave it to you? Anything at all?'

Robert shook his head slowly. 'I was only ten. It's a long time ago, Nick. I remember I was playing in my room – tidying up my cupboard, if I remember rightly, when he came in and said he had a special surprise for me, something that none of my chums would ever have.'

Robert began to gaze into the distance, as though trying to picture the event that had taken place over fifty years before. 'I just remember how excited I was.' He gave a little laugh. 'My father told me he had discovered it in a secret tomb, which hadn't been seen for a thousand years before he came across it. Said it told the story of a great warrior from the Middle East who ruled over half the world, long before the Romans. I was hooked!' He looked back to Nick. 'Later, of course when I came across it one day in my late teens, he told me the truth ... that he had bought it from a street trader in the Middle East when he was stationed there on some special assignment during the war. A town called...'

'Kallia,' interrupted Nick.

Robert looked at him in amazement. 'How did you know that?'

Nick shook his head. 'It's not important at the moment. Is there anything else you can tell me about it, anything at all?'

Robert shrugged his shoulders. 'Not that I can think of. I took it out of the bag and looked for a long time at the little eagle on the surface. It was so simple but so beautiful. It made it seem as though the scroll must be important.' He smiled. 'But it looks just like an old piece of brown leather.' He looked at Rachel and laughed. 'Bit like an old worn chamois, actually. If it wasn't tied up it would probably have been used by your mother!' Rachel laughed back.

'Tied up?' Nick interrupted again.

Robert looked back at him. 'Yes. With a sort of strap, a leather one, but thicker than the scroll itself. It has a little emblem thingy on it.'

'What does the ... *thingy* look like?' asked Nick.

'God, Nick, I can't remember. It's all faded anyway. I think it's a ... star or something. Yes, a sort of white faded star'.

'Could it be like a triangle on top of a circle?' Nick looked around the room.

'What are you looking for?' asked Rachel, desperate to know what was going on.

'A pen and some paper, quick!'

Rachel opened the small drawer in the cabinet next to Robert's bed. They were in luck. 'Here,' she said, thrusting the pen and a rather scruffy piece of paper into Nick's hands.

Nick drew the emblem, which by now he had engraved on his mind.

Robert looked at it for a few seconds. 'Well ... yes, I suppose that could be it.'

'I knew it!' exclaimed Nick, throwing the pen down onto the bed.

'Will you tell me what is going on please?' asked Rachel.

'It's the Qumran Brotherhood. Their sign. It's exactly what I thought', said Nick, a look of triumph on his face. 'I have a counterfeit. It's a copy of the real thing. What your father was given really was ... is ... one of the Dead Sea Scrolls.'

Nick realised what he had said, and glanced back out of the room. He had forgotten for a moment Cardinal Cornelli, Henry and the men in black. Robert and Rachel stared at him in silence, hardly able to comprehend what he had just said.

He put his hands on Rachel's arms. 'I have to get to the scroll ... the real one ... before it's too late.' He turned and looked at Robert. 'How do I get to ... what's his name?'

'Brown,' replied Robert. 'John Brown. He's in Kent. Here, I will write down the directions. Give me the pen.'

'I'm coming with you!,' said Rachel, as firmly as she could.

Nick let go of her arms. 'It's too...'

'I'm not leaving you this time!' she said, glaring at him. 'You might need some help, and anyway Dad was just saying before you arrived that I should have a break in the country.' She smiled triumphantly. As far as she was concerned the argument was over.

The monitors leaped to attention at Benjamin's touch. Arial's face looked tense and nervous, magnified by the size of the central screen that Benjamin was staring into across his desk.

'Do not let him out of your sight. Your role is almost complete.' Benjamin's voice sounded almost hypnotic to the young accomplice.

'I will follow him wherever he goes, Benjamin. He will not escape my gaze.'

'I am trusting you with the most important task I have ever given,' added Benjamin, his speech slow and deliberate. 'Our people depend on you.'

Arial straightened his tall, athletic frame until it was taut. He could feel his heart beating, hard and fast. He hoped it did not show.

'I will not fail, master. God is with me'.

Chapter 28

As they left the ward, Nick glanced down the corridor and caught sight of two men, both dressed entirely in black, standing chatting to each other just beyond the elevator doors about twenty yards away. He stopped and took hold of Rachel's arm, then slowly stepped back into the ward. He was convinced they hadn't seen him.

Rachel stared at Nick. 'What is it? Is there someone there?'

'Let's just say I'd rather they didn't see us leaving.'

He stuck his head back out into the corridor. They were still there, engaged in what looked like a quiet but intense conversation. He looked down the other way. A blank wall. Only four doors, two on either side of the corridor, one of which seemed to be another private room. Two others looked like cupboards. The fourth, the one almost directly opposite, had a 'store' sign pinned to one of the two double doors.

'Stay here. I'll be straight back.'

Before Rachel could protest, Nick quickly crossed the corridor, keeping his eyes fixed on the two men as he did so. He pushed one of the doors open and stepped inside, gently closing it behind him. He looked around the room. Although it was fairly large, most of the shelves seemed to be completely bare. The odd packet of dressings together with some plastic pipes, whose use Nick didn't want to even imagine, lay scattered on some tables under the frosted window at the far end of the room.

He moved down toward them and stopped as he reached

halfway. A break in the shelving on his left revealed three rows of pegs on the wall behind. He was in luck. Five white doctor's jackets hung limply on the middle row. He quickly grabbed two of them and briefly examined their lengths, putting on the larger one. On a small table beside the wall were a number of Perspex spectacles. He picked two pairs up and stuck one of them into the spare jacket before placing the other on his face.

As he returned to the door he could hear voices outside. He listened for a few moments, and then heard them become quieter, deciding that they had moved away, back along the corridor. Slowly he pulled open one of the doors and leaned out into the corridor. He caught sight of Rachel, her gaze fixed onto the door, as he imagined it had been for the whole time he was in the room. For a brief second her face looked puzzled, before she realised it was him.

Nick looked down the corridor. The men were still there, but had moved apart. One was now sitting in a small waiting area off to the right and opposite the elevators. The other had moved further down the corridor and was reading something on a noticeboard pinned to the wall.

Nick calmly walked out, and crossed the corridor back into the ward.

'Here. Put this on,' he said, handing Rachel the spare coat. 'And these,' he added, tapping the coat's pocket.

Rachel took the glasses out and looked at them. 'A fashion statement these are not!' she remarked.

'Let's just hope they do the trick. Follow me, and try to look ... natural.' He tugged at the jacket and then ran his fingers through his hair. Rachel shook her head. 'I'll try!'

They emerged out of the room and headed down the corridor toward the elevator. Five yards, then ten.

They were halfway toward their goal when the man at the noticeboard turned around and started walking toward them. Nick looked toward Rachel. She recognised the man and was now staring straight at him, her mouth open. 'Don't say a word!' said Nick, touching her arm. 'Look at me. Just keep walking.'

The man strolled slowly along the corridor. He glanced toward them, but clearly hadn't recognised either of them. Nick put his head down and kept looking toward Rachel, keeping sight of the elevator and the man in the corner of his eye. At last they reached the elevator. They stopped and Nick pressed the 'down' button.

Rachel's head was bent over, staring straight ahead at the grey metal door. Her heart was thumping. The man had now reached them. He walked passed them and Nick could sense him moving over toward his colleague who was still sitting oppose the elevator door.

For what seemed like an eternity the two of them waited on the elevator to appear.

'You OK?' whispered Nick, glancing toward Rachel. She nodded her head quickly but didn't answer. Nick glanced up at the illuminated panel above the elevator door. Four ... five ... six. They were on the ninth floor. The elevator was almost there. There was a rustling behind them. Nick could feel Rachel tense. He hesitantly turned his head slightly and saw a nurse standing with a pile of files, directly behind Rachel.

'Morning, Doctor,' the nurse remarked, smiling at Nick. He smiled back as best he could, but said nothing.

The nurse's expression changed. She moved slightly closer, as if trying to get a better look at Nick.

Tring. The elevator announced its arrival, Rachel reacting with a quiet gasp. Nick took her arm and, as soon as the door opened, led her straight in and stood at the back, head pointing at the floor. The nurse followed them in, her gaze now fixed hard on Nick's face, her suspicions aroused.

Nick leaned over and pressed the ground-floor button hard, several times. The nurse was still staring at him.

'Do I know you, Doctor?' she asked, her curiosity now getting the better of her.

'Oh I don't think so', answered Nick. 'Wrong ward.' He smiled. Instinctively, he glanced out of the door to check whether the conversation had been overheard. It had. The two men were now staring into the open elevator, their eyes fixed on Nick.

Come on, come on, Nick whispered desperately to himself. He reached up with his hand and ran his fingers through his hair, just as the door started to close. The two men reacted immediately, leaping out of their seats at the same time and diving toward the elevator door. Rachel, seeing their reaction, threw out her arm and hit the 'door closed' button. She didn't need to. The door closed in what seemed like slow motion, but was quick enough to foil the flaying arms of the two men.

The nurse turned round and caught sight of them just as the lift door closed, dropped the files and put her hands to her face.

Nick let out a sigh of relief and threw off his glasses. Rachel followed suit, removing her coat and throwing it on top of Nick's on the elevator floor.

Nick looked at the nurse who had now moved back to the door itself and was looking somewhat scared.

'Don't worry, we'll be out of here in a minute. Nobody's going to hurt you.' He tried to give her some sort of comfort. 'Could you return these to your storeroom, please'? He handed her the spectacles. 'They weren't a very good fit anyway.' He smiled at her. She forced a nervous smile back.

Rachel stood in front of him. 'Now what?' She had regained some of her composure.

'Let's just hope this lift is quicker than they are! When we get out...'

'Yes?' said Rachel, waiting for the plan. 'Come on. How about ... run?'

'No!' said Nick finally. 'That's exactly what they will expect. We would just give ourselves away.' He looked at the nurse. 'Remind me what's on the ground floor'.

The nurse stared back at Nick, still shocked by what had happened.

'Eh,' she stumbled 'Well ... nothing really. There are the entrance doors ... and a seating area. Oh, and the WRVS canteen, on the right, opposite the door leading to the underground car park.'

Nick thought about it. He looked at the lift's control panel. 'OK. Look. You won't get hurt, I promise. You have to trust me. Those two men you saw are after *me*, OK? When the lift stops on the ground floor, I want you to stay here and go down to the basement. When you get there, stay in the elevator and press ground immediately. Will you do this for me?'

The nurse looked at Nick then at Rachel. She recognised Rachel from the ward. 'Your father?'

Rachel gave her a nervous smile. 'Yes. Robert Stanhope. He's here because of those men. You have to believe us. We need your help'.

The nurse straightened up and relaxed. 'OK, but I'm calling the police as soon as I get out of here.'

'No!' said Nick quickly. 'Please, don't do that! It will put all of us at greater risk, especially Robert. I'm on my way to sort this out. I promise we'll be back later ... with the police if we have to.'

The elevator tringed again, announcing its arrival at the ground floor. Nick and Rachel remained motionless, staring at the nurse. They needed her help and there was no more to say. Their eyes pleaded. Finally she nodded and stepped aside as the door opened. She pressed the basement button. Nick grabbed Rachel's hand. 'Thanks,' said Rachel as the two of them burst through the door and out into the hospital foyer. They turned right. Sure

266

enough, two elderly ladies from the WRVS were standing behind a long counter holding impossibly large teapots and smiling at all passers-by.

Nick and Rachel ran to the end of the counter and lifted up the hinged section that gave access to the area behind. They immediately jumped through the gap and crouched down behind the counter. The two elderly women stared down at them in disbelief, rather than fear. Rachel looked up and smiled. 'Won't be a minute!'

One of the women was about to speak when there was a sudden commotion in the foyer. She looked around. The two men had emerged from the stairwell, and one was banging on the door of the elevator. The other, panting, was scanning the foyer. He looked toward the two women, who simply stared back in amazement.

The first man looked up at the elevator dial. The down arrow was flashing. He grabbed his colleague's arm and shouted something that neither woman understood.

They ran across to the stairwell leading to the basement and leaped down the first set of stairs.

As their steps echoed around the almost empty foyer, Nick and Rachel leaped to their feet.

'Thanks,' said Rachel to the two stunned women, as they emerged back into the foyer and ran, holding hands, out of the front door and into the brightness.

The lift door opened onto the underground car park, eerily silent. The nurse, her heart thumping, pushed her finger onto the ground-floor button and held it there, staring at it as if willing it to make the door close. She heard the sound of pounding footsteps. She pressed harder, now pushing her finger with her other hand, desperately wanting to see the door close. It started to move. The footsteps were getting louder, heavier. As the door reached halfway she heard a shout. She could not hear what was being said, but then a hand abruptly halted the door's progress. It started to open. She looked at the tall, dark figure, breathing heavily, slightly stooped, trying to recover from the exertion.

'Where are they?', asked the man, now joined by his partner. The nurse looked at them, terrified.

'They jumped out and headed over there!' she exclaimed, pointing her finger randomly into the car park.

The two men looked around. There was no sign of anyone. The first man looked back at the nurse.

'Please, that's all I know.' She pointed at the floor. 'Look, they've taken off the coats.'

The man looked at the floor. Suddenly, the sound of a car engine turning over could be heard some distance away, the exact location impossible to gauge in the echoey space.

The second man tugged at the first's arm, and they both turned and ran off in the direction of the sound.

The nurse pressed the button again and held her breath. Whoever had just got into their car was about to have a bad experience, she thought.

Chapter 29

The small, red light on Benjamin's desk gently flashed to indicate he had an urgent call waiting. The number 3 visible below the light told him it was from the field agents assigned to Nick Stephenson. He sighed. This could only mean a problem had once again affected his progress.

He spoke toward the screen on the wall. 'Ambassador, I am sorry to interrupt. I have an issue that I really must deal with immediately. Rest assured we will talk again soon. We are very close now, and your ... support will not be forgotten.'

On the screen a small, balding bespectacled man slowly nodded his head, his eyes facing downwards as though in supplication. 'You have my word, Benjamin, as always.'

Benjamin tapped the glass desk and the image disappeared immediately. He tapped it again, and the face of a much larger man, his face covered in sweat, his eyes darting from side to side appeared on the screen. Benjamin's fears of another problem were realised.

'Well? Have you lost him?' he asked as he leaned back in the chair.

Arial spoke. 'He ... evaded us, Benjamin. Yes, we have lost him. He was clearly trying to escape from us. He knew we were there.' The man gave a loud exhale as his shoulders sagged.

There was silence for a few moments as Benjamin stared at the man. Why was this taking so long to sort? He knew he had to remain patient, but events were now in progress that he could not stop. He could control things only for so long. If his hare was running now, though, perhaps the end game was about to be played out.

'Then it is as well that we have a tracer on his car,' answered Benjamin, satisfied that Arial had sweated long enough. Without saying another word he tapped the desk and the man disappeared. He pushed the seat back slightly from the desk and leaned down to his right-hand side.

Below the desk sat a heavy metal box, a keypad protruding from the front of one of two drawers. He punched a six-number code into the pad. Two green flashing lights appeared. He repeated the sequence, this time adding a seventh number. The lights flashed again, this time faster, and after a few seconds the drawer slid silently open. He carefully lifted out a small black book, a barely visible swastika engraved on the bottom left-hand corner. 'He placed it on the desk. He reached back into the drawer and pulled out a black velvet pouch, twelve inches long, and placed it beside the book. He looked at both for a brief moment and took a deep breath. In over 40 years he had only ever held these items around a dozen times. They were the centre of his world, the reason he was the man he had become, and yet there was a fear that he could not totally eliminate from his mind about the power they would unleash on the world. It was the only fear Benjamin had known since the loss of his father.

He leaned forward and pressed the buzzer on the speaker perched at the edge of the desk. A woman's voice was heard immediately. 'Yes, Mr Goldstein?'

'I need the helicopter. Five minutes. And get Weisman here. He's coming with me this time.' He let go of the buzzer.

Outside the Prime Minister's room, the two guards, personally assigned to him for protection by Benjamin and dressed from head to toe in black, stood quiet but alert either side of the large wooden door.

Moshe Rosenfeld stared once again at the scribbled notes on the paper in front of him, as he had done a hundred times in the last two days. The knot in his stomach did not ease.

Twenty-four hours notice ... Close border crossing ... Declare state of emergency ... Retrieve all Mosad agents ex-borders ... holding statement to Ambassadors ... seal prisons...execute 'foreign nationals' ...

He looked up, hoping that when he looked back the note would have gone. It hadn't. He read on...

House arrest internal dissidents ... faxed list to follow ... first attack will be from within. Do not crush.

Moshe shook his head. He had underlined the last three words. He took a handkerchief out of his pocket and wiped it across his brow. He knew he followed a long line of leaders, brave men, who had shown they were unafraid to confront their enemies and crush them with overwhelming strength and firepower, the bedrock on which the nation had survived. They represented the front line of Western civilisation, the free world, exposed to the huge but crude threat of the extremist Arab world, but even he was now cowering at the expected response that Benjamin had laid out in his letter.

He read on again, the palms of his hands now sweating onto the white cotton fabric...

... Cabinet to war room within 6 hours ... expect 500,000 casualties within 36 hours ... containment only as long as possible...

271

He took a deep breath and read the final line four times...

... nuclear response on B's command...

In all the years that he had been in contact with Benjamin, he now realised, there had never been any meaningful discussion on the real intent behind his sponsor's motives. Of course he had known that one day there would be a price to pay, but as the years had gone on Moshe convinced himself that Benjamin had merely spotted that he, Moshe Rosenfeld was the right man for the job, and the occasional military or hydroelectric contract being steered toward one of Benjamin's conglomerates was reward enough, he had rationalised, to keep him happy. All this stuff about a Truth Scroll was merely fantasy on Benjamin's part, a wishful, romantic nonsense they had once shared before Moshe had been required to deal with the real world. Benjamin's past, whatever dark secrets it might have held, served only to give him an aimless pursuit to fill the vacuum left by boredom for a man who has everything. Surely nothing would come of it.

Now he realised it was payback time and there was nothing he could do about it.

Whatever the power unleashed by this scroll, Benjamin clearly intended to use it to destroy the enemies of Israel. Moshe Rosenfeld was being asked ... no, told ... to unleash a holocaust.

Chapter 30

The drive from his flat, where Nick picked up the biscuit tin, took just over an hour. Rachel acted as navigator and remarked more than once that if she could only wear a pair of goggles rather than sunglasses it would be more befitting for the Morgan's image. She obviously pictured herself as a heroine from some 1940s war film, her hair blowing wildly as Nick sped along the motorway towards Brighton, with the hood down and the engine roaring.

They approached a forked junction and Rachel confidently pointed toward the road veering to the left. Nick looked at her for reassurance. She was biting her lip. Nick ran his fingers through his hair.

'Are you sure...?' he started to ask but stopped mid-sentence. There was, he thought, an obvious answer – no! He veered to the left.

There was silence for several minutes. Nick's mind was racing. What was he about to find? It had been the most extraordinary week of his life, and he wondered how it was going to end. He looked in his mirror. He couldn't be sure, but he was almost convinced he hadn't been followed. It had occurred to him that whoever it was who shared his interest in the scroll didn't seem likely to have given up and was perhaps just waiting for the chance to get him alone and exposed. He knew he was running a risk bringing Rachel along, but somehow she was giving him strength, and in any case she was as deep in as he was. At least this way he could keep his eye on her. Either way the two red lights he had jumped coming out of London would have put paid to anyone thinking of following them.

'I think it's next on the left after that garage,' Rachel suddenly blurted out just as Nick reached the entrance to the garage forecourt. He hit the brakes, spotting a side road no more than forty yards ahead. He spun the Morgan around the corner, the wheels screeching as the back end of the car fought valiantly to keep pointing in the same direction as the front. Nick didn't look at Rachel.

'Where the hell are we?' he asked, his voice suggesting both frustration and nerves.

'A place called Little Garth,' Rachel replied, staring down intently at her father's scribbled directions. 'The Blacksmiths should be just a few hundred yards down this road on the right.'

Nick looked around. There was open countryside on both sides of the road, flat and seemingly endless fields of green of every shade all around, broken only by the occasional magnificent oak tree towering high over the wayside like nature's equivalent of a motorway sign board.

As he rounded a gentle bend in the road, Nick spotted the sign for 'John Brown's Blacksmith's Shop', nailed to a tree at the side of the road. He allowed himself a wry smile. The name somehow seemed appropriate, was, in fact, he thought, almost a dead give-away.

The 'shop' was more like a run-down barn. There was a gravel parking area in front of it and a small cottage and two redbrick buildings behind. Nick pulled off the road and parked on the gravel forecourt in front of the barn's entrance door.

He turned to Rachel. 'Now listen to me carefully.' Rachel sat back in her seat like a child who was about to be warned about her behaviour. 'Let me do the talking, OK!

We don't know anything about this guy, and for all we know he's as up to his neck in this as we are.'

Rachel's gaze didn't leave his as he spoke, and Nick could see that there was some genuine fear in her expression. He reached out his hand and laid it gently on top of hers.

'And ... be careful!' he added, not really knowing what he meant, but understanding why he said it.

Rachel smiled nervously at him and grasped his hand gently.

'Come on then, let's find out what this is all about,' Nick said, pulling off his sunglasses and placing them carefully on the dashboard. He picked up the digestive tin and gave it an instinctive shake to make sure the contents were still inside.

The helicopter took off from the roof of the Truth Foundation and immediately pointed south. The tracker device bleeped strongly in front of the pilot as it eagerly relayed the Morgan's position.

'Where do you think he's going?' asked Weisman, still out of breath from rushing to the building from the British Museum.

'I have no idea, but I believe we may be reaching the final act of our play, Dr Weisman.' Benjamin smiled at him as if to reassure and calm him down.

'Shouldn't we wait for backup?' Weisman asked, aware of how resourceful and elusive Nick had proven.

'No time, Doctor,' answered Benjamin, clipping his seatbelt in place and pulling on the headphones. He touched his jacket just above the position of his heart. 'We have everything we need here.'

Weisman's eyes lit up. 'You have it with you ... here?'

Benjamin grinned and spoke through the headset to

the pilot. 'Don't get too close, but let me know when he stops. We will have little time to close in.'

'I understand, Mr Goldberg,' replied the pilot.

Chapter 31

The barn looked somewhat derelict, the silence of the countryside adding to the feeling that not only was there no one here, but that no one ever bothered to come here. Nick approached the large garage-style door and knocked it several times. After a few seconds' waiting he tried the large black handle, which made a rusty creaking sound but turned freely, allowing Nick to open it inward, catching a small bell suspended above the door as he did so. The sudden jingling noise from above startled both of them. Rachel uttered a muffled sigh before giving Nick an apologetic smile and a whispered 'Sorry!'

Nick pushed the door in as far as it would go, throwing as much light into the dark interior as he could. He looked around quickly. Ahead of him he could see a wooden counter, behind which, up against the back wall, were hanging various odd-shaped metal hooks and leather harnesses. It was clearly a working smithy, with anvils, tools, metal sheets and a number of small wooden benches spread out randomly all over the stone floor. At the far end could be seen the gentle glow of a fading fire on an open hearth.

'Hello? ... Anyone here?' Nick shouted.

'At least it's cool in here,' Rachel added, fanning herself with her right hand in an exaggerated fashion.

Nick ignored the comment. He was too concerned by the silence to be distracted by Rachel's apparent whimsical comments. They both walked further into the barn.

A sudden shaft of light at the far end of the barn

indicated that someone was about to enter, a fact confirmed by the creaking of a rusty door.

A tall dark-haired man in dirty blue overalls strode in, wiping his hands on an old rag as he did so and stopped two paces inside the door, staring at them in anticipation. He said nothing, simply continuing to rub his hands on the dirty cloth, the faint aroma of oil wafting across the room to where Nick and Rachel stood motionless.

Nick felt obliged to break the silence. 'Are you John Brown?' he asked awkwardly, but in as pleasant a manner as he could manage. The man didn't answer. 'I'm a friend of Robert Stanhope's,' Nick continued, trying to illicit some sort of response. 'This is Rachel, his daughter and I'm...'

'Nick Stephenson,' the man interrupted, suddenly seeming to relax and walking casually forward. 'I know who you are. I've been expecting you ... although not this fast. Follow me,' he answered as he continued to walk toward, and then past, them, out the door through which they had just entered. Nick and Rachel looked at each other, neither sure whether to follow or not.

'I don't like the look of this,' Rachel volunteered after a few seconds.

Nick moved to her side and took her by the hand. 'Maybe he's going to show us his prize begonias,' he joked, trying to make light of their tense situation. 'Come on, we're not turning back now,' he added, waving the digestive tin and leading her toward the open door.

They were momentarily blinded by the bright sunlight as they emerged from the barn into a large cobbled yard. Directly opposite, the man was standing in the doorway of another, smaller, brick-built building. On seeing them emerge, he turned and walked slowly into the building.

Nick looked at Rachel, smiled, and shrugged his shoulders. They crossed the yard and peered inside the building. It was much smaller than the barn and appeared to be open at one end, a number of hay bales sitting up against a chest-high wooden fence. The other walls were all solid, with no windows or doors, apart from the one they had just walked through. Propped up against one wall were several large metal drums, like the kind used to store oil. Against the other wall were a number of pens, clearly designed to house animals – horses or cows. Rachel screwed up her face as they entered – farmyard smells were not something she was used to or particularly liked.

John Brown was now standing behind a long wooden table, and to his side Nick could see a large metal box and what he recognised as an old safe, like the kind, he thought, that always seemed to appear in 1940s gangster films. They moved cautiously toward the table.

The man put down the rag. 'Mr Stanhope told me you were on your way,' he said, his face remaining expressionless.

'He called you?' asked Rachel, surprised.

'Yes, about a half hour ago. Told me ... I had something you wanted to take back to him.' The man suddenly appeared nervous.

Nick decided to take the initiative. It occurred to him that Brown was probably more concerned about the situation than they were. He guessed that Brown had no means of knowing about the story that was unfolding before them. But his cover had been effectively blown by Robert, and he didn't know whether Brown knew Rachel and himself from Adam and Eve.

'Look Mr Brown ... it is Brown, isn't it?' Nick paused. The man shook his head. Nick went on. 'All we want is the ... document that Robert gave you and we'll be on our way. We don't know anything about your arrangement with him.' Nick stopped and stared straight at Brown, hoping that the direct eye contact would persuade Brown that there was nothing to fear from them.

'Is there anything else I should know?' asked Brown.

'What do you mean?' answered Nick.

'Well, Mr Stanhope didn't sound too good on the phone,' he added. 'I do this as a hobby, you know'.

Nick tried not to snigger. Given the way he seemed to have fooled a lot of people, the last thing Nick was prepared to accept was that his last week of insomnia was down to this man's hobby.

Rachel intervened. 'My father called you from hospital, Mr Brown. He was taken ill earlier this week. We're just sorting out some loose ends for him and he was anxious to get his document back.'

Nick looked at Brown. 'Do you have it here?'

Brown hesitated for a moment, then seemed to take a deep breath and relax. Nick decided he had concluded that they could be trusted.

'Yes. It's in the safe.' He bent down to open the door. 'One of the hardest jobs I've done,' he volunteered as he removed a carefully wrapped package from the safe.

'Did Robert say what he wanted it for?' Nick asked, curious to know whether Brown had any idea what he was dealing with.

Brown stood up and placed what appeared to be a linen bag on the table in front of him.

'Just told me he wanted a copy to keep in his office. Said it was the first present he could remember his father giving him and it had too much sentimental value to leave lying around, but he wanted to have a copy as near to the real thing as he could achieve to remind him of it.' He looked at Nick with a clear sense of pride. 'I might not be the best at what I do, Mr Stephenson, but I try to make things as accurate as possible.'

He gave a brief smile and stood up straight with pride 'I've never had anyone complain about my work!' He looked at both of them, but realising there was no response forthcoming, he added, with a sense of failure, 'Mr Stanhope was going to collect it himself tomorrow.'

Nick moved forward toward the package lying on the table. He scanned the bag, noticing the very faint outline of what looked like a bird's wing wrapped around the folds of the material. He straightened it out carefully, revealing the shape of an eagle with outspread wings, delicately and beautifully inscribed on the fine material.

Nick spoke without taking his eyes off the bag. 'You have done a good job, John. Robert is very pleased and I am sure will want to thank you in person when he is feeling better.'

As he bent over to pick up the scroll Nick hesitated as he heard a sudden noise behind him.

'Stop right there, Mr Stephenson,' a voice said.

Nick turned and immediately caught sight of two figures, the smaller holding a gun that was pointed straight at his stomach. He had never seen a real gun before, and his initial thought was how *unreal* it looked, followed almost instantly by a wrenching feeling of fear. He had recognised the voice and, as his gaze rose to meet the man's face he straightened, the fear partially subsiding. It was Josef Weisman. Somehow in the back of his mind, as if a thousand years ago, he knew it would be. There was a strange comfort in seeing Weisman's face.

In an instant, after all that had happened, Nick felt he knew what he was dealing with. He didn't understand it, but finally the enemy was familiar and that gave some sort of comfort.

A taller man, who had been standing in the shadow behind Weisman, stepped forward, and Nick realised immediately that this was the person who was behind the whole thing, whatever that might be. There was no mistaking the badge of superiority. The man had an air about him, a presence that left Nick in an instant in no doubt that this scroll was indeed something of great importance. Finally Nick felt that he would get to the truth about the scroll.

Nick looked at Benjamin. Clearly this was a man who had complete control over the circumstances of their meeting. Nick had no means of knowing why, and how, they had come to meet at this point, but it seemed obvious to him now that he had been playing a game with him, wanting Nick to lead him to this point, and that the final endgame was now being played out in this small, insignificant barn in the remote English countryside.

Nick decided the best means of defence was attack. *Ignore him. Make him feel unimportant.* He looked away from Benjamin and instead addressed Weisman.

'Well, well,' he stated, as calmly as he could. 'It's about time you arrived. What kept you? Couldn't keep up?' Nick was terrified, yet at the same time completely curious about the turn of events. He was convinced the truth was about to be revealed, and for the moment didn't give a thought for his own ... or Rachel's safety.

Weisman smiled. 'It's a pleasure to see you again, Mr Stephenson. You've been busy since we last met.' He flicked the gun to his right, indicating that he wished Nick to move against the wall, and away from the table.

Nick glanced at Brown and then Rachel. He looked at the digestive tin in his left hand, and then nodded slowly at Weisman to indicate compliance. Very slowly Nick took one pace to his left and stood still. He weighed up the situation. *Wait and see how this develops.*

Benjamin moved forward and approached the little group towering over them. He looked at Brown. 'Now, I want you to move away from the scroll, please. Leave it on the table.' He glanced at Weisman as he slowly removed the small reference book and the black pouch from his jacket pocket and held them carefully in his hands.

Nick looked at Brown who was clearly physically intimidated and in no mood to question such an order. 'Now let's just discuss this,' Nick intervened in as controlled a manner as he could muster. 'Who are you anyway?'

Benjamin gave a wry smile. 'Someone who has been very patient with you, Mr Stephenson.'

Nick screwed up his eyes at the sound of the voice. It sounded so familiar... 'Have we met before?' he asked, his mind frantically trying to place the unusual accent and deep tone.

'Yes, and not in dissimilar circumstances. It seems I still have the controlling cards.'

Benjamin looked back at Weisman, now eager to get on with gaining what was rightfully his. He handed him the book and the black pouch in exchange for the gun. Nick could read the elation in the man's eyes as he took the precious parcel from his leader. 'Be careful with these, Josef,' said Benjamin in the manner a father would say to his son.

Weisman's eyes widened and he reached out slowly to take them into his possession. Carefully, he set them down on the table beside the package that Brown had produced. His gaze moved to Brown's linen bag. He let out an inadvertent sigh as his fingers reached out and touched the sandy-coloured pouch, his forefinger momentarily tracing the outline of the eagle.

Weisman looked up at Benjamin, a smile breaking out on his face. 'It is true... His sign is here...'

He carefully opened the bag and removed Robert's scroll and placed it on the table. He carefully folded the bag, before laying it, the eagle insignia facing upwards, back on the table beside the scroll. He stroked the scroll gently with the back of his hand, stopping to touch the small strap tied loosely around the centre, the sign of the Brotherhood clearly visible on the brown leather.

Nick's mind was racing as he took in what was happening.

He searched his memory as he tried to place the other man's voice. A bright light suddenly flashed into his mind. He remembered the pain and the pinprick in his arm. He ran his free hand through his hair. He heard a voice.

'It was you!' He pointed straight at Benjamin. 'You were there... You were trying to make me tell you where it was!' It was only a faint memory, but the voice was too distinctive even for his drugged mind to forget completely.

Benjamin looked back at Nick and scowled at him. 'Very good. Now, can we get on with it please? I have no time for this.'

He looked back at Weisman, who had unravelled the scroll, which Brown had placed on the table. He had carefully removed the contents of Benjamin's pouch and placed it down on the table beside Robert's scroll and was now busily looking through the book, his eyes darting back and forth between the three objects lying on the desk, as if cross-checking the three articles.

Nick had no idea what Weisman was doing. There was clearly something happening that was beyond his understanding, a final move that was not in his control. He'd had enough of Benjamin's tone and was beginning to feel he had nothing to lose anyway.

'I don't believe you have any right to take what is not yours ... whoever you are,' Nick said, suddenly feeling more annoyed with the situation than he had done in the previous six days.

'What *I* want are answers!' Nick added. He shook the tin at Benjamin. 'What do you want with some phoney, forged, mumbo-jumbo anyway?'

Benjamin looked at Nick and chuckled. 'Oh, Mr Stephenson, we both know the answer, don't we?' He moved forward and pointed the gun directly at him. 'You doubt my resolve. Don't! You can only guess at what is contained in this scroll'.

Nick stared back at him 'What is it then? Money ... wealth? All you see is a treasure, a fortune. I'm sure you've already picked out a buyer. Who is he? A Jew? Arab maybe?' Nick knew he was chancing his arm, but he didn't seem to have much to lose. Play stupid and he might at least keep him talking. And in any case, he had to know what it was all about.

Benjamin grinned at Nick. 'You know nothing!' He looked back at Weisman who was now shaking his head frantically, his eyes wide with excitement, a large grin on his face. He said nothing, but the merest hint of a smile appeared on Benjamin's face. At last the wait was over.

Nick had no idea what the exchange of looks was all about, but he guessed it wasn't good for their predicament. He decided to try one more time. 'Why? Why go to all this trouble? You know it's a fake?

'You think this is about money?' hissed Benjamin, the vein in his neck clearly bulging once more, his face contorted with anger. His patience was wearing thin. 'You think only of material things ... you little man! You are nothing!' he shouted, startling not only Nick, but also Rachel and Brown, who had now taken a step backward from the table.

Benjamin moved toward Nick who felt frozen to the spot. 'This is not about wealth, or fortune. It is history, Stephenson, *history*!

He moved back towards the table. 'Do you know what this is?' Benjamin pointed at the black pouch, and then quickly looked back at Nick's face. 'It is the Holocaust!'

Nick frowned, confused entirely by the ranting of the madman in front of him. Benjamin's face beamed like some grotesque maniac.

'Yes, Mr Stephenson. The Holocaust! But it's not only about the destruction of the Jews this time. It is a time bomb for the whole Western world!'

He laughed and looked away towards Brown and Rachel. 'Here we are, in this … shed, miles from nowhere, with the most important, the most potentially devastating piece of script that man has ever written lying in front of us…' He began to laugh again.

Nick looked briefly at Rachel. She had moved closer to the table, and was within arm's length of Robert's scroll and the other pieces of the puzzle. Nick stared at her, scared that Benjamin would spot her move and stop her in her tracks. She gave him one of her stubborn looks. Nick decided he couldn't stop her doing whatever she was thinking.

Nick shook the tin at Benjamin's face. 'You're mad! This is a useless piece of paper and you know it.' Nick was lost. He was now convinced that Robert's scroll was genuine, but its significance was still unimaginable to him, and its connection with these new items bewildering, but he was determined to keep Benjamin talking.

Benjamin looked back at Nick, his face betraying his impatience. Benjamin moved toward him slowly. His voice was suddenly calm again, and he grinned as he leaned close to Nick and delivered what he knew would be a bombshell to the man who had learned so much, and yet knew so little at the same time.

'I don't care what you think. Once your scroll is destroyed no one will ever know what it was worth, or what it meant!'

Benjamin stared intently into Nick's eyes, revelling in the total confusion now betraying itself on the twitching frown of his adversary. He had total control again.

Nick stared at Benjamin in complete shock. His mouth was wide open in disbelief, but he uttered no sound. Had he heard the man correctly?

'You're going to … destroy it?' He couldn't believe his own words. 'Why?' It was the last thing he had contemplated.

286

All this cloak-and-dagger stuff to get it ... and now this maniac was planning to destroy it? It didn't make sense.

He moved swiftly toward Benjamin, his curiosity once again now taking over from his fear. 'What is in this scroll?' He waved the digestive tin at him once again, knowing that the copy was still inside.

Weisman turned as Nick advanced. He stepped swiftly forward between Nick and Benjamin as if to protect his master. Nick stopped.

'Look, I led you here. You've been following me all week, you and your henchmen.' Nick stared at the man, who didn't flinch. 'Who the hell are you? ... And what's so important about this scroll?' He was feeling desperate.

He thought back to the Grosvenor Square office. He had to chance his arm. 'Tell me about Project Messiah.'

Benjamin's straightened up and took a deep breath. He now realised he had moved in on Nick at just the right time. His plan had become closer to exposure than he had imagined. Those around him were becoming liabilities and the information flow that he had so vigorously controlled was beginning to be compromised. He would deal with that later. He raised his chin and for a few moments looked straight at Nick, with a hint of a smile on his face.

Nick kept his stare fixed on Benjamin's eyes. 'All right, Mr Stephenson. Perhaps you deserve to know before you die.'

Nick looked at him in fear. He had reckoned on such an end, but somehow didn't believe it would come. He had to keep him talking.

'You had Cardinal Cornelli killed, didn't you?' Nick asked, deciding now he really did have nothing to lose.

'He was dispensable,' Benjamin answered, no emotion obvious in his voice. 'We had to keep you ... *contained*.'

Nick looked at him in disbelief, anger now releasing

itself in his voice. 'Contained? What the hell do you mean, "contained"?' He could picture Cardinal Cornelli's soft brown eyes staring at him.

Benjamin didn't flinch. 'We had to find the scroll ... the "real" scroll, and Cornelli was too close to the truth. You were what he ... and we ... had been waiting for. He would have known what you had. We knew only *you* could lead us to it, and nothing could get in our way.'

'And the man in the underground?' Nick added, his anger slowly building. 'Who was he?'

Benjamin paused, looking briefly at Weisman. 'He was one of the Brotherhood.'

Nick looked at him. 'The Qumran Brotherhood?'

Weisman looked at him and clenched his fists.

Benjamin interjected quickly. 'In spirit, yes, Mr Stephenson. He was a good man, prepared to die for his beliefs.' He reached forward and touched the shoulder of his accomplice, who was clearly upset at the mention of the incident.

'Are you?' Benjamin asked, looking back at Nick.

'That depends on what I'm up against,' answered Nick, his confusion becoming greater by the minute. 'Is this thing really worth dying for?' Nick asked, pointing at Robert's scroll, which remained lying on the table.

Benjamin turned toward the table and looked at the various items spread out on the table. He slowly nodded his head. 'Oh yes, Nick. At this moment in time it is the *only* thing worth dying for.'

He walked toward the table, his eyes burning brightly. He briefly touched the contents of the pouch that Weisman had emptied, then turned to Robert's scroll and picked it up. He turned back to Nick and held it in front of him.

'The so-called Truth Scroll,' he said slowly, sarcastically, a sense of triumph clearly evident in his tone.

Nick looked at him. 'It's just one of the Dead Sea

Scrolls', he said casually, trying to tease an explanation out of Benjamin. 'One of hundreds of the damn things.'

'Yes, Nick. But it could be *the* Scroll. Some say, the final testimony of the Brotherhood.' Benjamin stared at the scroll that he was now nursing gently in his hand.

Nick's mind was racing. What was the significance of this scroll? Was it really so important? More crucially, was Benjamin willing to kill three innocent people to protect its secret, whatever it was? He briefly considered admitting his complete ignorance of the scroll's significance on the basis that Benjamin could then let them go but decided that this seemed a remote possibility to say the least. He decided to try to flush out the answer with what he knew.

He thought back to what Robert had told him about the scroll. 'It's what the Nazis discovered, isn't it?' Nick said in an almost excited way, trying to sound like someone who had slotted the final piece of a jigsaw and suddenly saw the whole picture. 'Gerber was taking this back to Berlin, wasn't he? Why?'

Benjamin looked at Nick with a surprised expression. 'You have learned more than I thought.' He pointed the gun at Nick and moved toward him. 'Can you imagine what they would have done with this?'

Nick stared at him, still not knowing what the scroll meant, never mind what such a regime could have used it for.

Benjamin continued: 'Who knows what would have become of my race if they had got their hands on this scroll. The whole world could have turned against us. Imagine a world where the Americans and the British had turned a blind eye to the Nazis' atrocities against the Jews. No reason to fight!' He held the gun and the scroll above his head and shouted out loud, his voice echoing round the barn, his face contorted into a grotesque smile. '*Let them all die!*'

There was silence for a few seconds as his audience absorbed his words, then Benjamin slowly passed the scroll to Weisman and his face became serious. 'Do it!' he ordered, before looking directly back at Nick.

Weisman reached into his pocket and pulled out a small gold cigarette lighter. He held Robert's scroll out in front of him. He smiled at Nick, realising that this turn of events would leave his enemy in complete bewilderment.

Chapter 32

Nick fought with his mind to understand what was happening. He was living a nightmare, but one that was all too real. It was so fantastic that it had to be, literally, unbelievable, yet he was in the middle of something he knew he could not walk away from. If everything that had happened in the last few days was indeed real, he had to bring it to a conclusion and he knew that whatever that meant, it did not involve letting the men in front of him carry out their intention.

He glanced at Rachel who had a look of disbelief on her face. Nick understood. Was Weisman really going to set the scroll alight? This turn of events had indeed left them both completely dumbfounded. For a week they had hidden the scroll, they and others had been attacked, they had risked their lives and had begun to believe that they had acquired something of great value, and yet here was the moment their pursuers had finally got their hands on the thing they most craved ... only to set it alight? It didn't make sense.

'Why destroy it?' shouted Rachel, moving further toward Weisman before being stopped in her tracks by Benjamin's outstretched arm.

He laughed, realising that his tormentors had no understanding of the significance of their find, of the years of frustration he and his followers had endured, patiently waiting for this moment. He could not resist the pleasure of watching their disbelief as the future unfolded around them.

'Because this could destroy my nation,' answered Benjamin. 'It is the ranting of a madman, but it could have that power. It *must* be destroyed.'

'What madman? And what could be so powerful about an ancient piece of parchment, even if it is genuine?' Nick was now beside himself with questions. What was this man talking about?

Weisman opened the lid of the cigarette lighter and flicked the roller. The flame kicked into life. He held the naked flame to the edge of the scroll. It caught fire immediately. He smiled and looked back at Nick.

Benjamin moved in front of the burning parchment. He felt an urge to explain, to tell Nick the whole story, the man who now represented the people he would shock, control and finally bring to their knees. In defeating Nick Stephenson, he had defeated the Christian world.

'The Brotherhood lost its way, Mr Stephenson. In A.D. 68 the false testimony of the followers of Jesus Christ infiltrated even their closed and sacred circle. A number of them were fooled by these followers, and it caused the destruction of the Brotherhood.'

Nick took in what Benjamin was saying. He thought back to his first visit to the library with Rachel, and the conversations with Henry. Although there was still something missing, it was beginning to become clearer in his mind.

'This scroll ... somehow confirms Christianity, doesn't it?' Nick asked. Benjamin ignored him and looked around at the scroll; the thickness and tightness of the bound parchment caused it to burn very slowly.

Nick pursued his thoughts, now accelerating as the parchment burned. 'It questions the whole basis of your religion. The Qumran Brotherhood realised Christ was the true Messiah!' The Truth Scroll – that's what it meant. Marten's found a scroll that would have given Hitler all the power he would ever need. Nick thought about what he had just said. Almost under his breath he added, 'Oh my God!'

Nick looked at the tall man in front of him. He was now sure that this crazy lunatic was the leader of whatever sect or fanatical religious organisation that had come upon this information. But how could they be so sure that this scroll was the one? If Robert's father had given this to him over fifty years ago, how could they possibly have known this was the one they wanted?

He stared at Benjamin. 'How do you know about its existence?'

'It is mentioned only in one other scroll,' replied Benjamin, smiling, his eyes now fixed on the contents of the pouch lying on the table, '...and that is in the possession of the only true sons of Abraham.'

'The Shomrei Emet,' said Nick, scowling.

Benjamin tensed up at the words. 'We are not the cold-blooded terrorists they would have you believe. The truth is all that matters!'

'The truth? What the hell are you talking about! You're not protecting the truth, you're destroying it?'

'No! It is heresy! Lies! Once we know that this ... deception, this sacrilege of a scroll that you have so carefully hidden can no longer be exposed to an uneducated world, we can provide them with the *true* Word, the one that our forefathers rightfully believed in. It is *the* Word and it will be heard. And my race will have its true and deserved place in this world! We have waited a long time for this moment.'

Benjamin turned and strode over to the table. He carefully placed the contents that had earlier been extracted back in the black pouch, replacing them in his inside pocket.

'So the scroll in the papers ... on the news reports ...

it's not this one at all. It's . . .' Nick was finding this hard to believe.

'It is in the possession of a priest who is about to call a press conference and announce to an anticipating world that Jesus . . . was . . . *is* a fake!' announced Benjamin triumphantly. He tapped his jacket pocket. 'The original is with me, but by the end of today thousands will be in circulation throughout the world. The four Gospels of the traitors will become mere historically interesting fakes. The Canon merely awaits my call. Once your scroll is destroyed there is nothing to stand in our way. I have waited a very long time for this moment, Mr Stephenson.' He looked intently at the burning parchment. 'And now it is gone.' He gave a contented smile. 'God didn't create a perfect world, Mr Stephenson. As soon as he put *us* here he saw to that.'

'A priest? . . . Canon Howe?' Nick looked bemused.

'Yes.' Benjamin replied, as if pleased Nick had spotted the subtlety of the ploy. 'Who else to add credence to the truth but a servant of Rome itself?'

'But why would a Roman Catholic priest support your contention of Jewish supremacy?'

'Because even he has realised how twisted the Word has become, how poisoned the Church has been by the Scriptures, and how the course of history has been tainted by centuries of lies. He has spent most of his life working with and interpreting Scripture. He too believes he has the chance to correct a great wrong and change the course of mankind's beliefs.' Benjamin was in full flow. 'He too can become a prophet!'

Nick looked at Benjamin in disbelief. 'You've brainwashed him! He is no more of a latter-day prophet than I am the first man to walk on the moon!'

Nick thought back to Benjamin's earlier words. If it was true that there was another scroll that purported to 'expose' Jesus, then the one Nick possessed must be extremely powerful and must somehow rank above every Gospel written after Christ's time. Why was it so important that this scroll was destroyed? Suddenly it was becoming clearer to Nick what Benjamin was doing. What he was trying to do.

He looked at the burning parchment. 'Why are you afraid of what this says? Who wrote these words?'

Benjamin gave an evil-looking grin, knowing he was about to release the most incredible piece of news Nick would ever hear. But somehow he thought he deserved it. It would do him no good anyway. He was about to die. He moved toward Nick and smiled.

'You would know him as John the Baptist. The eagle was his sign, his signature.'

Nick looked at him in disbelief. He caught his breath, unable to believe what he was hearing. The eagle had been a Nazi insignia, but all the time it had been hiding the true identity of the scroll's author. He remembered Henry's words – *the eagle has been a symbol shared by many tribes and even individuals through the ages…* The last few days had been like a dream at times, but this capped it all.

Nick tried to regain his senses. He had to keep the man talking; he had to think this through.

'You mean John the Baptist joined the Qumran Brotherhood and managed to persuade them that they had been wrong for … two hundred years?' He could hardly believe what he was saying, the words seeming to hit him in slow motion, even though they were coming from his own mouth. He could hardly start questioning his own beliefs and morals at this moment, to think whether he cared or not about whether this was all true or important to him, or anyone else, but he knew somehow, deep down, that he could not let this maniac destroy something that others might decide was worth fighting for.

Nick gave a sarcastic laugh and moved toward Benjamin, realising that he had to keep on the offensive if they were to have a chance of escaping alive.

'How do you know this? Have you or anyone else read this scroll?'

Benjamin began to look agitated again. 'It is the only reason there could have been for the Brotherhood's destruction. The Baptist was an infiltrator, a fanatic, who tricked them into believing that their own writings proved his assertions.'

'But the Gospels...' Nick began, but was quickly interrupted.

'... were written decades after Christ's death by men who had never even met him! Only John the Baptist wrote down the *words* of Christ. But he twisted them! He was smart enough to have four others write down *his* words. Four people couldn't *all* have got it wrong, could they? He even wrote of his own apparent torture and death ... and very conveniently, if somewhat heroically, took himself right out of the picture. He set out to destroy Judaism, and he almost succeeded. He created a split in the Brotherhood, from which it never recovered. Jesus was no more than a pawn, brilliantly used by John. But his plan backfired, and once he was found out and killed, the others he had persuaded about Jesus actually believed in John's stories! They started a breakaway sect, and today you know it as the Christian Church.' Benjamin looked almost relieved to have told the story to Nick, who rooted to the spot, trying hard to separate truth from the mere ravings of a madman.

Nick glanced at the burning bundle in Weisman's hand, the parchment now well alight at the edge. He ran his hand through his hair. He was completely confused and

296

stunned by what he had just heard, but even more determined to stop the scroll's destruction.

'You haven't answered my question,' he shouted, moving to one side. 'Have you even read this scroll? Do you know what it says?'

'I don't have to read it, Mr Stephenson. We have the Master Scroll. It is all we need to prove to the world that Jesus was little more than another radical of his day, a mere foot soldier, and an illiterate one at that. Why do you think there is no first-person account by him? Wouldn't that have been so much more convincing? Why didn't *he* write down his teachings? Every other real prophet did. The Master Scroll will show the world that Christianity is founded on the world's biggest con trick ... a *public relations* stunt, little more than the the embittered fabrication of an outcast, John!'

Nick could feel the frustration rising in Benjamin. A challenge to his long-held belief was not what he wanted to hear. He had to keep pushing.

'You don't know *what* it says, do you?' retorted Nick. 'Rumour and ... old wives' tales, that's all this is. You have no proof at all. And what about this ... Master Scroll. How can it possibly be seen as anything other than just another old piece of worthless tittle-tattle?'

Benjamin's eyes narrowed, and his jaw tensed. 'Do you have to have everything spelled out to you? The Master Scroll is just that. It is the Brotherhood's constitution, their written act of faith. It has the signatures of all the recognised leaders of all the Tribes of Israel at the time of their greatest challenge from the outcast. The Brotherhood knew they faced their greatest threat, and it was decided that they must create a documented witness to the falsehood that was sweeping through their nation like a plague, and which John had cleverly planted among other races beyond Palestine in an attempt to crush the

Jewish people. It proves beyond doubt that John, and the four who conspired with him, were little more than religious terrorists, plotters who sought to overthrow their leaders and seize power for themselves.'

Nick gave an involuntary laugh. This was becoming more ridiculous with every revelation. He knew he had to keep Benjamin occupied while he thought his way out of the predicament.

'How did you come by this Master Scroll then? You found it lying around in an attic somewhere, I suppose?'

'Do not mock what you cannot start to understand,' replied Benjamin as he moved menacingly toward Nick. 'My father gave me a piece of paper on the night we were separated, many years ago. On it was an eight-digit number. I had no idea what it meant, but I memorised that number as though my life depended on it. I knew that my father would somehow one day reveal its meaning.'

He paused, as though his mind had wandered back to a distant but defining moment in his life.

'When I was eighteen, I received a letter from a rabbi who, I later learned, had helped me escape from the Nazis. It explained that my father had been taken one night, but that he had left a message that was to be passed to his son on a certain date should he fail to return. The message told me that the number I had been given would unlock a safe deposit box in a Swiss bank. In it I would find something that would define my life and the means by which to change the course of history.'

Rachel, who had been standing transfixed by the story unfolding, stepped forward. 'What was in the box?'

Benjamin looked at her. He felt a great burden lifting from his shoulders as he told his story for the first time. He wanted to tell it, his own testimony. It felt like a cleansing, and he knew that they would never be able to repeat it.

'The Master Scroll, Marten's notebook, and a banker's draft for one million dollars. A letter from my father explained the meaning of the scroll and listed the names of a number of contacts, sons of prominent Jews in Germany and other countries, who were to be made aware of the contents of the scroll by word of mouth as the Nazis began their purge. I had been chosen to lead our people from the wilderness. Marten's death had not been in vain. In the months before his ... murder, he had time to record the words that he had translated from both scrolls, their contradictory stories. He sent his rider, Gerber, off with your scroll, knowing that if it reached Berlin his Catholic leader would use it to destroy the Jewish state for ever and with it take control of Western Europe.'

Nick looked at Benjamin in disbelief. 'Hitler was a Catholic?'

'Oh yes, Mr Stephenson, and one who was never excommunicated by the Church of Rome. Why not?' He smiled as he let the words sink into Nick's and Rachel's minds before continuing. 'But Martens was a far deeper and more committed scholar of ancient parchments than his master could imagine. He could not destroy either of them, and he knew that only God could decide which the world would finally learn of.' He looked at Nick and smiled in victory. 'Today *He* has decided.'

Rachel smiled nervously and looked at Nick. Benjamin sounded totally convincing, even if the whole story sounded far-fetched. She did not want him to feel he had gained the upper hand.

'Sounds a bit dramatic ... and completely stupid!' She laughed, then, facing directly toward Benjamin, slowly and very deliberately changed her tone to one of contempt. 'But it also sounds a bit like one scroll against another to me. How do *you* know which one is right ... if either?'

Benjamin looked back at her and smiled. 'When you have

spent your life pursuing the righting of a great wrong, you do not doubt the fundamental basis of your belief. My father's letter explained of the existence of the so-called Truth Scroll. It has been the thorn in our side for fifty years. Gerber was not yet dead when he was found lying beside the dirt track. He gave just enough information to those who found him to let them know of the scroll's content, and eventually my father tracked down Marten's notebook. We knew that the scroll was out there, and we could not risk releasing the Master Scroll until we had found it. We knew that if it were ever to emerge, it could destroy everything. *Casting* doubt would be enough to *create* doubt.' He turned toward Nick. 'We have been very patient, Mr Stephenson. It is time for us to reap the reward.'

Benjamin looked at the burning parchment that was now crackling with the intensity of the heat. 'Give it to me,' he said to Weisman as he reached out his hand. Weisman carefully handed the blazing document to him.

He looked back at Nick. 'Once this lie is destroyed, the Master Scroll can never be challenged. The people of Israel will be free to take what is rightly theirs, and the Western nations will pay for their patronising tolerance of our great nation. Only we are God's people!'

'You're crazy!' shouted Nick, shaking his head. He had been trying to think through the consequences of what he was being told, even if he didn't believe a word of it.

'If you could prove what you say, and even if people believed you, all you would do is create chaos. The very foundation of Western society could collapse...' Nick stopped himself. He had suddenly, in one moment, realised this man's true intent. 'That's what this is all about! Power! You're after power, control! You're the one who has been manipulating the press...'

Into Nick's mind flashed the newspaper headlines and television coverage of the last few days. He realised that this man had been able to manipulate the world's media. He shuddered at the thought of the extent to which Benjamin had been able to mobilise such a vast upswell of opinion and interest in such a short space of time. He realised he was dealing with something way beyond his comprehension. And yet, this was a mere human being in front of him. He had to do something.

But he was beaten to it. Rachel had listened to the exchange with growing alarm. She decided the scroll, whatever it was or said, was too important to be allowed to be destroyed.

She suddenly ran toward Benjamin shouting as loud as she could, only to be stopped physically by Weisman as she reached to within a few feet of the burning parchment. Benjamin, startled by the sudden move turned toward her and held out the burning Scroll to his right-hand side. Nick reacted instantly, partly to divert attention away from Rachel, and partly to stop Benjamin's blatant destruction of something he was now convinced was too important to be destroyed without at least a fight. He kicked up his right leg and caught Benjamin's forearm, at the same moment smashing the biscuit tin hard across Benjamin's face. Robert's scroll was sent flying through the air in what seemed like slow motion before it fell, still burning, onto a pile of hay laid out on the floor against the back wall of the barn.

Benjamin let out a scream and clutched his face.

Nick looked at the burning document and the flames now gathering pace quickly in the dry mass of straw. 'Get that fire out now!' he shouted at Brown.

Brown, who had stayed motionless and was completely mystified at the exchange, hastily grabbed an old towel from the bench and started beating at the flames. He held his arm up to protect his face from the heat, but the wild beating seemed to simply fan the flames. The

301

fire spread rapidly heading toward the paraffin barrels in the corner of the barn.

Nick, meanwhile, had dropped the digestive tin, pushed Benjamin aside and rushed toward Rachel, who was still being held by Weisman. Seeing Nick heading straight for him, Weisman threw Rachel back toward the bench, and swung his arm at Nick, catching him on the side of the face and knocking him clean off his feet.

For a few moments Nick lay, dazed, on the stone floor, the crackling sound of the fresh, burning hay only feet away from his head. He glanced toward Benjamin, who had by now recovered his composure and was on all fours, searching for something in the straw lying on the floor of the barn that was rapidly becoming engulfed in smoke and flames. As he started to rise, a swinging boot caught him on the side of the face, and he caught sight of Weisman out of the corner of his eye scowling as he lunged at Nick in a blind fit of hatred.

Nick fell back to the ground, blood streaming from the corner of his mouth. Rachel let out a scream, as she struck Weisman on the back of his head with a spade she had found propped against a side wall. Nick wiped his mouth and looked up from the ground.

The long summer heat had merely accelerated the rate at which the small barn was being devoured by the flames all around it. Nick saw Benjamin stumble toward the door, and watched as Brown intercepted him and grabbed his jacket from the side. As he did so, Nick saw the digestive tin fall to the ground from Benjamin's grasp, the contents half spilling out. He got to his feet as quickly as he could and groggily headed toward it.

Just as he reached the tin, he heard a sudden loud crack above his head. A timber joist barely four feet above him was alight, the flames flowing along and round its knurled surface.

'Look out, Nick!' Rachel shouted, covering her eyes from the now intense heat inside the barn.

Nick looked up at the rafter and started stumbling backwards. He felt the back of his legs hit something solid, and he started to tumble. As he did so, his eyes caught sight of the tin to his right hand side. He reached out his hand, just as his world went suddenly dark.

Chapter 33

Nick opened his eyes slowly, painfully, as the sunlight shone back into his world. He looked around. At his side lay one of the barrels that had been cut in half vertically creating a trough shape.

'What happened?' he stuttered. 'Where am I?'

'Thank God. You're all right', replied Rachel, smiling down at the blackened face resting on her lap. She glanced at the barrel. 'Just as well you fell back into that. Mr Brown pulled you out in it, just in the nick of time. Once the paraffin in those other barrels caught fire, that was it!'

Nick slowly pulled himself up into a sitting position and looked across the grassy field toward the burning structure that was now almost completely flattened. The smell of the paraffin caught the back of his throat, causing him to cough. He started to recollect the evening's extraordinary turn of events.

He looked round quickly to Rachel. 'Weisman ... and the other guy?'

Rachel shrugged her shoulders. 'After your "friend" hit you on the back of the head, the roof of the barn started to collapse. There was nothing I could do. I was trapped, so I jumped over the fence and tried to come back in through the door, but it was stuck. Mr Brown, here, saw you fall and let go of Weisman. He pulled you out of there, Nick, just before the barrels exploded. There's hardly anything left of the place, and what there is has basically ... well, melted together in the heat.' She looked at John Brown, reliving the horror of the scene. 'We didn't see Weisman or his accomplice come out.'

She turned and pointed over Nick's shoulder to a flat area of grassland behind him. 'It looks as if they came by helicopter. It took off while we were dragging you out. They may have been in it ... or still in there.' She looked back at what was left of the barn, her head suddenly feeling heavy with exhaustion.

Nick didn't know what to say. He smiled, reached up, and kissed her gently on the forehead.

Brown looked at the smouldering mess and shook his head. 'It took me over a year to build that shelter.' He looked at Nick. 'Just as well you fell into the manger though,' he said slowly, shaking his head.

Nick and Rachel looked at each other, Rachel silently mouthing the word, a look of disbelief on her face. They turned to Brown.

'The what?' asked Nick.

Brown looked back at them. 'To feed the animals with,' he continued. 'You know? As in the French – *manger* ... to eat.'

He didn't understand the look of disbelief on their faces.

Epilogue

Nick pressed the 'set' button and the stopwatch started running. The Morgan pulled away sharply from the parking space, clipping the edge of the footpath as Nick threw it around the first corner. He smiled. This was going to be a fast one!

As he pulled out of Chelsea Harbour and into the never-ending flow of London traffic his mind started to wander. The last three months had been some of the happiest he could remember. Rachel was the main reason, of course. Their friendship had grown deep, and most evenings now involved Rachel in some way. The overnight stays were now becoming a regular thing, but not in any mundane or taken-for-granted way. He didn't feel threatened or tied down. In fact, the more he saw of Rachel now, the more he wanted of her.

The fact that Robert had now recovered fully, and his financial problems were resolved, had also helped. His old partner knew he had been foolish to risk all he had, but finally securing a pre-let on the entire building had ensured Robert a handsome return on his investment. Nevertheless, it had made Nick swear to himself never to put his hard-earned money into property.

His mind flitted briefly back to the field in Kent, as it had done many times. No bodies had been discovered, and Nick found himself once again imagining what had happened to the man he now knew was Benjamin Goldstein. His sudden disappearance had made the front page of *The Times*. Rumours of kidnapping and suicide abounded.

and he and Weisman had even been linked to the murder of the Chilean Director of Cultural Affairs.

He had thought long and hard about contacting Father Howe. Benjamin's story was so fantastic that Nick knew, without Roberts scroll, or the copy, he could never prove whether it was true or not. Of course, the Master Scroll had never been released … if it ever existed, and no press conference took place. The press had a field day with 'The greatest hoax of our times!' It seemed that quite a few prominent financial and media types had lost their jobs over their stupidity in ever believing there could be such a thing. Eventually, Nick had phoned the Ecole biblique, only to be told that they did not, and never had had an office in London, and that Canon Howe had disappeared suddenly. Nick's attempts to trace him elsewhere had been completely fruitless. Wherever he was, he had never bothered to show his face again.

Nick slowly ran his fingers through his hair.

Now that Robert had retired and Nick had taken over the business, the sense of responsibility had mushroomed inside him. He realised how lonely he had become before, but only because he now had someone to talk with, someone he *wanted* to talk with. Perhaps this feeling of responsibility was more than just about the firm.

The Morgan purred across London like a caged tiger desperate to escape its constraints and stretch its legs in a long sustained burst to freedom. As he turned the corner into High Holborn, Nick caught sight of the crane towering above the gleaming new steelwork, now up to the ninth storey and already reshaping the street scene around it.

Approaching the site, Nick smiled as he had done every morning for the last two months at the site board standing proudly over the pavement. The irony of it never ceased to amuse him:

Another Forster Development
High-quality Offices up to 100,000 sq ft
Let to:
Bank of Israel

As the Morgan came to a sliding halt just inside the compound gate, Nick reached out to the dashboard and hit the stop button. He was seventeen seconds outside his best.
